MOON TRACKS

MOON TRACKS

Travis S. Taylor
Jody Lynn Nye

BAEN

Copyright © 2019, by Travis S. Taylor and Jody Lynn Nye

A Baen Books Original

Baen Publishing Enterprises
P.O. Box 1403
Riverdale, NY 10471
www.baen.com

ISBN: 978-1-4814-8383-4

Cover art by Dominic Harman

First Baen trade paperback printing, March 2019

Distributed by Simon & Schuster
1230 Avenue of the Americas
New York, NY 10020

Printed in the United States of America

10 9 8 7 6 5 4 3 2 1

Chapter One

"Incoming!" a voice broke above the hubbub of the crowded hangar.

Barbara Winton gawked as a half-meter-long remote-controlled dune buggy leaped over the shoulder of a man and hurtled straight toward her. She dodged out of the way just in time. The small blue car hit the ground, bounced high a couple of times in the low lunar gravity, and sped off between the feet of a woman beside her with the hum of electric motors and squeaks of the ten-centimeter-diameter rubber tires against the concrete hangar floor.

"Sorry!" The owner of the voice, a young Hispanic man with hair dyed blue, slipped out among a group of women wearing light green jumpsuits. He grinned at her, then sidled off in pursuit of his toy.

"No problem!" Barbara called after him. She shook her head and her brown hair floated a bit in the Moon's low gravity. That hadn't been the first model car to try to run her over. Barbara returned to her search, talking into the collar mike connected to the personal data engine microcomputer mounted in the pouch on her purple jumpsuit sleeve. "Team Solar Wind? Where are you?"

They weren't answering. "No wonder, with all the noise!" Barbara said to herself under her breath.

Barbara inched her way through the packed hangar, peering at each of the racing teams in turn, trying to spot the badges that identified the quartet of people she was seeking. The tall girl referred again and again to the holographic images rising from her personal data engine's screen, showing the faces she needed to find.

"Turn ninety degrees to the left and walk forty-five yards," Fido, the voice of her PerDee, said. "Their ID signatures are coming from that direction."

"Thanks, Fido."

"You are quite welcome, Barbara," the data engine responded.

Barbara swiveled to the left, ducked underneath the swinging arm of a man excitedly pointing out a feature on the oversized vehicle behind him, and started homing in on the IDs. She wasn't used to such numbers of people bounding all over the place like happy grasshoppers. While there were nearly seven thousand people on the Moon, a number which was growing every day, it was never *crowded*, but it sure seemed that way at the moment.

The hangar, a vast dome of transparent aluminum oxynitride, gray carbon nanotube-reinforced plascrete, and good old-fashioned steel beams, arched high overhead, with shuttles and tools winched almost up to the ceiling, out of the way. For once, the huge enclosure wasn't open to the Moon's vacuum, so she didn't have to wear a full environment suit. Instead, the hangar had been pressurized and heated to play host to an amazing array of people from all over Earth, cool new technology, a *loud* cacophony of music, and megatons of excitement. Armstrong City, her home for the last few months, was about to play host to the greatest race humanity had ever witnessed: a race around the Moon.

She was not only going to witness it, Barbara thought with pleasure, but she would be right in the thick of the action. She would be one of the actual racers.

As the newest member of Dr. Keegan Bright's Bright Sparks, a group of young scientists handpicked by the scientist and video star from thousands of hopeful applicants to join his lab on the Moon, Barbara had had the opportunity to work on the most exciting experiments in the most extreme lab ever. So far, she'd helped to work on two space telescopes—nearly three—among other fantastic projects that nudged at the boundaries of human knowledge, but the moment that the colony founder, the billionaire philanthropist Ms. Adrienne Reynolds-Ward, had announced the eleven-thousand-kilometer race around the surface of the Moon, she and her five fellow Sparks could think and talk of nothing else. Prizes would be awarded for placing, but the big thrill was the chance to build their own Moon buggy. The Sparks had fired messages back and forth to one another, in their personal lab, all eager to add their own ideas for constructing the ultimate race car.

Still, in the back of Barbara's mind, the prize money danced like a glistening beam of light. Ms. Reynolds-Ward was offering one million dollars as first prize. Barbara had done the math. After the vehicle's expenses were covered, each of the six Sparks would have a share amounting around one hundred thirty-five thousand dollars. With the salary and bonuses she earned as a Spark, she needed hardly any of that sum on the Moon. Instead, she wanted it to help her parents back in Iowa. The family farm where she grew up was always on the verge of going bankrupt. That prize money could go a long way toward covering outstanding expenses and taking the pressure off her folks.

Being a Bright Spark was certainly starting to help. She had had no idea when she learned she was going to become part of the team that she would be making *money*. Just getting to go to the Moon and work with Dr. Bright and the Sparks was reward enough. Then she discovered how *much* work was involved. They kept her busy with research and filming, making certain that the webisodes were uploaded on time as required by the contracts with their sponsors. She felt the rewards for all that hard work were ample. For the first time in her life, she didn't feel like she was sacrificing something important when she splurged a bit on a new outfit, an actual book and not a digital one, or even a hairdresser in the hotel salon to give her a really good cut, something she almost never did before. That turned out to be a terrific mood-raiser as well as enhancing the shape of her face. Dr. Bright's video team gave her the thumbs-up when she had shyly shown off her new haircut. Being raised on a struggling family farm had taught her the value of things and of hard work and had instilled in her a frugality that was difficult to overcome, even with her new and recurring paycheck. She wanted to win, so she could send that prize money home.

The Sparks' entry into the race, which they were still working to complete, had started as a mishmash of ideas thrown out during a brainstorming session in their combination classroom/laboratory/control room/storage space/catch-all-for-everything-they-did room, Sparks Central.

Gary Camden and Jan Nguyen, so alike in appearance and thought they were called the Nerd-Twins, were doing most of the construction, with input from the others based on their specialties, but at a distance. Barbara had studied and worked a lot with power systems, so the Nerd-Twins were constantly calling her, or waking her up in the middle of the night, to ask questions about maximizing distance they could travel versus weight on the *Spark Xpress*.

She didn't particularly like the name, but Neil was ecstatic about it.

"It has buzz!" he had exclaimed. "The net's going to love it!" He was right, of course. Once it was mentioned on the vlog, the name had gone viral. People asked about progress every hour of the day, from all over the world. She wished she had more answers to give the fans.

The buggy was coming along, she thought. While nobody but Gary and Jan had seen it, the Nerd-Twins had assured them it would be raceworthy and on time. Barbara was actually starting to worry about that part. She was afraid the pair had bitten off more than they could chew and were letting their pride keep them from asking for help.

Barbara could only imagine what the *Spark Xpress* must look like at this point. It was probably way more cobbled together than the racers she was currently seeing and some looked, well, *very* sketchy. Most of the vehicles parked in the hangar had a homebuilt, garage-mechanic, enthusiast-designed, hand-tooled appearance, though none of them looked anything alike. Team Fire Bird, whose team was sponsored by a Russian-Asian power supplier, seemed to have two massive smokestacks rising behind its crew environment on its red-and-white buggy. Barbara knew they couldn't be real smokestacks, since the Moon had no atmosphere, but she was curious as to the purpose they served. Any questions she asked the four drivers, all female, all about six feet tall and model-gorgeous, were met by blank stares, and not all that friendly, either.

Barbara refused to take their attitude personally. After all, she was a competitor in this race, too. She continued to be as welcoming and hospitable as she could, answering questions, giving directions, and posing for selfies. Lots of selfies. Almost too many selfies.

A scale model of a bright yellow-and-blue buggy hurtled across the floor, aiming for her legs. She jumped to avoid it, flailing her arms to keep upright in the light lunar gravity.

"Sorry!" a handsome blond man a little more than her own age of sixteen called, bounding toward her. He grinned. "It's only a hologram." He waved his hand over his own microcomp, and the buggy vanished. His mouth dropped open as he recognized her. "No, aren't you Barbara Winton?" He had an intriguing accent.

Barbara managed a smile, wishing she felt as confident as she hoped she looked.

"That's me," she said. She put out a hand to shake his.

"*Bozhe moi!* How amazing to meet you! I'm Tomasz Salenko. I'm a big fan! Please! Pose with me." He threw his free arm around her and tossed out his PDE, which hovered into place in midair, then zoomed all about them recording data. On its platform, a holo of the two of them formed. "I will post this on the Internet now! So nice to meet you! I can kiss you? On the cheek? I have had all my inoculations."

Barbara felt her cheeks burn. Nobody had ever asked her if they could kiss her like that before, well, if you didn't count Danny Larsh, but that was in the second grade.

"Yes, if you want," she said, feeling shy.

Tomasz planted a smacking salute on each side of her face and let her go. "This is better than I thought! I have met the new Spark and kissed her!" He withdrew and snatched the small device out of midair. His fingers played busily on the small screen. "Posted!"

Barbara gave him a sheepish grin and fled, almost bumping into the Russian models. From the extreme interest on their faces, they must have watched the entirety of her interactions with Tomasz. One of the women raised an approving eyebrow at her, nodded her head and smiled knowingly at her. Barbara guessed that until Tomasz had made a fuss, the Russian women hadn't thought of her as anyone special, but once they realized she was a celebrity, they finally acknowledged her presence. Barbara just nodded and kept moving. She found all the attention kind of embarrassing, but it shouldn't have surprised her. Their mentor, Dr. Keegan Bright, had warned her before the first shuttle landed.

"People are going to recognize you," Dr. Bright had said, a grin spreading over his handsome and famous face. "They're going to feel like they know you, when they really don't. A lot of what they think about you is what they think about themselves. Take that with a grain of salt and don't let it bother you. If you need to take a break away from the crowd, just do it, but remember that our success depends on everyone pulling together. I'm going to need you. The whole colony is going to need you. As the home team, you're hosts, and that's why Ms. Reynolds-Ward waived your entry fees and is offering to help you find sponsors—unrelated to her business interests, of course. So we all owe what extra time we've got to the event. Help the visitors get used to being on the Moon. You know plenty that they don't, no matter what they think. Be good ambassadors, and don't burn yourself out."

Her fellow Sparks, Dion, Jan, Gary, Neil and Daya, had all nodded, as if they already knew what Dr. Bright was saying, but Barbara had a feeling that the briefing was intended for all of them, too. She knew nothing like this race had ever happened in the history of Armstrong City—or ever, for that matter. Humanity's first lunar colony was young. No crowd this large had ever descended on it before.

The Armstrong Peninsula Hotel, newly repaired and refurbished since the shuttle crash a few months back, was strained to the walls with hundreds of visitors: racers, dignitaries and the press. Regular colony residents with extra beds or floor space to share had been pressed to put up some of the overflow. Several storage tubes had been emptied out onto the lunar surface and converted into makeshift living quarters. Many of the better-funded teams thought ahead and brought their own inflatable living quarters and set up headquarters for themselves just at the edge of the city, where the mayor had given them access to cleared and graded areas designated for future growth. Barbara had toured a few of those camps. They had air, water, power, and data hookups out there, but that was about it. She was grateful that security concerns prevented housing anyone else in the Sparks' quarters. Even the underground lake had campers on the shore.

So far, almost everyone had been great, and reasonably cooperative, except when it came to showing up for their physicals and gear check. Barbara didn't really blame them for that. After all, who wants to get poked by a doctor when they could be out looking at the Moon! But it was her job to track down the teams who still needed this final check out.

"Team Solar Wind?" she repeated again and again over the common communication frequency that everyone should have been monitoring. She could hardly hear her own voice. "Team So—" A blare of trumpet music drowned out her words, followed by raucous laughter.

The arrow indicator issuing from Fido's emitters enlarged to the size of her head, meaning she was almost on top of her quarry. At last, she spotted Team Solar Wind near the enormous metal sliding doors and nudged her way past a circle of engineers admiring a huge blue buggy with treads deeper than her arm could reach. The East African team stood in a knot under the ladder of their own gigantic vehicle, holograms splashing color on their faces and chests. Barbara rolled her eyes.

Like everyone else, including her, Team Solar Wind was playing M-Tracker, the augmented-reality seeker game that made its players home in on the faint sound of music to capture phrases of songs, or "tracks." Once all matching tracks had been collected, the program put them together to construct a whole song from a licensed music catalog containing thousands of titles. The game was a recent development on a recent Earth favorite, although it hadn't appeared on the Moon until around the time that the teams had started to arrive. It was irresistible fun.

She and her friends had immediately started playing, chasing down the musical notes that appeared in augmented reality all over the colony, trying to construct entire songs from the single lines and phrases audible in one's personal earpiece. Once you managed to complete a song, the full version downloaded onto your PDE's playlist, so there were actual stakes to succeed. TurnTables, the source of capture tools like staves, clefs, rests and other musical notation as well as bonus tracks, began to appear around Armstrong City, and provided a forum for Battles of the Bands between groups of players whose track playlists had reached viable levels. Since there were nine or ten "Crews" a player could join, ranging from Classical Crew to Spacepunk Crew, the resulting noise in the hangar overwhelmed practically all other sound, especially her hails. Someone had to have planted a TurnTable pretty close by. It was shooting tracks out in all directions for some fifty meters at least.

"Baby, yeah, spin it spin it spin it, to the next dimension with you . . ." a throaty female voice chanted. The cut repeated over and over.

"You got one! That's Needa Meier's 'Quasar.' I have to have it!"

yelled the shortest of the East African team, a round-faced man with dark brown skin and a shock of hair dyed in streaks of platinum and gold. Barbara recognized him as Charlton Mbute. He waggled his hand over his own microcomputer, as if he was fingering an instrument, desperately trying to interact with the jumble of bright red notes that arose from the emitters at each corner. The cluster of notes seemed as if they were about to coalesce, then vanished. "Noooo!"

His friends, a rangy man and a woman about twenty years older than the other three, laughed. Charlton turned in place, stretching his device out in hopes of catching another one.

"Hey, Team Solar Wind!" Barbara shouted. The quartet ignored her.

"Did you get the lost chord?" his nearest companion asked, a slim woman with ebony skin, a long neck and knife-edged cheekbones, Lois Ingota. She held out her own smartphone. The holo above it danced with swirling motes of numerous colors. "Look! How wonderful! This place is full of songs!"

"But no more Needa," Charlton said, with sad eyes. "I needa Needa! I'm missing just that last cut to make the whole song."

"They are not listening, Barbara," Fido said.

"Guess I'll have to play pied piper," Barbara said. Fido looked like everyone else's smartphone, but was a dozen times more powerful. And to top it off, his operator turned out to be extremely gifted in programming such things. "Fido, can you research which is Needa Meier's lost chord?"

"Yes, Barbara," said the perky voice. "I have access to the M-Tracker database."

"Really?" Barbara almost goggled in astonishment. "How can you do that?"

"One of Dr. Bright's former Sparks is a M-Tracker lead programmer. Some of the code was written while she was here. I have a back door."

Barbara swallowed the urge to ask Fido for hacks on the songs she hadn't managed to complete yet. That wouldn't be fair.

"Can you reproduce the hologram?"

"Naturally, Barbara."

"Good. Play it on your screen. When I start to move, drag it toward the main door."

Red lights in the shape of musical notes pinged up and down in midair above her wrist.

". . . Transdimensional transcendence, light transference commence . . ." The phrase repeated itself over and over from the small speaker. *That was a tongue-twister*, Barbara thought. *No wonder it was the missing piece of the song.*

"Look!" she shouted, shoving into the midst of the laughing group. "Look what I've got!"

Charlton's eyes went wide as he heard the lyrics ringing out.

"That's it!" he said. "That's the rare one!" He all but lunged toward Barbara. She backed up a pace.

"Oh, it's getting away!" Barbara said. The notes seemed to leap off her wrist. Team Solar Wind never thought twice. They set out in pursuit of the missing musical phrase, scrambling with their own PDEs held out before them. Barbara had to open out her stride to stay ahead. She weaved in between people and vehicles, heading toward the hangar's exit. She glanced over her shoulder to make sure Solar Wind was still with her. The small man bounded eagerly beside her, his teammates in his wake.

As soon as they got out into the gray-enameled hallway and the door sealed behind them, Barbara let the holo fade.

"Noooo!" Charlton moaned, spinning back and forth. The light gravity sent him bouncing from one side of the corridor to the other. "I almost had it!"

"Oh, well," Barbara said brightly, tucking her hand through his arm and steadying him. "Well, you can go look for it later. In the meantime, you're due for your physical examination. I'll take you to the medical center."

Lois Ingota's long-lashed eyes crinkled as she put her hand out to grasp Barbara's. "You're Barb! We have, like, thirty messages from you. I'm sorry. There was a live TurnTable right there. It's just so much fun to play!"

"It is," Barbara said, steering them down the corridor toward Dr. Singh's office. "What Crew are you in?"

"Oh, I'm Jazz," Lois said, tossing her close-cropped head. "The others are all Spacepunk. Do you like being up here?"

"I love it. If I spill something I usually have just enough time to catch it before it hits the ground," Barbara said. The others laughed and then started peppering her with questions as they walked. She was glad that they were ones she had already answered a million times. Charlton caught another few cuts of assorted music as they went. Barbara had to keep him from veering off down another corridor in pursuit of faint notes. She had read or seen videos about people becoming addicted to games like M-Tracker but she always had assumed those people had a predisposition or weak will for such things. Psychology wasn't her area of expertise. She did like playing the game, but didn't let it get in the way of more serious fun.

At the door of the medical center, a very petite girl with brown skin and a long dark braid herded Team Solar Wind into the waiting room.

"And you're Daya!" Lois said, looking down on her with delight. "Oh, this is like being in a show! Will we meet Dr. Bright next?"

Daya smiled at them, but she was all business.

"Perhaps later. He has his show to record, but perhaps you can meet him after the welcome ceremony," Daya said. "Who would like to have their exam first?"

Out on the Sea of Tranquility, in the center of the Armstrong City complex, Dion Purchase held onto his younger teammate, trying to keep him from charging at the motley group of visitors bounding around the park. Neil Zimmerman's narrow, pale, freckled face was red inside his bubble-shaped helmet. He fought to get loose from his bigger friend's grip. With a football player's build, Dion easily kept him back.

"Come on, little brother, they're not hurting anything," the African-American youth said over their private channel. "Just go on with the broadcast, okay? We need to get it done stat."

In fact, the twenty or so figures in white EVA suits and helmets looked like they were having a blast, romping up and down the long plexiglass walkway that terminated at a wire-stiffened American flag. All around them, puffs of regolith dust that they had kicked up along the edges of the thick surface gave structure to the laser-projected notes flickering here and there like multicolored fireflies. The suited people bounced after those like cats chasing butterflies in a meadow. Over the in-helmet general frequency, snatches of music rose and fell as though someone was tuning an old-fashioned radio.

"They shouldn't be out there like that," Neil said, unable to concentrate on the script that scrolled up the inside of his faceplate or the presence of the cameraman or the lighting and sound technician. "They're playing that stupid game! They don't even care that they're walking on *history*." He started to bound out toward the crowd, but Dion pulled him back again.

"You play the game, too," Dion said. He kept a firm glove on Neil's shoulder. "You're just as nuts about it as they are. So am I."

"I know! But this is something they ought to respect." Neil lifted his chin in defiance. "That's where Neil Armstrong and Buzz Aldrin stepped out onto the Moon for the first time! Those are their footprints. It's practically sacred land. That's what today's vlog is about! How can I talk about it when these guys are bouncing all over it like it's a gym floor?"

Dion shook his head.

"Look, little bro, the memorial is meant to be walked on. The floor we laid out arches upward to protect everything underneath it, including all the junk as well as the cool stuff. Daya designed it that way. The plastic is unbreakable and virtually unscratchable, especially over Armstrong's first footprint. It was a race to get the site under cover in time, before the shuttles started landing, but we did it, and it's safe forever now. The wall around the lunar laser ranging retroreflector array will keep anyone from bumping into it and moving the mirrors. I don't mind having fun. I'm glad that M-Tracker has gotten going up here! I don't know about you, but I was dying of envy whenever I saw videos over the Internet. I think even the Apollo astronauts would have gotten a kick out of seeing people playing where they landed. Remember, Apollo 14 brought a golf club and balls up here."

"I know! I helped Dr. Bright put glass over them myself in Fra Mauro when we enclosed the laser reflector over there." Neil shot a killing glance toward the crowd. "At least the race won't go that way. If I could get ahold of the person who planted a TurnTable out here, I'd make him polish the glass on his hands and knees! And they're blocking the flag! I wanted it in the shot. We've got to get them off there!"

"They've got a right to play," Paul, the tall, thin cameraman said with a shrug. He hoisted the rig on his shoulder. Ann, the sound and lighting tech, planted the two stalks holding her spot and fill lights and their batteries in the regolith off the edges of the plexiglass. She lifted her chin to signal that she was ready. "Let's get going, okay?"

"No, it's not okay!" Neil said. "Let's get these jokers off." He shook off Dion's hand and bounded toward the crowd. "Hey, all of you! This is a historical monument!"

"You mean a hysterical monument?" a girl's voice said over the general frequency. Dion was too far away to tell who was speaking yet. "It's a rave, baby! Come on! You can dance with me."

A space-suited woman with a shapely figure that won a nod of approval from Dion bounced out of the mob of players toward Neil. She ran a gloved hand over his helmet as if stroking his hair and spun him in a circle.

"Don't be a sourpuss," she said.

"Don't you know what this site is?" Neil asked, raising his voice to be heard over the bursts of music. Dion admired that he was trying to control his temper. "It's where humans first landed on the Moon. It's important!"

"That's cool," said a man with a tuft of wiry black hair sticking out from under the fabric coif inside his helmet. He joined the throng gathering around Neil. "I'm getting awesome tunes off this spot! Maybe the history people are smiling down on us. Or up. Do you think it's up, Cantia?"

The shapely woman laughed.

"We're just hunting tracks, cutie," she said.

"Couldn't you do it somewhere else?" Neil asked, visibly holding onto his temper. "Out of respect?"

"Get lost," another man said. He had a heavy, fleshy face with a pendulous lower lip. He poked Neil in the chest with a gloved forefinger. "You don't get to tell us what to do. We know the rules. You're just another racer."

"Another racer? Don't you know who I am?" Neil asked, breasting up to the man.

"You're a kid! Now, get lost!"

The rest of the group crowded around them as the man shoved Neil in the chest. The push sent the skinny teenager skidding on his backside down the plexiglass walkway. The others gasped. The man looked stunned. Dion figured he really hadn't worked out lunar gravity yet. It had looked pretty spectacular.

"You didn't have to do that!" Neil barked.

He jumped up and stormed back toward his goggling aggressor, who held up both hands as if to ward him off. Dion bounded over to separate them.

"All right, all right," Dion said, in a soothing voice. He put a hand on each of their chests. "This doesn't have to get ugly. Come on, Neil."

He took the boy by one arm and steered him back to his mark at the end of the walkway.

"He pushed me!" Neil yelped.

"He won't do that again," Dion said. "Look at his face! He didn't expect that kind of result."

Neil glanced at the throng. Some of them had gone back to track-hunting, but a few of them started swinging one another in a circle or pushing each other around to see how far they'd fly, accompanied by whoops of joy.

"That does look like fun," he admitted. "I just get so few chances at extravehicular activity that I guess I didn't think about what it was like the first time in low-gee."

Dion grinned. "So, they can become part of your vlog for the day."

"Yeah!" Neil brightened. "Einstein, make a note in my prompts, okay?"

"As you wish, Neil," the PerDee on his wrist said.

"We ought to get on with it," Ann said. "We need to be back inside in an hour for Dr. Bright's broadcast and the opening ceremonies. And, I have to get releases signed by all those people."

"Aw, all right," Neil said. He took his position on the walkway with his back to the flag at the end, and smiled at the camera. Ann turned on the lights and adjusted them so they didn't glare off Neil's helmet. "Testing, one, two, three," Neil continued. Ann held up her thumb to indicate that she was picking up the transmission from his suit microphone. "Hi! This is Neil Zimmerman. I'm live out on the Sea of Tranquility, where the project that Daya Singh and I have been telling you about for the last few weeks has finally been completed." Neil stepped to one side so Paul could focus down the ramp in the direction of the American flag, as if held aloft by an imaginary breeze. "Under this sheet, which measures fifty meters by twenty meters, are the first steps taken by a human being on the lunar surface. That's been here for a while, but we've incorporated interactive points with videos and links to historical footage. Daya designed it, and all of us Bright Sparks built it, so we could protect that moment in history for all time and make it relevant. . . ."

"Wait a minute," a voice interrupted him. "Did you say Bright Sparks?"

Neil glanced around, looking for the speaker.

"I forgot we're on open channel," Dion said.

The others had stopped playing in the regolith. They bounced over the surface to surround Neil, Dion and the crew. Protectively, Dion put himself between the oncoming mob and Neil.

"Sparks?" the heavy-faced man said, his eyes wide with wonder. "Did you say Bright Sparks? Dr. Bright's kids?"

"That right," Dion said, keeping his tone measured. "I'm Dion Purchase."

"Oh, my God, man, that's awesome!" He picked Dion up in his arms and gave him a huge hug, no easy task considering Dion's size. "I've watched you guys since I was a kid!" He let Dion go and grabbed Neil.

"Hey!" Neil squawked, enveloped in the newcomer's arms.

"Sorry, sorry," the man said, setting him down so hard he bounced. "I didn't know you were *that* Neil Zimmerman."

Neil preened. Privately, Dion grinned. "You watch my vlogs?"

"Every day, man! I never miss an entry. What's going on here?" The man peered at the camera and flapped a glove at it. "Hi, Mom!"

"Hey," Dion suggested, knowing an opportunity for goodwill when he saw it. "Maybe you should interview them, Neil."

"Oh, yeah!" the shapely woman said, shooting an approving and appraising look at Dion. "How about it? I didn't know who you were. I'm so sorry. I'd love to be interviewed!"

Neil cleared his throat and turned toward Paul's lens.

"So, I'm out here in the Apollo 11 Memorial Park in the center point of the Armstrong City complex." He pointed to the sky, and the lens tilted upward. "As you see, it's open to the vacuum of space, but down here is the monument to the first moments when two human beings walked on a new world for the very first time. Now, with the Moon buggy race about to start, we've, uh, we have a whole lot of new people coming to appreciate this historic place. What's your name?"

"Nev DeLeon."

"Stephan Zhe."

"Cantia Frerent," the woman said, with a sideways glance toward Dion.

"Teddy Davis," said the young man with the tuft of black hair. He had a gentle drawl. To Dion's eyes, Teddy looked about the same age as Neil, but was probably a few years older. "This is the absolute best! I read about Armstrong and Aldrin in school. I didn't mean to show disrespect. We're Team PolymerAce. We'll be racing for the prize!"

"Of course you are! So are we. What makes you think *you* have a chance?" Neil questioned each one like a crime reporter investigating at the scene, and did a pretty good job, Dion thought. He could tell that the younger Spark was determined to get some interesting quotes from them, but equally eager to get them off his patch so the crew could take the long shots that they had lined up. Dion stood back, letting Neil handle the interviews. He could tell by the way Teddy talked that he commented frequently on the Sparks' online site, but he wasn't sure he could match the youth to any of the handles he had seen.

Neil got a few good quotes from each one, then tied it all up like a pro. ". . . Well, I'm going to be following you all via BrightSat, my EMdrive mobile satellites, and broadcasting live to everyone on Earth. So you'd better get back in there and get ready."

Another hologram, this one of four men and women in black jumpsuits trimmed with gold, rose from Dion's sleeve-mounted PerDee.

"Looks like you get your wish, little brother," he said, pushing the images so they appeared on Neil's device, too. The faces were the ones right in front of them. "Dr. Singh wants Team PolymerAce inside pronto. Time for their physicals."

"Hey!" Teddy protested. "I want to stay and watch the Sparks do the rest of their broadcast!"

"C'mon," Cantia said, with a grin, taking Teddy's arm. "We should have done it yesterday. Thank you, Neil. It's been a slice."

"Yeah!" Nev said, still staring at Paul and the camera. "That was great! Could I get an autograph or a selfie?"

"Later. We have to work, for a change."

Smiling, Cantia herded her teammates off the plexiglass. Neil relaxed visibly.

"Great!" he said. "We can finish this right."

"Sure can," Dion said, smiling down at his young colleague. "Then you need to get your butt down to the gym. I've reprogrammed the centrifuge just for us."

Neil's momentary look of triumph turned to despair.

"No, Dion! I did my exercises yesterday! Why?"

Dion shook his head and dragged his small colleague out onto the plexiglass walkway, planted him on his mark, and turned both of them to face the camera. Paul and Ann immediately began recording the long shots and tracking footage they wanted to fill in around Neil's narration.

"We need the edge," Dion explained. "All these people have their Earth muscles. They've got an advantage we lack. We exercise in the centrifuge and on the treadmill twice a week just to keep from losing tone and bone mass, but it's not the same. Remember how Barb was when she first got here? She could lift me over her head. Now, she's still strong, but it won't be long before she's just like the rest of us. These visitors from Earth have more stamina as well as strength."

"We don't need strength," Neil said, drawing his brows down over his nose. "We've designed the devices to work with us the way we are! Besides, Daya and I aren't going out on the race track."

Dion shook his head.

"Tech is smart, but what happens when tech fails? We've been there too many times." He saw the expression on Neil's face change as he remembered. The younger Spark hadn't been out on the far side with them when he and the other three older Sparks had been stuck during a coronal mass ejection, but he'd been back in Armstrong, where things got a whole different kind of hairy. Paul shot Dion a thumbs-up. Dion nodded. "Come on, little bro."

"I still think mind is better than matter," Neil said.

"You try using mind control to change a tire," Dion said, taking him by the shoulder and bounding with him toward the airlock that led back toward Sparks Central. "When you make that happen, I'll believe."

Chapter Two

Dr. Keegan Bright beckoned Cisca Small to follow him through the crowd toward the front of the hangar. He was a medium-sized man in a plain khaki-colored jumpsuit, but when people noticed his shock of blond hair, blue eyes, muscular shoulders and jutting chin, they stared, grins breaking out on their faces. They all knew him. He'd been a video star for a couple of decades, a pilot, an astronaut, an athlete, an inventor and a teacher. His daily science program was a staple of STEM education worldwide. Most children had watched his show while growing up. A large number of them still watched it as adults.

"I envy these kids," Cisca said. A brown-haired woman with dark, curling hair, freckles, warm brown eyes and an infectious smile, and standing two centimeters taller than he did, Cisca had been one of his earliest students. Keegan regarded her with affection. It seemed like only yesterday she'd graduated from the Bright Sparks program and started her own computer game company. He had known she could go far with her grasp of programming and artistic talents, and here she was. "I mean, when we did six weeks up here, it was a lot more primitive than it is now. How many people live here?"

"About three thousand permanent residents. At any given time, though, there can be almost seven thousand people moving in and out of here," Keegan said, pitching his voice to be heard over the hubbub. He naturally fell into lecture mode. "Now, with the race we are nearly twice that, and our infrastructure can't handle it long-term.

We're pushing the life-support facilities to the max just to accommodate the guests, but it's worth it. There's redundancy on redundancy."

"I know that's the way you like it," Cisca said.

"It's the best way," Keegan said. "What did I always tell you and your bunch? The more backups we have, the more certain we can be of recovering in case of an emergency. This is also a good trial run when we start to expand Armstrong City and open up colonization to the other planned settlements. Ms. Reynolds-Ward has been fielding interests from other countries and corporations willing to sponsor development. There's a Chinese settlement starting up in the southern hemisphere right this minute. We could have eight more cities up here in the next twenty years. The mining project I told you about is just one of the joint efforts to help bring in funding. And you're helping a whole lot by expanding M-Tracker up here."

"Out of the pure altruism in my heart, Dr. Bright." Cisca laughed, her voice a musical ripple. "I'm just doing what I love, and making money off of it the way you always taught us to. Your input's been amazing. It's made the game more interesting on Earth, too. I see it expanding clear around the Moon, too, and Mars one day."

Keegan shook his head. "The biggest problem here on the Moon is that there is no network infrastructure yet. On Earth, pretty much the entire planet is connected. Even in the most distant archipelago, you can get a connection through satellites. Here, we don't have global coverage."

"Yes, that is a wrinkle," Cisca said, narrowing an eye. "What do you suggest? Satellites?"

"Some, yes, but perhaps more advanced tech. I have some ideas I'll send you that we can discuss further once the race is over. I'm not the only one with ideas. Leona, in fact, would like to create a twin sister that is a siren and have her placed out in the middle of nowhere in order to attract attention, as a tourist spot to create a new location for economic growth."

"A siren? Hmmm . . . sounds intriguing."

"Yes, I thought so too. And I *still* don't know how Leona had the original thought. That is a step in passing the Turing test, you know."

"You think she might be true AI?" Cisca asked, with growing enthusiasm. She glanced at Keegan's PerDee.

"I don't know yet." Keegan shrugged. "Getting there, perhaps. I just don't know. She's got a planet's worth of memory to bump around in. I've got to run her through some more tests."

A stocky, blonde woman with a camera rig on her shoulder backed toward them through the crowd. Beside her, their secondary sound technician, Abi Khalem, helped steer Yvonne Walotski away from bumping into anyone, while picking up wild sound. The shielded microphone slung over the slim, short man's shoulder looked like a fur-covered cucumber. In their wake came Jackie Feeney, the producer of Keegan's show *Live from the Moon*, speaking low into a head mic and monitoring her floating PDE as she pointed out shots she wanted the crew to take. She spotted Keegan and came over.

"Hey, Jackie, you remember Cisca?" Keegan said, gesturing toward his guest.

The producer's honey-colored eyes widened with pleasure as she recognized the newcomer. She grasped Cisca's hand.

"I sure do! How have you been doing?"

"Great! I see that M-Tracker has taken off like mad!"

"You don't know the half of it," Jackie said, with a grin, resettling her headset in her thick, dark, wavy hair. "I can hardly get my crew's attention half the time because they're off chasing some exotic piece of music that you released. That's some clever design. TurnTables are popping up all over the place. How do you program where they end up?"

Cisca glanced toward Keegan. He shot her a cautious look. He knew how the combination battle arena/supply centers got where they were, but a trade secret like that wasn't something to share with so many ears and recording devices close by.

"It's part of the fun," Cisca said, very casually. "But we're proud to be one of the sponsors of the race. We hope that M-Tracker fans will pick a favorite team to root for. We're running sweepstakes on our sites and in the app for special tracks to celebrate the Great Moon Race."

Jackie had been in the entertainment business long enough to take a hint. She nodded.

"Can we record you saying that?" she asked, gesturing to Yvonne.

"Yes!" Keegan said. He drew Cisca so she stood beside him facing the camera. Abi attached a small microphone stud to her jumpsuit lapel. He waited for Jackie's nod, and started asking Cisca about her company's game, her involvement with the race, and her time as a Bright Spark. He currently served on the advisory board of the M-Tracker, so he knew plenty more than the general public did, including up-and-coming features that were bound to draw in millions more players than it already had.

While most of his attention was on the interview, Keegan was keeping half an eye on the proceedings going on around him. Twenty-six teams and their vehicles had arrived over the last couple of weeks. As far as he knew, that was the whole bundle. Not that he was disappointed; the turnout proved to be bigger by half than he, the mayor and Ms. Reynolds-Ward had hoped. Each team of four drivers had come with a minimum of half a dozen support staff, engineers, health professionals and representatives of their sponsors. Fans had managed to grab the last few remaining seats on every shuttle and were wandering around, taking selfies and issuing citizen-journalist blogs, videos and vlogs onto the net. If anything was going to help normalize the idea of living on the Moon, this was it. A hundred engineers were finishing up the final touches to get the vehicles space- and roadworthy. Keegan and some trusted colleagues both there on the Moon and back on Earth had been reviewing the designs all along. They'd rejected a lot of hopefuls, winnowing down the entries from a few thousand. These last couple dozen were the successful applicants, who had displayed sound engineering and multiple redundancy on the safety features. A million things could go wrong, racing across a void in the cold vacuum of space, limited gravity, and widely diverging temperatures between lunar day and night, but everyone was taking the difficulty seriously. Like NASA, no one wanted their part of the design to fail first.

"Well, let's take a look at some of the entrants," Keegan said. "We've got some video from our camera operators plus our dedicated vlogger, Neil Zimmerman. You want to take a look and give us your input, Cisca?"

"I'd be delighted, Dr. Bright," the programmer said, smiling. At Keegan's nod, Jackie sent her tablet floating in front of them, displaying a three-dee slide show of the entrants. "Wow, look at that!"

"That's *Jade Dragon*," Keegan said, as the rendering of the enormous, light green vehicle turned over to show every angle of its three sets of paired wheels. "They're using passive solar collectors built into all the upper surfaces of the buggy to feed that massive drive system underneath the living quarters. They could do over two hundred kilometers per hour on Earth. Look at that front spoiler."

Cisca shook her head. "Doesn't look like a winner to me. Those tires look too small to go through the regolith. They'll end up plowing instead of driving." The image changed to a brilliant blue vehicle with treaded tires four meters in diameter. "That one looks just like a twentieth-century dune buggy!"

"That's Team Amazonia," Keegan said. "You're a year too young to remember Aldonis Maranha, but he runs an energy company that he started while he was in the Bright Sparks program."

Cisca grinned. "I guess a lot of us got our businesses going while you mentored us, Doc."

Jackie made a "wind it up" gesture with her forefinger. Keegan took the hint and turned back to the camera.

"All these teams come with a fantastic array of ingenuity. Their vehicles are plenty different. We put as few requirements on the designers as possible. They have to be self-sufficient as far as life support, and that includes living arrangements, plus food storage and preparation, bunks, sanitation, and air purification. They must be ground-based. No flyers or rockets permitted. And they have to keep in mind that if they're using solar energy, that part of the race will take place during the dark phase with neither sunlight nor earthlight.

"As for the racers, we put a few more requirements on them," Keegan continued, with a grin. "They have to be human. Not mechanicals. We had one group contact us who wanted to do the whole race with android avatars controlling their buggy from Earth. Uh-uh. Sorry, you literally have to have skin in the game. Each team consists of four people, all of legal age—which is eighteen up here— and healthy enough to withstand the rigors of the race. Now, I want to be clear: Healthy doesn't mean what you might think of as 'able-bodied.' We've got one team consisting entirely of bike racers who competed in the Paralympics last year, and do not underestimate them. They're awesome."

"I came up in the shuttle with Team Podracer," Cisca added, with a nod. "My company is one of their sponsors."

"Dr. Bright, we have some footage of Team Podracer in training," Jackie said. "Let's take a look at that now."

Keegan held out his sleeve, so that Cisca could watch the video on Leona. His PerDee's handheld unit was more of a remote connection to Leona's entirety. While she was fully functional on the handheld alone, she was, as Keegan was finding out of late, much "more" when she was connected to the larger supercomputer and quantum processor blades at his laboratory. He still wasn't certain how much "more" she was. Her experimental program that he had turned loose in the mainframe was developing on its own, with only occasional input from him. Leona was turning out to be something new, but he didn't want to talk about that on a worldwide broadcast.

"Leona, open up the video of the team training on Earth's lunarscape in Nevada," he told the PerDee. Team Podracer's test vehicle hammered over terrain much like the dunes and craters outside Armstrong City, except for the brilliant blue sky. It recovered from hard bounces and slides down sandy slopes with split-second timing that elicited "oohs" from Cisca.

He admired the Paralympians getting involved in this race. They might even have an advantage that the others didn't, since they were used to fighting their environment to get around. He had noticed in the beginning that a couple of them had a kind of chip on their shoulders about it when he talked with them about their application, treating "able-bodied" almost as an insult. After a few exchanges, he had made it clear that he didn't care how many functional limbs a person had, as long as their heart and neurological functions could stand the environment. They had to sit through the rad-monitor and suit-check lecture the same as everyone else, and it turned out that they were enjoying the light gravity just as much as the other teams. Once they'd oriented a little, they turned out to be delightful, brainy, motivated kids, just like the others.

Keegan narrated the video as they watched the cyclists, three women and one man, climb in and out of the mockup of their buggy's cabin.

"Those developed shoulder and arm muscles are going to be a real advantage up here," he said.

"I understand you're going to be checking out the relief stations on the racecourse," Cisca said.

"That's right," Keegan said, tickled at how neatly Cisca took over the role of interviewer from him. He tapped Leona, who threw up a gigantic hologram of the Moon between them. The sphere rotated slowly for the camera. On the gray, pockmarked surface, a curving red line appeared, studded with blue circles. "The race begins a couple of days from now. The judges and I are going to be doing a final flyover to make sure emergency repair and hospital facilities are in place, then I'll be back for the starting gun."

"Will you be providing coverage all the way through?"

"Well, no, not me. I've got a project that has been scheduled since before the race was announced. I'm going out with a team to a mining site out in this area," Keegan said, pointing to a cluster of craters not far off the track a little shy of halfway around the lunar globe. "But you bet that I'm going to watch all the updates. This is going to be as exciting as it gets."

"And . . . cut it there, guys!" Jackie said. She came over to Keegan and Cisca. "That's all the live color we need for now until the opening ceremonies. I've got zillions of images and short videos from Neil. That camera app of his is getting a workout. And one of his drones almost came down on the mayor's head a little while ago. But it's all great stuff! I'm funneling it all through the LFTM website. I'd love to have you back in a while for more commentary, Cisca."

"Great!" Cisca said. She leaned over and kissed Keegan on the cheek. "I have to get back and check on the TurnTables. We've got a few more going in this afternoon."

"Have you found anything yet?" Gary's voice interrupted the new playlist resounding in Barbara's helmet. He sounded to her as though he was right beside her, when he was out of sight a hundred meters or more away.

"Stop the music, Fido," Barbara said. Her favorite playlist died away at once. She straightened up as best she could in the low area. "I'm still looking, Gary. Are you sure what you're looking for is in here?"

"Something's got to be in either your pile, my pile, or out beyond that first crater ridge," he assured her. "I mean, the lists of what people have stowed isn't too organized, but it's usually reasonably accurate."

She held the heavy tarp up over her head as if she was in a tent and scanned the pieces of equipment and cases lying on expanses of clean-swept lunar rock, the settlement's cold storage. The flashlight on the suit helmet above her forehead lit up the mounds and drifts of spare parts. It looked like the back room of Santa's workshop, except the snow was gray.

Tarps like this lay all over the lunar landscape, a few meters up to several kilometers from the Armstrong City complex. The ones closest to the spaceport were covered in layers of regolith dust, anywhere from a few centimeters to a couple of meters deep, but the rest usually had only light dust from the heat/cooling cycle of the Moon stirring it up. Anything that wouldn't be needed for a while, or was too valuable or too much trouble to recycle or repurpose, and that could tolerate the temperature swings from near zero during the long lunar nights to really hot during the long lunar days, ended up out here. Barbara, who had grown up on a farm, was used to seeing outdated or broken machinery that got parked out behind a barn or in a storage shed and hauled out to be harvested for parts to fix a different piece of equipment. She found it fascinating what people kept out there, anywhere from complete computer mainframes down to boxes of paperback books in sealed plastic bags. Dr. Bright assured her that if allowed to warm up, the books would almost certainly hold together, depending on the type of glue used in the binding and the quality of the paper. The list for this collection area said it included office furniture, bunk frames and refrigeration units, but it looked like leftovers from a water treatment plant instead.

It felt pretty late to be scrounging more pieces of equipment for the *Spark Xpress*, but Gary had assured her that they only needed last-minute additions.

The design phase had been a lot of fun to begin with. They were all excited about building a buggy that could win a race against all the other teams. Dion, the most senior Spark and resident mother hen, could drive any vehicle, so he was designated as chief pilot for the racer. He and Jan, a natural tinkerer and engineering student who was Barbara's bunkmate, had started drawing their wish-list components in the air, where they were rendered into visual designs by the three-dimensional laser projector emitters on their PDEs. Gary, a genius at fabrication and Neil, who had a knack for visualizing things in three dimensions in his head, started putting in their two cents, changing the design to reflect *their* visions. The four of them had thrown together the plans for a cross between a monster truck and a Conestoga wagon before Barbara and Daya Singh, a budding physician, called for common sense. Barbara knew that Dr. Bright watched over them from the get-go, but never interfered except to let them know that he could find them sponsorship funding for up to two million dollars credit. Anything above that, they were on their own. The truth was, that amount was a drop in the bucket for any prototype manufactured by a corporation, but the Sparks were expected to be capable of working miracles with limited resources.

Within a few hours, they had a practicable design. The Nerd-Twins had set to work creating the initial chassis, and called for several components to be made to order for the buggy. With the race only months away, there wasn't enough time for all of them to be ordered from Earth. Custom components were usually not a problem for the Sparks, but they had never built something so large in such a short amount of time. Teams on Earth had the advantage of being able to drive to a vendor for parts or have them shipped overnight. On the Moon, if it couldn't be three-dimensionally printed or scrounged it just wasn't available for many months. Within a day or two, Gary and Jan had realized that they would fall behind schedule in no time. There was no way they were going to finish a design like the one they had all come up with in the time and budget available. They had to throw the original design into the pipedream file and start over.

That was when Barbara's years on the family farm had truly paid off. She knew if she put practical limitations on the team, they would find a way to make their dreams work anyhow. She made them sit down and write out the *actual* needs and requirements the vehicle had to meet. They spent hours creating what she had called the requirements lists.

In its final form, the "mission requirements" list contained eleven items. Their buggy had to:

1. Circumnavigate the Moon,
2. House four human occupants for the duration,
3. Be pressurized to one atmosphere,

4. Maintain comfortable temperature range between
   nineteen and twenty-five degrees Celsius,
5. Be large enough to house all supplies needed
   for the duration of the mission,
6. Have communications with BrightSats and
   other communication systems available,
7. Be capable of motivating as fast as possible
   while being safe for occupants,
8. Be capable of traversing difficult terrain
   (boulders, cracks, loose soil, hills, etc.),
9. Have a radiation safe zone (perhaps under
   water and batteries),
10. Have safe egress and ingress capabilities
    (pressure doors and hatches),
11. Carry spares for irreplaceable parts.

From those requirements, Barbara told the Sparks, they would derive the engineering details. And they did.

That was where the engineering stopped and the scrounging started. They needed a compartment at least two meters high and three or four meters in length and width at a minimum. As he was the closest to two meters in height himself, Dion had actually asked that they look for something slightly bigger that would allow for more head room. It wasn't easy, until Dr. Bright had sent them to the outskirts of town to repair Lunar Weather Station One Hundred Seventeen. Here they found some of the Armstrong City's original shelter tubes which had lain unused for decades. The tubes were corrugated aluminum covered with degraded multi-layered insulation blankets. A few damaged solar panels still hung from them. They were roughly two-and-a-third meters tall, cylindrical, and about four meters long, perfect for the main cabin of their racer. They even had an air-sealed door on one end. Barbara had since wondered if it was purely luck that Dr. Bright had needed them to fix the sensors out there or if he had known about the tubes all along. At least, it seemed serendipitously lucky that it had been Weather Station One Hundred Seventeen that needed repair, and not any of the other four hundred or so of them spread out on the Moon.

The team had chosen the habitat tube with the least damage and trucked it back to the Sparks' hangar. Gary and Jan had then gone right to work. It took the better part of two weeks to strip it down and repair it, but it would have taken a lot longer to build something from scratch or order something from Earth, and their budget would have gone straight out of the airlock. After that, the Nerd-Twins threw the other four Sparks out of their workshop, only surfacing to ask for a component to be manufactured or found, as now. They insisted that they could work faster without the others underfoot. Barbara chafed at being locked out, but she understood their process.

"I'm not finding anything like you described," Barbara said, pulling up one tarp after another. "Are you sure there are any seat frames in this section? This is mostly like pressurized tanks, plumbing, and electrical conduit."

"Tanks?" Gary's voice sounded excited. "How wide are the tanks? Anything around a meter wide?"

"Um, yes?" Barbara said, turning back toward an oblong bubble she had noticed on the way in. "That blue one. I'd say it's a meter across, and about three long. Fido, send him a picture."

"Yes, Barbara," the PerDee said. "I have sent a high-definition image."

"That'll be perfect!" Gary crowed. "Stay there. I'm coming over. I can see you on Turing's GPS."

"You haven't told me what it's for," Barbara said.

"This is for the seats! I can make these into swivel chairs. If I cut that in half on the diagonal, I can shape the parts into bucket seats and pad them with lightweight expanding spray foam and then cover them with some sort of fabric or neoprene. I'll figure that part out later. What you found was made on Earth and meant to be self-supporting, so they're stronger than metal I can shape here in lower gravity. Half the work is already done for me. There you are!"

Barbara jumped as Gary's shadow fell across her. She looked up as he bounded toward her, his helmet hitting the tarp with every step. Barbara grinned.

"I still have to get used to not hearing anyone coming up on me."

"Sorry," he said, his long face contrite. He shook his head to get his fall of shining black hair out of his eyes. "Show me the tank."

She led him over to the heap of equipment. Together, they moved a couple of desk frames, a double bunk bed, and a plastic saucer sled off the hot dog–shaped container. Gary crowed with glee, and used Turing to measure the precise specifications.

"Yeah! This will work great. Can you help me get it back to the workshop?"

"I wish you'd let the rest of us see what you're doing," Barbara complained, as she hoisted one end of the tank. In spite of the insulated gloves she wore, she could still feel the tang of cold in her fingertips. The metal tank had been under the tarp for no telling how long and had cooled to below minus one hundred fifty degrees Celsius. Touching it without the right type of gloves on could instantly cause frostbite to the level of losing fingers. Barbara shook her head. The simplest tasks on the Moon that most people would never have to worry about were the most dangerous. Her EVA suit's gloves were designed to work in space and could protect her fingers from its hazards. She shifted so the bulk rested on her palms. "You keep hiding parts of the buggy whenever we go into Sparks Central! Dion and I are going to be helping to drive the *Spark Xpress*, and we all have a stake in winning this race!"

Gary sounded sheepish. He glanced back at her over his shoulder.

"Jan and I want to surprise you and Dr. Bright. And the fewer people who know what's going into our design, the better."

"We're not going to tell anyone," Barbara said, feeling hurt.

Gary's sensitive face creased.

"I never thought you would, but design specs are leaking out all over the net. I'm even wondering if someone is bugging our PerDees."

"How could they do that?" Barbara asked. "Dr. Bright would know if there's a tap on our signals." She was horrified to think someone might have access to the complex memory banks of the microcomputers. All of the PerDees contained extremely sensitive proprietary and personal information. Some of the blueprints and designs could be worth millions of dollars, maybe much more, in the right hands. Dr. Bright could get into a lot of hot water from his investors if that information were stolen. So could they.

"I'm not sure," Gary said, shaking his head. "I'm pretty certain I saw logins during times none of us was accessing the data."

"No way!" The thought made a cold lump of fear congeal in

Barbara's belly. "If that's true, we need to tell Dr. Bright and have someone check the system."

"I don't know who to trust in such a situation."

"You can trust Dr. Bright."

"Maybe. I don't know!"

"Well, *I* still need to know how the build is going."

Gary opened his mouth to answer.

"Hey, you two! C'mon back!" Jan's voice reached them. Barbara looked up.

"What's going on, nerd?" Gary asked. "Barb found just what we need for the drivers' seats. We have to take it back and cut it."

"It can wait! The opening ceremonies are about to start!"

"Can you meet us at door fifteen with a hoverdolly?" Gary pleaded. "We can be there in a couple of minutes."

"Yes, but hustle! I want to put on a clean jumpsuit for the event."

"On our way," Barbara said. She hoisted the tank and pushed aside her concerns. "Let's get going. I want to see it all!"

Chapter Three

Even with the buggies and equipment pushed back to the far wall, the vast Armstrong City hangar had become even more crowded. Everyone wanted to see the festivities close up, not on scopes or screens. Bloggers and reporters sat or stood on either side of the dais, already talking or tapping in on their screens, giving a play-by-play to all the billions of people back on Earth. Noise rose to the ceiling. Music coming from the M-Tracker TurnTables added to the din.

Dr. Keegan Bright squeezed through the crowd, making way for Cisca to join him up beside the platform. Everyone was so excited and distracted, he had to nudge people aside from time to time in order to get past them. He hadn't seen a crowd this big since he had moved to the Moon. As gregarious a person as he was, he still felt a little claustrophobic.

"This is huge!" Cisca said. "A little basic, though."

"It's not pretty, but it's the only place in Armstrong City big enough for the announcement," he said. The mayor had already arrived, and was chatting with a couple of reporters from Australia's news media. Ms. Reynolds-Ward wasn't there yet, but her aide, Percy Sheldon, stood next to the steps. When he saw Keegan, he gave him a preoccupied, pursed-lip smile. A few of the sponsors, from JSA, the National Science Foundation, and a superconductor company, chatted to one another behind the dais.

"Impressive!" Cisca said, glancing around. "Everyone's dressed in their team colors. This is going to make great television."

Automatically, Keegan scanned the crowd for Jackie and the crew. Jackie must have read his mind, because she waved to him from the front row, where she had a view of the action and of her camera operators. Yvonne and Paul had staked out opposite corners of the stage. Neil ranged back and forth with his PerDee, taking videos and still shots. Keegan hadn't spotted the other Sparks yet. They had voted to wear purple jumpsuits, or "ultraviolet," as Gary put it. Officially, they weren't supposed to represent *Live from the Moon*, but there was no real way for them to separate themselves from the Bright Sparks program. He had given them no help on their design or financing other than pointing them toward potential sponsors and letting them use the lab and equipment to build their racer. Regular watchers would understand. These kids took complete ownership of their work and did what they had to do. He had been keeping a quiet eye through an app on their PerDees to make sure they hadn't run into trouble on anything. Apart from a couple of minor hiccups, they didn't really need him. There were a couple of things he wouldn't have done in the design, but chances were good that they'd be no problem. That was, if they finished building it on time.

A loud tap coming from the hall speakers raised a loud cheer from the crowd. Ms. Reynolds-Ward entered the room, her hand hooked through her husband's elbow. She waved to the onlookers as she walked up the steps of the stage. A slim woman in her fifties with a long, narrow face and curly salt-and-pepper hair, she had a conspiratorial kind of smile that suggested that you and she understood the same things. Keegan gestured to the visitors and dignitaries to mount the stage with him. He made his way to the hovering microphone drone at the center of the dais and held up both his hands.

"Hey, everybody!" he called. "This is about as Live from the Moon as it gets!"

No one paid attention. The noise in the vast chamber threatened to swamp his voice. Keegan glanced toward Cisca and drew his finger across his throat. She brought a fingertip down on her own PerDee. The TurnTables immediately went silent, to the shock of the M-Tracker players. Most of them glanced toward the stage and sheepishly put their various smart devices away.

Keegan grinned. It was good to have friends in the right places.

"Hey, I want to welcome everybody to the Moon!" The crowd cheered loudly. "I'm Dr. Keegan Bright. Most of y'all have seen me on my show, *Live from the Moon*. All of us who live up here are working toward making life on other planets accessible to human beings. It's a lot of work. Some of it's dangerous. That's one hostile environment out there. We're evolved on a nice, temperate planet with breathable atmosphere, normal gravity, liquid water and livable temperatures.

"But you all know we humans are capable of much more! We set out across oceans without knowing what was on the other side. We dug down into the planet to see what's there. We set out from Earth in little capsules mounted on the top of rockets full of high explosives, and look at us today! We have established a foothold on another world, and it's growing in size every single day. But it isn't all hard work and no fun. We are here to have fun, right?" The crowd bellowed its approval. "This race is going to be fun, right?" The cheers got even louder. Again, he smiled and waited for the crowd to settle. "Welcome to the first ever, hopefully not the last, Great Moon Buggy Race!"

The crowd went more than wild at that, yelling, dancing, and singing. Finally, Keegan held up a hand, signaling them to quiet down.

"According to my algorithms, this created great video," Leona said to him through the wirelessly connected ear patch he wore just behind his left ear. Keegan nodded.

"Now, the teams that are assembled here," he gestured toward the audience, and heard Jackie order Paul to turn his camera onto the crowd, "are pioneers of a new kind. Every single group has designed *and built* a race car, a Moon buggy, capable of circumnavigating this hostile little globe, and conquering it in a way that none of our astronauts have yet done. I've taken a look at the plans for each of your buggies and, let me tell you: they're brilliant, and every one of them is as different as can be.

"I can't tell you how much I'm looking forward to seeing how you all do on this race. I'm proud of you all. I'll be back in four days to start you all off, and I'll be proud to stand at the finish line and see the winners come in. In the meantime, please allow me to introduce Armstrong City's patron and founder, Ms. Adrienne Reynolds-Ward."

Keegan gestured her forward. The drone microphone automatically lowered itself so it was a few centimeters from the tall woman's mouth. Ms. Reynolds-Ward beamed.

"Welcome, everyone! I'm so proud to have such an amazing turnout today! I'll be honest: When we announced this race on Dr. Bright's show six months ago, I thought we'd have about five buggies, if that. I'm absolutely amazed to see more than twenty teams here. This is going to be so exciting. As Dr. Bright said, I'll be waving the starter's flag in four days . . ." She glanced at the wall chronometer. "Forty-six hours from now. We have some wonderful prizes for the entrants and winners. Each of our entrants will be given a 'goody box' full of packages, gifts, and prizes from the race's many sponsors. For the winners that get on the podium, there is even more!

"For third place, our bronze medal winners will receive two hundred thousand dollars, a week-long VIP-status stay free at the Armstrong City Hotel and Casino that includes round trip fare from Earth, plus a guest appearance on *Live from the Moon with Dr. Bright*. Our silver medalists will receive three hundred thousand dollars, two weeks VIP status at the hotel and fare plus a guest appearance on *Live from the Moon with Dr. Bright* and entry fees for the next year's race waived. And finally, our gold medal winners will receive a full month at the hotel with VIP and concierge status, a guest appearance on the show, entry fees waived the next year, and one million dollars cash!"

The crowd broke into cheers. Ms. Reynolds-Ward held up her hand.

"But really, my friends, what could be a better prize than to be the first winners of a race around the Moon?"

The applause and shouting rose until it filled the hangar. Keegan beamed. The founder grinned back.

"For those of you who don't know much about Armstrong City, I organized the funding that put it together with a brain trust chosen from the finest engineers and social scientists in the world. Looking around at what we have now," she sent her eyes around the high-ceilinged space, "you can't believe how primitive and Spartan it all was when it started. We had a few space-built habitats and one single generator in the beginning. Now look how amazing it is! And you can be a part of its future. We're starting off now, with a contest that takes all the innovation that young, motivated minds can bring to it. . . ."

As she unspooled the city's history, Keegan felt a thrill of pride. He had come up several times during the planning and construction stages, and consulted on pulling the habitat together, but the driving force had been all hers. He let his eye drift over the crowd. More of his former students than Cisca were present, some as drivers and some as support staff, even a few in the press corps. Every time Ms. Reynolds-Ward said something complimentary about them, a lot of the team members high-fived or hip-bumped one another. Off on the right side of the stage, he spotted the current Sparks standing in a cluster.

They were dressed in their new purple jumpsuits, all right, but instead of being pumped by the speeches and the excitement of the coming race, they looked upset. Well, five of them looked upset, and Barbara Winton looked confused.

He followed Neil Zimmerman's pointed glare to a team dressed in chocolate brown a short distance away.

Then he saw her: a slender young woman with long, straight, black hair that hung to her shoulders. She wasn't cheering or smiling like the others in her team, but then, she hardly ever did smile. Dr. Bright was pretty certain that the girl was born with a serious look on her face and had come out telling the doctors a more efficient way to handle her delivery.

Pam.

Pam Yamashita. One of his most difficult Sparks—some might even say one of his few failures in all the years he had been running the Bright Sparks program. He felt like slapping himself in the forehead. He had seen the name go by on the manifest from SolStar as a member of their driving team. He knew she was coming, so why did it feel such a shock to see her there in the flesh? He felt a little discomfort, but for her sake, not his. She was one of the few people not cheering, but then, she'd never been very demonstrative. He needed to make a point to see her. After all, she was a Bright Spark, even if it was for only a year or so. And even if she hadn't gotten along with the team that well.

The founder beckoned to the air, and a massive hologram of the Moon rose behind her, filling the entire ceiling of the hangar. People let out gasps of wonder. As it turned, Ms. Reynolds-Ward used a handheld laser pointer to display the racecourse, narrating the names of the pitstops and emergency evacuation points. Most well-known lunar sights, including the fully finished and operational Aldrinville radio telescope, rolled by, to the cheers of the audience.

She outlined the race's rules, which Keegan could recite by heart. "For safety, all buggies are required to a minimum of two teams of two, spelling each other, two of you sleep while two drive/navigate. Life-support systems have minimum standards you need to fulfill— and we will check!—but beyond that, the sky is the limit, so to speak. In fact, the sky *is* the limit. The vehicles are not allowed to fly. They can go airborne over jumps and such, but you cannot maintain powered flight of any sort." She ended with a slide show of some of the vehicles that had been entered, although neither SolStar's or the *Spark Xpress* were included.

Keegan smiled inwardly to himself. He had expected the Sparks to keep their cards close to their vests as he had taught them, and he shouldn't have expected anything less from Pam. Maybe she wasn't his "failure." Maybe she was just a success of a different sort. Keegan kept telling himself that one day he'd actually believe it.

"Now, let me introduce the mayor of Armstrong City!" Ms. Reynolds-Ward turned the podium over to Mayor Jaime Petronillo. Also fiftyish, with a prosperously plump figure and a brilliant smile in a broad face, he looked like the absolute cliché of a politician, but underneath it, he was a hardworking man who loved his job, was great with people, and never stopped telling Keegan that he felt like the luckiest man alive.

"Hello, my friends!" Petronillo said, holding out his arms to embrace the whole assembly. "So, how are you today?" The crowd screamed back at him. Their excitement had built about as high as it could go. "Wonderful!"

Keegan tuned him out, watching the Sparks.

"Leona," he whispered, "monitor their conversation. I want to know if it gets too hot over there."

"Yes, Dr. Bright," the PerDee's AI voice said in his earpiece.

". . . And I will be at the starting line with our esteemed founder and Dr. Bright. See you back here in . . ." Petronillo checked his smartphone. ". . . ninety-five hours and thirty minutes! Good luck, and may the best team win!" The mayor threw up his hands. The crowd cheered. Almost the whole crowd.

As the groups around them scattered back to their vehicles to get them tuned up and ready for the beginning of the race, Barbara looked at her colleagues with dismay. Dion's hunched posture told her that the normally easygoing youth was on the defensive. Neil looked as if he was about to breathe fire.

"What's bothering you, roomie?" she asked Jan in an undertone. All of them were wearing their earpieces so they could hear one another over the crowd.

"Her," Jan said, lifting her chin toward the team in brown, who had also remained standing in place when the crowd dispersed.

Barbara glanced over at the visitors, two men and two women wearing the logo from SolStar. She studied their faces. It took a moment, but the oval face and high cheekbones of the shorter woman struck a match in her memory.

"Oh," she murmured, in surprise. "That's Pam."

The other five Sparks seemed to shudder. As if she heard her name, Pam walked over to them.

"Aren't you going to say hello?" she asked. "It has been a while, friends."

"Hello," Jan said, in the flattest voice Barbara had ever heard her use.

Pam's face was almost expressionless. Barbara wondered if the word "friends" had been a commonplace greeting for her, or if she was being ironic. What had passed between them had obviously rubbed her friends the wrong way, but Barbara didn't know why or how.

Pam Yamashita had been the last Bright Spark to leave the program before Barbara joined it. She hadn't been part of the group for very long—Barbara cudgeled her memory to remember how many months. In fact, she couldn't remember a lot about Pam, even though she read the blog and checked into the Sparks' website daily. Pam had hardly ever posted, and when she did, her entries were heavy on technical detail about one or another of their projects. They didn't give much insight into her personality. It was pretty obvious that something she had done had rubbed the others the wrong way. Barbara had tried to draw out her companions on the problem, but none of them really wanted to talk about it. Had it been that bad?

"What are you doing here?" Neil asked bluntly and, in Barbara's opinion, a bit rudely even for him.

Pam's lips twisted into an expression that was neither a grimace nor a smile.

"I'm here with SolStar. I'm the captain of their racing team. You can't put up a sign on the Moon that says no admission, Neil. At least, not yet. But, I'm sure if anyone could do it you'd be the one to try."

"We're not trying to tell you never to come back to the Moon," Dion said, though his deep voice was devoid of its usually warm tones. "It's a free Moon, as far as I know."

"Just not to talk to any of you, is that right?"

"No!" Gary said. His cheeks reddened. "You don't get it. I guess you never will."

"Perhaps not," Pam said, evenly. She turned to Barbara and stuck out her hand, looking her up and down curiously. "I'm Pam Yamashita. You're the new one, Barbara Winton? I've seen some of your work already. I'd say were it not for you, the team would have been in trouble out on the Aldrinville site. Good work. Pleased to meet you."

"Um, thanks. How do you do?" Barbara replied, automatically taking her hand. Was the compliment sincere, or was Pam taking a dig at the others? Barbara knew she was overanalyzing. Pam's demeanor seemed stoic and odd to Barbara, but that didn't necessarily mean she was cold. People were all different in their own ways. "SolStar—isn't that one of the companies that supplies technology to the space program?"

"Not the NASA one or to Reynolds-Ward Industries," Jan put in, as if that were an insult. Barbara knew that wasn't true. Anyone who was interested in the Armstrong City project knew the names of the major suppliers. SolStar was huge in global commercial space. Had it not been for SolStar, Ms. Reynolds-Ward wouldn't have been able to build Armstrong City as she had. It had taken all of Ms. Reynolds-Ward's company's efforts as well as the rest of the commercial launch industry to develop a steady flow of traffic to the Moon. Competitor or not, Barbara didn't believe that one company or even government had the resources to make traffic flow to the Moon and back in a profitable manner by itself.

"Yes," Pam said, her dark eyes level. "It is one of Ms. Reynolds-Ward's rivals. Ironic, isn't it, how rivals must also sometimes become allies for the greater common good?"

"Yeah, whatever, Pam. You didn't think so when you were here." Barbara was surprised by the venom in Neil's voice. He seemed more upset to see Pam than any of the others were. He whispered into the link in Barbara's ear. "You're her replacement."

"Yes," Pam said, with a frosty little smile. "You *are* my replacement. I hope *you* do well, Barbara."

The other Sparks seemed to writhe in embarrassment.

"You shouldn't have access to our private frequency," Neil said, crossly. "Are you hacking us?"

Pam raised one thin eyebrow.

"That is a serious claim, Neil, which has serious legal implications. Once again, you prove that intelligence and maturity don't always go hand in hand. I certainly am not violating any laws or ethics. Why shouldn't I be on the Sparks channel? It's still in my PerDee. I'm certain most of the Spark alumni on the Moon are tuned in. There are a lot of us here. You didn't think about that, did you? I was one of you. And Dr. Bright has always said once a Spark, a Spark for life." She nodded knowingly at the circle of disapproving faces. "Well, it's good you figured it out now before something *embarrassing* happened to you. Dr. Bright should have warned you. Perhaps . . . he didn't think he needed to." She lifted the small device from a pouch on her brown jumpsuit front.

"Dr. Bright let you keep it?" Gary asked.

"Ada's mine," Pam said, closing her long fingers protectively around the flat silver case. "She has a lot of my personal stuff in her memory. I deleted all the confidential files per the nondisclosure agreements I signed when I joined and confirmed when I left the program, so you don't have to worry about that. I suspect many of you have not thought through the legalities of the documents you signed to be here as a Spark. Have you, Neil? Believe me, I have. You have nothing to fear from me."

"I'm not afraid of you!" Neil barked. The end of his nose had turned red.

"Ada?" Barbara asked, dying to defuse the tension that filled the room. "For Ada Lovelace?"

"Ah, yes." For the first time, Pam's expression warmed. "Yes, that's right. Did one of them tell you?"

"Um, no. They wouldn't have to. I celebrate Ada Lovelace Day on October thirteenth every year. The first computer programmer was a woman, Lord Byron's daughter."

"That's right." Pam seemed surprised that she knew. "Yes, that is why. What do you call yours?" She gestured at the PerDee in Barbara's sleeve.

Barbara felt a little embarrassed at her choice. It had seemed almost automatic in the beginning. Now it sounded silly.

"Fido," she admitted.

"Yes, Barbara? How can I help?"

"Nothing, Fido," Barbara said. "Forget it."

"I like dogs, too," Pam said. "If I recall, Jan is a cat person. Right?"

"Meow." Jan snarled at her like a cat ready to pick a fight with a bulldog. Pam regarded Jan with an expression like a scientist studying a slightly uninteresting insect.

Pam didn't look like a hostile monster. In fact, all of the hostility was coming from the current Sparks. Barbara wished she knew just what had happened between them. Pam was trying to be friendly. She almost liked Pam already.

"Don't let her take you in," Daya said suddenly, over the in-ear frequency. The smaller girl's chin was up in defiance, as if daring Pam to say something. "She doesn't care about other people, only *herself* and *her* future."

Barbara felt torn. She had no real reason to dislike Pam—yet. Still, she didn't like the way her friends were treating Pam. Her parents had raised her to be civil even to people she didn't like. The middle of a public auditorium was no place to air past grievances. Didn't the Sparks realize that any stray argument might end up on the Internet? The time to discuss old problems was in private, and not four days before they took off on a long and difficult journey.

She studied her friends as though she had just seen them for the first time. All her life, she had put the Sparks on a pedestal. They seemed perfect people, living enviable lives, doing fantastic experiments and living on the Moon, sharing everything with the world. Since she had come to join them, she had begun to see their flaws, but accepted them without a thought. She wasn't perfect; why should they be?

Maybe Pam wasn't all wrong. Part of Barbara thought that her friends' manners could use an upgrade, but part of her knew that she wasn't there to rescue them from themselves. Her dad would have told her that they were all people with jobs to do, and they just needed to get back to work.

"Okay, nice to meet you, we've got work to do," she said to Pam. To the Sparks she said, "Come on," urging them toward the door and away from Pam. Neil and Jan looked as though they felt like continuing with the argument, but Barbara didn't give them a choice. She herded them like goats out into the corridor. She wanted to say something to the tall, lone figure left behind near the stage, but her friends needed her now. "We've only got four days before the race, and there's a lot left to do."

Chapter Four

"I just finished printing it out, and I was about to assemble the parts," Neil told Barbara and Dion, standing in the middle of the lab that housed the three-dee printer. His freckled face was flushed with frustration. He thrust an accusatory finger toward the door. "Then, *they* came in here speaking that weird code the two of them talk to each other, and they loaded up *every last piece* of the new BrightSat and took off with it! I asked them what was going on, and Jan just said that they needed it for the Moon buggy." He shot an angry glance at the big, scarred metal worktable, where a few tools and bits of circuitry lay scattered on its surface, the rolling stool beside it, and on the floor.

"I don't know, Neil." Dion looked at his youthful friend and then over at Barbara as he spoke. "We kind of gave them carte blanche to do whatever is needed for the racer. There isn't a lot of time left."

Neil's face twisted.

"Yeah, but, I mean, I know that, but they can't just come in here and take something that is already slated for something else! I was going to use that bird for reconnaissance during the race. And Dr. Bright wanted me to use it to map out that mining expedition for him." Neil looked pleadingly at Barbara. "Barb, can't you talk to them? They'll listen to you."

"I understand your frustration," Barbara said, "but we said they can take whatever they need. How long will it take you to reprint out all the parts for a new one?"

"Print out a new one? *Again*?" Neil ruffled up his dark hair with both hands. "It took a *full day* of printing all together. Before that, I had to spend a day and a half setting up the models. I mean, now the software is already in place, so it would just be waiting for the printer and keeping the print materials loaded on the spools while it runs. But I don't automatically get to jump the line. That counts as outside help. I have to wait my turn behind half the engineers doing routine maintenance. So another whole day, then maybe a day to assemble it. If there's a problem with any of the components, I have to get back in the queue all over again. Can you please just get it back?"

Barbara frowned. With the race just a few days away, she could understand why the Nerd-Twins had to commandeer anything that would facilitate getting the buggy finished, but they really needed to hurry up. Their secrecy seemed understandable at first, when any slip meant that their design could leak all over the world, but it had hit a point where it interfered with preparations. She wished she knew just how far from finished Jan and Gary were on the buggy. She made her decision.

"I'll go see them. Besides, we need to do a test drive. I hate to take the car out until it's had all the kinks worked out of it. It's time they showed us what the buggy looks like and how it works. We still need to train on it. And we've been assembling a whole lot of gear. I have to figure if we can pack everything in it we're going to need. I hate being unprepared so close to the race. I'll let you know what they say." She turned to go. Dion caught her wrist and turned her back toward Neil.

"Hold on," Dion said. "What did you just say *you* were going to use that one for exactly, Neil? Reconnaissance? For the race?"

"Well, I don't want to talk about that yet." Neil looked like a kid that just got caught with his hand in the cookie jar. He squirmed. Dion narrowed an eye at him.

"You're not gonna tell me that Dr. Bright told you to wire the BrightSat for surveillance, are you, little bro?"

"Neil." Barbara put her hands on her hips and tapped her foot on the floor giving him a stern stare down like her mother used to do her. "Out with it."

"Out with it?" Neil fixed her with his most charming, wide-eyed and innocent expression, which was all the proof she needed that he was up to something. Barbara had figured out over the last months that Neil sometimes had a problem with thinking rules didn't apply to him. It often got him in trouble. She wanted to head him off if she could. "Out with what?" His voice broke on the last syllable—further proof, if either of them needed it.

"What are you up to, dude?" Dion asked, gently. "Come on. You need to let us in on it. Maybe we can help out."

Barbara started to add her own appeal, but she held back. One of them had to be capable of playing the "bad cop" if necessary. Dion was good at appealing to Neil's sense of camaraderie without being heavy-handed.

"Okay, okay, I'll tell you." Neil looked over his shoulder like somebody might be listening in and his voice lowered slightly. "The sat is standard EMdrive propulsion and power and all, but Dr. Bright wanted a more accurate laser imaging and ranging system. He wants to map the surface at his expedition down to the changes in surface details to within a centimeter. So, he gave me this payload package that included a high-dollar laser radar system. You'd be amazed how tiny that thing is." With both hands, he sketched a box that would fit on one palm.

"Sounds cool," Dion said, looking impressed.

"Yeah! I'd show it to you, but it's gone!" Neil's voice was full of bitterness.

"Go on," Barbara urged him. "I can tell there's more."

"Well . . . during check-out of the payload, I realized that it could measure tiny surface vibrations by mapping the little laser speckles on the surface and how they change with time. There is also a really interesting effect on the returned beam when interfered with the reference beam. I read up on it a whole lot. It's called heterodyning. Probably more along your or Jan's expertise, Barb." He opened his eyes with wide innocence toward Barbara, clearly hoping to appeal to her vanity. She wasn't fooled, but the technology did interest her.

"So you can measure tiny surface vibrations. So what?" Dion asked.

He wasn't getting it yet, but Barbara understood. She had done exactly what Neil was about to do, with a much less state-of-the-art system than he had. On their farm at home in Iowa, her family had used drones to map the soil and moisture content. They had also used them to watch for off-nominal vibrations on their aging fleet of combines and tractors, hoping to catch mechanical failures, like a bearing going out before it cost them an entire month's profits to fix a seized motor. Heterodyning had considerable versatility in its application.

Just like that, Barbara got exactly what Neil had in mind, and she didn't like it. She fixed him with a neutral gaze, and waited to see how much he was going to tell them.

"Well, think about it, Dion," Neil said confidently and unconsciously mimicking the way Dr. Bright did when he was trying to get the Sparks to reach a conclusion he already knew the answer to. Barbara had to admit that he channeled Dr. Bright quite well. "Tiny vibrations on surfaces are created by all sorts of things like motion, temperature changes, and sound."

There it was. *Sound.* Barbara's hunch was right. He was planning on using the BrightSat to spy on people's conversations. It was so typical of Neil that she had to bite her tongue and count to ten before she spoke.

"Neil," Barbara said at last. "Seriously?"

"Why are you looking at me like that, Barb?" Neil's eyes widened, and he gulped hard.

"You *know* the rules. It's cheating to listen in on private conversations. Does Dr. Bright know what you are planning to do with his lidar system? Hmm? No, I bet he doesn't, and I'll bet you didn't bother to tell him. You knew he wouldn't approve. You can't put the Bright Sparks at risk like this, Neil. What if the other teams caught you cheating? *We* would probably get disqualified, and it would look really bad for Dr. Bright. It could ruin us. It could ruin *him!* Is that what you want?"

". . . Uh, no. . . ."

"Wait a minute," Dion said, looking from one of them to the other, as though he had missed something. "Come on, you're being too hard on him. Is that it? Little bro, are you planning to use the satellite to listen in on the other racer teams' private conversations?"

Neil didn't say a word. His face turned so red his freckles disappeared.

"Of course he is." Barbara just shook her head. She knew how hurt Neil felt, but he had to learn to think about how his actions affected the others. "I really want to win this race, but that's not the way I want to win. You talk to him, Dion. I've got to go deal with the Nerd-Twins. I'll see if I can get the satellite back."

Barbara bounced quietly down the corridor toward the Sparks laboratory and classroom, then diverted toward a side passage at the southwestern side of Sparks Central. She still felt aggravated at Neil, but Dion could deal with that. She had a lot of questions for Gary and Jan.

Because of the amount of technical work that took place in Sparks Central and the other labs in Armstrong City, a fully heated and pressurized high-bay loading and receiving dock had been built along the outer periphery of that zone and led into an exterior air lock accessible to ground vehicles. Dr. Bright had managed to have a section of the loading bay partitioned off for him and the Sparks to use for larger projects, and for staging experiments that wouldn't fit through the personnel air locks. Over the last few months, that had turned into the construction site for the *Spark Xpress*.

Barbara cycled through the double doors leading into the bay and made her way toward the edge of the meter-and-a-half-high loading dock. Since the racing teams and all the press and visitors had arrived, pressurized space had come to be at a premium. Dr. Bright had had to fight to keep the dock from becoming temporary housing. Stacks and stacks of gray shipping containers, boxes, and pieces of heavy equipment were stored along the walls of the high enclosure, leaving just enough of a path between them for fork lifts to drive through. Walking paths had been cordoned off with yellow-and-black-striped "Caution" tape. The chamber smelled of regolith dust, concrete, and the sharp acid odor of batteries. The *tick!* of every step she took on the sealed floor echoed off the hard walls. This had to be almost the only place in the city where she couldn't hear M-Tracker music playing.

Partitions made of reinforced beige plastic separated storage from the open delivery area. The Sparks construction area was at the right, sharing the external bay wall with the heavy exterior door. Boxes and packages of supplies, some of them broken open and sprawling their contents, were jammed along the partition. Barbara chuckled at how messy the normally tidy bay looked.

She took a light jump off the edge of the dock and stretched into a long, arching ballistic trajectory over the forklift lane and the caution tape. She bounced, almost flying, a range of almost five meters before she hit the concrete floor, smack in the middle of the walking pathway. Barbara laughed out loud. Being able to leap across such distances with so little effort would never grow old. She loved being on the Moon. She loved working for Dr. Bright. She loved being a Bright Spark, even if it did mean herding cats sometimes, making them all move in the same direction, on time, and by the rules.

Long before she had come to the Moon, previous Sparks had walled off their construction lab with available and scrounged materials instead of the commercial beige sections, so the partitions—made of half a dozen different pieces of extruded plastic, metal sheeting, even old wooden pallets—extended upward to about three meters. The ceiling of the high bay was another ten meters above the top of the wall. Barbara noticed the ceiling-mounted crane that served the delivery vehicles was tracked over the center of the Sparks' lab and the thick metal cables were hanging taut as if something heavy were attached to the end of them. A tingle of anticipation ran up and down her body. The *Spark Xpress*! Their racer was in there, receiving the finishing touches. She had to see it.

"Fido, cycle me through the door." She stood just outside the hinged, people-sized portal, and waited for the electric lock to click open. The red light on the control panel flashed green, and the display read "Hello, Barbara Winton."

"You are free to enter, Barbara," Fido told her as the door clicked open. She passed through, pulling it shut behind her to make sure the lock closed back. Above her head, a doorbell chime sounded.

"Thanks."

"You are very welcome, Barbara."

Beyond the door, the previous Sparks had designed a tiny foyer about two meters by two meters with a wall blocking the interior view of the bay. A screen of Dr. Bright and the various iterations of Sparks on the wall cycled through pictures at random. Barbara noticed a lot of Neil's handiwork in the collection of images. She grinned as she spotted one of herself from her first week on the job, out at the Aldrinville telescope site.

She heard voices, then slithery, scrambling noises like mice in the walls. Before she could turn the corner Jan appeared in front of her. Jan's normally neat black pigtails were askew, with a lock of shining hair hanging down over her forehead. The pockets of her rust-red coverall bulged with machine parts and tools.

"Hey, roomie, can I help you with something?" Jan stood right in front of her, blocking her entrance. Barbara shifted to one side to pass her. Jan matched her move.

"Yes, Jan. Yes, you can." Barbara sidestepped, only to have Jan do the same again. She felt her temper heating up. She didn't feel like dealing with more nonsense. They had a race to run! "Neil said that you took the pieces of the new BrightSat off the table right in front of him."

"Well, we needed the parts," Jan said reasonably. "Look, why don't you come back later, and we'll show you what we did with them?"

"Why don't you show me now?" Barbara asked, matching her roommate's forced cheerfulness. "I'm dying to see the buggy. You two are brilliant designers. I'm looking forward to showing off the vehicle to the other teams. With all the ideas you've been throwing around in their brainstorming sessions, it has to be spectacular."

Jan hesitated.

"We're not really ready to show it to you yet."

"Not ready?" Barbara echoed, keeping her temper in check. "The race is less than two days from now! I want everyone to have time to practice driving before we get out there on the road."

"We will," Jan promised. She looked tired and, unless Barbara was reading her wrong, frightened. Her natural tendency to worry rose up, making her belly feel tight.

"What are you hiding?"

"Nothing. Nothing, really, roomie. But we're not quite ready yet." Jan leaned more into her path.

Barbara exhaled gustily. She realized that she'd been doing a lot of that lately with the team. She wanted to trust Jan, but she just sensed something fundamental was wrong. She steeled herself.

"Ready or not," Barbara said. She looked Jan in the eyes, walking forward so that her roommate would have to move or be run over. "Here I come."

"But, wait, uh, Barb . . ." Jan jumped out of her way, and all but ran alongside her toward the bigger chamber. "You can't just walk in! Not yet!"

Barbara turned the corner and felt her heart stop beating for a moment.

"Oh, my gosh!" she breathed.

"Not ready" was a colossal understatement. Before her was what ought to be the team's Moon-race vehicle, but looked more like a disconnected disaster.

The room always looked like a bomb full of machine parts had gone off in it, but in the run-up to the race, the mess was a thousand times worse than usual. Hanging from the crane cables was the habitat cylinder, now cleaned up and covered with shining, new multi-layer insulation blankets. On the top half, the blankets had solar panels printed into them. Connected to one end of the cylinder was a structure made of metal framework and transparent polycarbonate material that looked a lot like a squatty rocket nosecone. Through the windows, Barbara could see instrument panels, steering wheels, controls, and places for two seats, meaning that it was the cockpit. From the clear dome lying nearby, the meter-diameter hole in the middle of the top of the tube must be a location for the topside viewing bubble the team had discussed. An opening had been cut out of the cylinder right in the middle of the long axis on the side facing her. Next to the opening, on a pair of wheeled metal dollies, was what looked like the fold-down door of a small personal jet airplane, but it wasn't attached yet. Barbara couldn't imagine where the Twins had found an atmosphere airplane door on the Moon. In the corner of the room, seats and bunks were stacked up, and long wires and very thick power cables ran up into the opening and inside the vehicle.

She looked around for wheels, but discovered there weren't any. Attached to the habitat tube in four locations were struts that jutted out a meter and a half from the main compartment like the legs of an alligator. Lying on the floor beside each strut's end were large shiny metallic screen balls with hexagonal holes connected honeycomb style throughout and across the surface of them. Barbara recognized the geometric shape of the grid on the balls as a "buckyball" or buckminsterfullerene shape, which was the configuration of the carbon-60 molecule. With an engineer's eye, she figured that each of the balls were intended to be cupped on the upper half by structure and connected to a large electromagnetic motor. The balls would function much like a ball caster on a shop cart, and could travel in whichever direction they were motivated to do so. The large motors would electromagnetically drive them the same way spokeless electromagnetic wheels and electromagnetic bullet trains were driven. It had been one of the five designs that the Sparks had brainstormed. Barbara admired the design, and guessed that the fabrication of those had taken up most of the Twins' time. But, still . . . !

This was why the rest of the team had not been able to vet the racer design. Barbara chided herself for carelessness. She was nominally the team's leader. Never again would she sign on to a project like this where the details were kept from the rest of the team. She should have sensed trouble when the Nerd-Twins offered no preliminary or critical design reviews, even after months of asking.

"Oh, my gosh!" Barbara gasped again. "You two are not even close to being finished, and the referees have to see the vehicle in thirty-seven hours! Don't you want to win the race?"

"Of course we do! More than anything!"

"Then how could you let the project fall behind like this?"

"It's okay, roomie. We're going to make it," Jan said, sounding unsure of herself for the first time since Barbara had known her.

"No." Barbara turned and met Jan's eyes. "Jan, you won't make it. At least, you won't make it alone."

"But . . ."

"But, fortunately, you're *not* alone." Barbara scanned the mess. It was bad, but she'd seen worse in her days on the farm. It was time for help. Had she been at home, this is the point where her mother would call her aunt and tell her uncle and the nephews to come running with tools in hand. Now wasn't the time for chastising and blame. Now was the time for rolling up her sleeves and getting to work. "Fido, open a channel to all the Sparks, please."

"Yes, Barbara."

Still keeping her eyes fixed on Jan's, she chose her words carefully.

"Sparks team, this is Barbara. We're not going to meet our deadline for final assembly at our current pace. I need all the Sparks to report to the Sparks' hangar in the loading dock immediately, and be prepared to work through the night."

Jan looked resigned, but she nodded.

"That will help," she said. She sat down on one of the assembly pieces and wiped her forehead with a cloth from one of her coverall pockets. "We've been working flat out. We thought we could make it. Really."

"Hey," Gary's heavily muffled voice came from inside the cylinder. "Is Barbara in here? I just heard the message go out on Turing."

"Yes," Jan replied, with a guilty look at her roommate. "She's here."

"Oh!" Gary's voice dropped to a subdued tone. "Um, well, okay. Can you get that seventeen-millimeter ratcheting open-end wrench I asked you for? I can't hold this battery in place all day!"

Jan jumped for the tall rolling tool chest a couple meters to her right. Barbara could see all the drawers at different stages of open, and several wrenches lay strewn about on the floor near it. One with a "17" on it caught her eye. It was in Jan's side pocket on her jumpsuit. Barbara chuckled a bit.

"What's funny?"

"I think you were looking for this." Barbara reached over and took the wrench from the pocket. She slapped it into Jan's palm. "Don't leave Gary hanging."

"Wow, I knew I had that wrench a minute ago. I must be losing my mind. I guess I'm just tired." Jan looked back at Barbara with a sheepish expression. "We should've called you sooner."

"Woulda, coulda, shoulda," Barbara said, waving a dismissive hand. "Never mind. I'm here now. What do you need me to do first?"

"You did it." Jan sighed, this time with relief. "Sent for the troops. Once they get here, you can assign work to everyone. You're better at that than we are."

"Jan!"

"Coming!"

Wrench in hand, Jan crawled into the cylinder.

"Hover mode, Fido." Barbara reached into her sleeve pocket, extracted her PDE and tossed it in the air in front of her. The little microcomputer whirred as its mini turboprops kicked in and stabilized its position hovering in front of them.

"What can I do for you, Barbara?" Fido asked.

"Fido, I need you to fly all around the *Spark Xpress* inside and out as well as in this room collecting imagery. I then want you to take the three-dee model that Jan is about to send you of what the vehicle is supposed to look like and compare them. Create a list of missing parts. Understand, Fido?"

"Yes, Barbara. Woof!"

"Good boy. Go." The little device shot away from her. She turned to Jan, who emerged from the main body of the *Spark Xpress* with her hair even more disarranged than before. "You do have a model, right?"

Now Jan looked indignant. She took Ms. Scruffles, her PerDee, out of her coverall pocket and poked at the screen.

"Of course we do! On its way to Fido now."

Within an hour, the other three members of the team had finished their outside tasks and had arrived at the hangar, ready to work. All of them were as shocked as Barbara had been, but they dug into the jobs that needed to be done. Daya fed a steady stream of small parts and the occasional drink of water to Gary, who lay on his back under the control panel in the cockpit. Barbara grinned at the small teen's thoughtfulness. Daya had also brought along a box of individually wrapped snacks, a rack of refillable water bottles, and a thermos of coffee on a hoversled. That would keep them going for several hours at least.

The bay hummed with activity. Barbara had gone over the images that Fido had collected and compared them against the design document Jan had sent her. It took a while to break the combined file down into a list of tasks, but she was determined to get it right. They had no time for error. Fido was counting down the hours to the time they needed to have the buggy ready for its final inspection. They all had the list in their PerDees, and went on to the next item they were best at as soon as they finished the one they were working on.

Barbara couldn't see any gaps in expertise. If nothing went wrong, they ought to be able to finish, but no one was going to get any sleep.

"No, Neil, I need you to focus on getting the software drivers for the buckyball controllers finished and then we'll upload the environment code," Jan said, behind her at the computer station in the corner near the divider wall.

"Dion, a little more to the left there," Barbara told him from the top of a ladder against the flank of the buggy. The left-side rear buckyball motor housing was heavier than it looked. It kept wanting to roll over from the weight of the motor sitting on top of the ball. Shoulder to the arched metal "leg," Dion was doing his best to hold it in place while she threaded the bolts through the flange to hold it in place on the strut. "Whew! I can't imagine doing this in full gravity."

"I know, right?" Dion agreed, turning his face up to her. "This thing must weigh seventy kilos *here*."

"Almost . . . right . . . no . . . back a hair, there!" She slapped the bolt through the hole with a *clanking* of metal to metal and then quickly reached in with her other hand to slide a washer and a locking nut onto the thread. "Finger-tight will have to do for the minute."

Dion moved and the whole assembly shifted with an alarming groan.

"Can you thread another one in?" he asked. "I can't hold it much longer and it's gonna fall without another bolt in there."

"Hold on. Almost there." Barbara put two fingers into her breast pocket for the second bolt. It flipped out of her fingers, but she caught it on its long slow fall. *Lunar gravity*, she thought with a grin. Not wanting to make the same mistake, she held the washer and nut pursed between her lips until she could angle the bolt through the hole on the opposite side of the flange from the previous bolt. She spat the parts in her hand and worked them onto the bolt as best she could. "Okay. I think you can let go now."

The framework creaked as he let go, but it held.

"Whew, man, my fingers are worn out!" Dion clenched his fists and opened them several times.

"Then it's a good thing we only have three more balls to install." Barbara smiled at him. "Let your fingers rest while I tighten up the rest of these bolts." She took a wrench from her back pocket and went to work. Below her, Dion worked his shoulders and arms like an athlete limbering up, then held the ladder as she leaped off to the floor.

The doorbell chime sounded, indicating that someone else was entering the hangar. Barbara glanced toward the curtain wall. It had to be Dr. Bright. He was the only other person whom the system would admit. Or, so she thought.

Instead, from around the barricade came two men and a woman, all in their mid-to-late twenties. Barbara, having been a longtime fan of Dr. Bright and the Bright Sparks, recognized them instantly. The dark-haired woman with the bright smile was Cisca Small, a former Spark programmer turned multimillionaire game designer. The eldest of the three, a tall man, even taller than Dion, had long brown hair pulled up into a ponytail and wore virtual reality glasses. Barbara couldn't believe it. Calvin Book had been one of Barbara's favorites when she was in grade school. Dr. Book was now a particle physicist at the Large Hadron Collider Group. She knew he was working with Dr. Bright to get funding to build the largest atom smasher ever made on the Moon. Barbara hadn't even known he was up here. The third man was average in height with dark hair in a military cut. Major Thomas Beddingfield Jr. had graduated from the Sparks only about five or so years earlier and left to go to the Canadian Space Academy. He flew a space shuttle for the Canadians and had been on the first manned team to a near-Earth asteroid.

"Can we help you?" Daya scrambled from her spot next to Gary and intercepted them just as they rounded the corner. All of the other Sparks stopped what they were doing and looked up as well.

"Well, Daya, the real question is how we can help you? You asked for our help," Cisca told her softly. She glanced up at Barbara. "What can we do?"

"We're here," Dr. Book added, with a boyish grin. "Put us to work."

"I am not certain where to use you," Daya stammered. She glanced at the others. "Barbara, do you?"

"Sure thing." Barbara stepped toward them, her hand out. The newcomers shook it heartily. "Hi, I'm Barbara Winton. Wow! When I called 'all the Sparks,' I wasn't thinking that any of the Sparks alumni were listening. Please, thank you for coming, but we certainly couldn't ask you to help us now. I'm certain you are pretty busy yourselves."

"Well, Barbara, you don't need to make excuses," Major Beddingfield replied. "We're Sparks. Put us to work. We can see you need it."

"Are you sure?" Barbara asked, almost unable to believe her

luck. She looked from one to another, but they all looked willing and able.

"You heard the man," Dr. Book said as he flipped his VR glasses up on his forehead as he used to do so many times on the show when she was a kid. Barbara almost giggled at the familiar gesture. "All the other racing teams have a group of techs working with them. Why shouldn't we?"

"Very well, then." Touched and pleased by the inclusive "we," Barbara turned and looked about the room at her stunned colleagues. Jan looked mulish, but Dion's hopeful look urged her to accept the gift. They really needed the help. She turned back. "Ms. Small, you're a programmer. Talk to Neil there and see what he doesn't have time to do right now and do what you can."

"Certainly, Barbara, and it's Cisca," the game designer said with a warm smile. Neil, wide-eyed with excitement, beckoned her over.

"Thanks . . . Cisca." Barbara turned to her next helper. "Dr. Book, while I'd love to sit down and ask you lots of questions about your brilliant knowledge of the universe, what we really need right now is some muscle. See these big metal buckyball wheels?"

"I do, young lady," he said. Again, she giggled, feeling like she was seven again.

"Okay, Dion and I will each work with you and Major Beddingfield, if you don't mind," she added, addressing their third guest. "Dr. Book and I will finish up on the back wheels, and Major Beddingfield and Dion can do the front." Barbara saved up all the details to tell Dad and Mom on her next call home. It was so good to have people she could trust to do what needed to be done, and who would feel comfortable asking for clarification if they didn't know something.

"Not at all, and it's Calvin and Tom, Barbara," Major Beddingfield said, with a smile, as he picked up a wrench.

"We'll get right on it, then find something else to do. Could you have your task list sent to our PerDees?" Dr. Book asked.

"Right! I don't know why I didn't think of that," Barbara said, abashed. "Of course! Fido, send the task list to *all* the Sparks' PerDees."

"Yes, Barbara."

Pings from the newcomers' microcomps told her they had the

file. Beddingfield nodded over his, then stuck it into his thigh pocket.

"So, um, don't just stand around then," she said, with a laugh. "Get to work, Sparks! And thank you all so much."

"No problem, Barbara," Major Beddingfield said, with a cheeky grin that showed off his handsome jaw. "We got this." He followed a starstruck Dion toward their assignment. Barbara felt just as swept away as he did. Hearing their customary phrase from the lips of one of the most distinguished alumni was kind of exciting.

"Once a Spark, always a Spark," Cisca told her, giving her a friendly pat on the shoulder. She sat down on a swivel stool beside Neil, who passed the keyboard to her.

"Neil, Cisca is only here to help you get caught up on the software. Don't try to wheedle M-Tracker cheat codes from her. Stay focused on getting things done!" Barbara said.

"Me?" Neil asked, with one hand on his chest to protect his innocent heart. "I wouldn't dare!"

"Uh-huh," Barbara said, with a skeptical twist to her mouth. "Daya, don't let him get sidetracked."

"That is a full-time job nobody wants, Barb," Daya said, pleasantly, sorting the scatter of tools that Gary had been using in their proper places in the rolling chest. She went to pick up the coffee carafe to offer the newcomers. "But don't worry, we'll keep him straight."

"Roomie, I sure could use you on the power converter circuitry." Jan stuck her head out of the habitat tube. "And with the control stations, and the lighting, and, well, everything." Her voice rang in the hollow space as she climbed back inside. "And I'll need several pairs of hands to get that door on."

"We'll help with all of that just as soon as we finish with the wheels," Barbara promised. "Come on, uh, Calvin. Do you need a pair of gloves?"

"Got my own!" the scientist assured her, pulling a pair from a pocket on his cargo pants. "I'm ready to tackle that other buckyball mount if you are."

Barbara smiled at him. It seemed to be true that there was no cloud without a silver lining. Getting to work with one of her early favorites was a treasure she would remember for a long time to come. They had a lot of hard work ahead of them, but it was going to be *fun*.

"Okay," she said. "Let's do it."

Barbara had no sooner gotten back down to her knees and had her arms up inside the framework where the buckyball motor housing flange met the strut when the doorbell chimed again. And almost as soon as it did, a thought flashed into her mind. She had sent the call and the list out to *all* of the Sparks on the Moon without realizing it. That meant that *all* of the former Sparks on the Moon would get that call. That meant that. . . .

"What can we do to help?" The familiar voice sounded in the room like the squeaky wheel of a shopping cart as four more people turned the corner into the hangar. Barbara's heart sank.

Neil sprang up from the software terminal station.

"She can't be in here!" he shouted.

Chapter Five

"How's the preparation going for your mining expedition?" Jackie asked over her oversized tea mug at the table in the studio dressing room.

"Pretty well," Keegan said, running over lists in his mind. He shoved his gigantic insulated coffee cup from side to side as he thought and blew air through his lips. "The engineers are already on site in an inflated temporary habitat. It's light there now, but it'll start to darken soon after Calvin and I arrive. We'll be bringing a ton of lights for the tunnels. We've got the loan of the mineral company shuttle for the duration, and we'll live out of that. In the meantime the engineers are living in what's going to be the lab. I'm excited about the reports that the miners have been sending me. You can't believe the finds they've already located, just where I thought they would be. I wish I was there right now!"

"What about the Sparks? Aren't they way behind?"

Keegan smiled.

"Barbara can handle them. I have faith in her. I know the project got away from them, but she's cracking the whip now. They'll get to the starting gate on time, and she'll keep them going all the way to the finish line."

"This is too much for Barbara all at once, Keegan," Jackie said gruffly. Keegan felt like squirming. He hated it when she scolded him like that. This discussion ought to have been settled weeks ago, almost as soon as the race was announced, but Jackie kept bringing it up. It made Keegan wonder what, if anything, she had observed that he was missing. He trusted her instincts.

"I don't know, Jackie," he replied, swigging lukewarm coffee and trying not to yawn. He had to stop using caffeine instead of sleep. Bad luck had piled one of his individual projects on top of overseeing preparations for the race, so every minute had to count for two. "Looked to me like Barb handled the confrontation just fine, on both sides. The Sparks are going to have to learn how to deal with people being different than they want them to be. I know I had to with Pam. I'm *still* not sure I did it right."

"But, it is still a lot to deal with, and after Aldrinville. . . ."

Keegan held up a hand.

"Stop right there, Jackie. That was months ago. Barb was nothing less than superb at Aldrinville, and I think Pam might have been right about a few things she said. I have had nightmares about what might have happened to the other Sparks if Barbara and her good common sense hadn't been out there with them. I know that we couldn't have gotten to them in time to save them. They're all smart, but they do tend to go off in their own directions without someone to direct them. Barbara figured out just what to do when it needed to be done. And that emergency telescope to connect with Mars— pretty darned good. She has a cool head, and she's growing into a good leader."

Jackie gave him *that* look.

"I hope it wasn't just beginner's luck. Now you're letting them drive a self-supporting buggy around the Moon! That has never been done before, by anyone. It's all right that most of the contestants are adults, but the Sparks aren't. They're kids! They're the youngest team in the race. Even Dion has never been out on his own for that long, with all the pressure a trip like that involves. What kind of strain are you putting on Barb if something goes wrong out there? She's strong, but is she as tough as Pam? *That* girl is a survivor, no matter how poorly she got along with the others."

Keegan had pored over almost any situation a team might run into over the eleven-thousand-kilometer course. He had run scenarios past Leona, dozens of them, and even in the worst cases, the percentage for success was greater than the one for failure. He shook his head.

"You know what? I think Barb is tougher than Pam. She's tougher, but has a bigger heart than anyone I've ever met. And I don't mean a soft heart; I mean *heart* heart. The kind of heart that wins championship games and wins wars. The kind of heart where you have to dig down deep to keep going and, when most people will stop and give up, that big old heart just won't let you. And you'll drag your team along with you. Like the military special forces, she won't leave anyone behind. I think growing up on a family farm with such a great support network as well as intelligent direction molded her personality into being that way whether she knew it or not. She can handle it."

"But she's not the Sparks' mother, Keegan. She's not their sister. She's not their guardian. She's not even their babysitter, although I think at times that is why you chose her because she will do that for you."

"What? Babysit the Sparks?" Keegan felt stunned. Jackie wouldn't say something she didn't think was true. Had he really, perhaps unconsciously, chosen a new Spark that he could trust to be the "adult" when he wasn't there? He examined his motives with all the honesty in him.

No. He had been looking for a real leader for them. He'd needed to choose a self-starter, a person of action, and a person who could think through the holistic view where the other Sparks, talented as they were, couldn't. Barbara Winton had shown him over and over again that she always kept in mind the greater picture and the greater impact of even the smallest actions. The way she forced the team to sit down and write up a "requirements document" for the racer was a testament to that ability of hers, playing on everyone's strengths, including her own. She'd been taught planning by her parents, and understood how to use her resources with the least waste.

"No," he said, at last. "That's not true. I just don't want to micromanage them and mother-hen them. They have to find their own way. Having a peer leader is better than having me tell them what to do. Otherwise, the Sparks program would be no better than any other classroom on Earth. Or any other lab. Barbara is kind of 'first among equals,' that's all. I want them to be able to argue with her and add their own suggestions, not to step back as they would with someone like me who is in a position of authority. They will learn to find their way."

"Not without guidance, as smart as they are. For all intents and purposes here, you *are* their guardian. And maybe me, and even Leona, are *in loco parentis* to some degree. Sometimes, nothing takes the place of a grownup like a grownup. Don't make Barbara take on that responsibility as well. It's yours." Keegan had been making shows with Jackie for almost twenty years, since they had been teens, and she had always been able to sense what the cast and crew needed.

Jackie made a face. "I think that was one of your problems with Pam. She didn't slot nicely into the consulting leadership role. She's formidable in her own right. There's nothing wrong with that, but she's not a team player or a consensus builder. That young woman has a streak of independence. She fought back against your attempts to shoehorn her into that position. I've had a lot of time to consider the dynamics of those months, and I don't think she was wrong."

Keegan chuckled.

"You're right. The Sparks need me center stage. And Pam is intimidating, to say the least. Heck, sometimes she even makes me uneasy because she is just so stoic. And you know me—I'm not uncomfortable around anybody. From a professional standpoint, I don't know that she was my greatest failure. I mean, she's become amazingly successful, and she's only twenty years old. In the end, that is the main purpose of the Sparks Internships. Trouble is, her sense of loyalty or family or team that just never seemed to be there for the rest of the Sparks. That's the lack of a team captain's heart I was talking about. I don't know if she has that 'dig down deep and save the day' part to her. I just can't tell. Well, not my problem any longer. I'm glad to see her doing well. This current crop of Sparks is my prime concern. I'm proud of what they're doing, and you're right: I am their grownup. If I've been shuffling off too many of my responsibilities onto Barbara, I'll take them back."

He leaned back in his desk chair and sipped at his coffee mug with the *Live from the Moon* logo on it. Jackie had given him that mug the day they signed the contract with Ms. Reynolds-Ward and the rest of the sponsors. That day that led him to creating the advanced internships that brought Sparks with him to the Moon. *In loco parentis* pretty much defined how his life had developed since then. The program *had* been successful. He missed the days of just adventuring and doing crazy-cool science projects sometimes, being able to jet off by himself to work on an experiment for weeks or months without worrying about other obligations. But he wouldn't give up the Sparks for anything, either. He wondered if that was how parents felt about sacrificing their normal lives for their kids.

"All right, I've beaten you up enough," Jackie said, leaning back in her own chair. "The M-Tracker game is great for the show. It provides its own soundtrack! All the comments on the vlog want to know what's coming next. What have you and Ms. Cisca planned for the game? I'd hate to lose momentum on covering its development."

Keegan felt the grin spread across his face. In his imagination, a map popped up, a line of shining dots running across the landscape. Immediately, he pushed it away, just in case Jackie really could read his mind.

"You won't lose track of it," he said easily. "We've got some special surprises for the race teams."

"What, right out on the racecourse?" Jackie asked, her eyes lighting up. "Are you sure the buggy drivers can handle the distraction?"

"Oh, they don't have to go running off after a TurnTable if they're in the lead. And if they can't keep their mind on the job, they deserve to lose a little ground, don't they?"

"You're not doing this just to give the Sparks an edge, are you?" she asked suspiciously.

"Who, me?" Keegan asked, doing a creditable impression of Neil professing his innocence. "No. They won't go off course at all. But I can't tell you more than that because I don't *know* more than that. I may be on her board of advisors, but Cisca has to keep some proprietary information secret even from me. I think she's conferring with Leona, though." He glanced at her PerDee, flat on the table, a much less sophisticated unit than he and the Sparks owned. "Are you still playing?"

"You bet! I just completed a really ancient classical cut. 'Sympathy for the Devil,' by The Rolling Stones. I never thought I was going to find that first line."

"Excuse me, Dr. Bright?" Leona's voice interrupted them and her avatar popped up from the projectors on his PDE sitting beside his hand. Today, she had scaly red skin and big, bright green eyes, her interpretation of what a Martian might have looked like.

"Yes, Leona? What can I do for you?"

"Several of the older Sparks have entered the Sparks' hangar and are volunteering to help the team assemble the racer. Barbara is putting them to work. I estimate the added manpower will have them finishing the task ahead of the deadline by several hours."

"Hey, see, Jackie? Barbara can handle it." Keegan sat up in his chair and rubbed his chin. He realized that he hadn't shaved that morning. The details of the race, the show, and the mining expedition were weighing on him. He wasn't even certain when he ate last. Fortunately, his last two broadcasts of *Live from the Moon* had been live-action only, following him around as he took care of issues for the race. Jackie had filled in holes with spots the Sparks had videoed.

"Thanks, Leona, that's great news!" Jackie said. She reached for her PerDee. "We should get some footage of that. Cooperation between past and present Sparks will make great video. Besides, the other race teams have had tens, even *hundreds* of engineers—real degreed engineers, Keegan, not just interns—working on their buggies."

Keegan frowned. He sat his mug down and tapped a control on his computer. The hangar imagery came on his wallscreen. "*Wait.* Which Sparks?"

"Cisca, Calvin, and Thomas are there presently," Leona replied. "It would also appear four more are on their way."

"Quit beating around the bush, Leona," Jackie scolded the AI, seeming to forget that she was talking to a computer. "Who?"

"Pam is among them," Leona answered, after a moment's hesitation. Keegan was astonished by the sound of sheepishness in her voice. Every day, new additions to her persona that he *didn't* add kept popping up in the most unique ways. He really needed to do a more thorough Turing test on her, as he thought she might be getting close to indistinguishable from sentient. But that would have to wait.

"Pam?"

"That is not going to be pretty, Keegan." Jackie whistled in disbelief. "Maybe this is an olive branch?"

"I'm certain Neil and Daya won't take it that way. And Pam's the captain on a rival team. Oh boy, oh boy." Keegan just shook his head back and forth and sighed. "I'm not sure this is what we need right now."

Jackie stood up.

"I am. I already told you what we need right now," she said firmly, with one of her eyebrows raised. She reached for her PerDee to summon the video crew. "And you know I'm right."

"Okay, okay, I submit! You're right, Jackie. Or, at least, you were right about one thing." Keegan stood up, too.

"And that one thing is?" Jackie asked, a skeptical eyebrow rising.

"It's time for some grownup interaction, Dr. Bright style."

"But, she's on another race team. This is cheating!" Neil protested, hands planted firmly on his hips. He looked small and insignificant confronting the tall girl, who regarded him with amusement and dignity.

"Neil, just, just calm down." Barbara stood between the two of them, patting the air, frustrated beyond all reason. She didn't know why the Sparks hated Pam so and, honestly, she didn't care anymore. "We have a matter of hours to finish a tremendous amount of work and we don't have time for nonsense."

"Nonsense! It's not nonsense!"

"I don't know, roomie, I have to agree with Neil," Jan said as she crawled along the unattached fold-down door on her hands and knees. "Is it ethical for her to be here? Is it violating any of the rules?"

"Don't be silly, Jan," Pam said, her face calm as usual. "Barbara's request was for help from *all* the Sparks available. I am a Spark. There was and is plenty of cross-pollination between many of the teams. Yours may be the only one that has *not* reached out to any of the others, and that is not a matter of pure geography."

"Is that true?" Barbara asked Jan.

"Yeah . . . but why her?"

"I have expertise you need," Pam said. "See some sense. Getting to the Moon is difficult. Circumnavigating it has never been done on such a scale. We each need to accept all the help we can get or it will not be safe out there. When we are far from Armstrong City, we will be one another's backup in case of emergency. If you need help, I will give it willingly." The tall girl tossed her head. "Whether you believe me or not, I don't care any longer. But you were my friends and I would hate to see something happen to either keep you out of the race or to put you in harm's way."

"Good enough for me," Barbara said. She knew her father would have done the same. "I'm glad to have your help." Pam gave her a thin smile. Barbara knew from having watched videos of her as a Spark it was as warm as her expressions ever got.

"Not good enough for me." Gary had joined Jan by crawling down the stairs as well. He wore a blusterous expression. "I, *we*, Barb, we don't trust her."

Dion loomed up beside her. Barbara could tell by the look on his face that his loyalty was torn. Regardless of Neil's histrionics, Dion had probably been the most upset by Pam's behavior before she departed, whatever that had been. He protected and looked after all of them like a big brother. Barbara dithered, trying to decide what to do. Time was running away from them. She welcomed the help, but how could she get her companions to accept it?

The doorbell chimed, distracting her attention toward the door. Barbara groaned. More visitors had arrived.

But this was different. Around the corner bounced Paul and Yvonne, *Live from the Moon*'s two camera operators, their lenses pointing toward the group in the bay. Jackie was behind them, monitoring the shots on her PerDee and whispering directions in her headset that the crewmembers were getting through earbuds. In her wake came Ann with the lighting frame, its spotlights pointing back to the door. Paul turned his lens. Then, illuminated by the brilliant while lights, Dr. Bright turned the corner, beaming at the camera. Barbara felt a thrill run through her. She still got excited when she saw Dr. Bright, even after all these months on the Moon with him. Then her heart sank. He was coming into the middle of an argument she hadn't figured out how to solve.

"This is a special live edition of *Live from the Moon*," Leona's voice filled the room. Her current avatar appeared on one of the wallscreens as she spoke, complete with red skin and bulging green eyeballs. "With special guests from previous Bright Sparks teams. Ladies and gentlemen, please welcome Dr. Keegan Bright!"

With a hovering fill light following him and the spotlights in his face, Keegan had to peer through the brilliant illumination as he made his way into the crowded workroom. Faces turned toward him, all lighting up as they recognized their mentor. He could tell by the expression on her face that Cisca, who had always been the quickest thinker in the room, caught onto what he was doing in a split second. He knew he could count on her.

"Dr. Bright! Come in!" She caught Barbara's eye and gave her an encouraging thumbs-up. "Come see what we've been doing!"

Keegan turned to Yvonne's camera, giving Paul a chance to change position and get another angle of the workroom. The cameraman moved swiftly and silently staying out of the other camera's shot.

"I know you have been dying to get a look at the Sparks' buggy. Well, so have I!" Keegan said. "Let's just take a moment and visit with the crew of the *Spark Xpress*. Let's stop off first with Neil Zimmerman. Neil, you've been working on programming the controls and coordinating the communication between the base here at Armstrong City with the Moon buggy. Can you give me a rundown on how that's going?"

At the sight of the camera, Neil's face changed from indignation to his lecture expression. As Keegan and Jackie had predicted, he went all showbiz, abandoning his ire. One thing for sure about Neil was that when the camera was on him, he matured instantly by many years. Instead of his childish indignation and battle with Pam his demeanor became that of a true Spark.

"Thanks, Dr. Bright! Well, here are the control systems, linked to the central and backup computers on board, the monitors and the camera array...." He took Keegan on a tour of the components, even if it meant he had to step over pieces that hadn't yet been installed.

"... The buggy will be able to communicate directly to our console in Sparks Central and to my BrightSats. I built one," and there he shot a brief but annoyed look at Gary, "especially for the race but it turned out that we needed the parts for the *Xpress* so we cannibalized it. I've got another printing out right now and it should be ready in time to give us a bird's-eye view of the race from the start."

"Well, that's excellent, Neil," Keegan said as he patted the young man on the shoulder and gave him a reassuring nod. He kept moving and gesturing quickly to maintain the energy in the room. "Hi, Daya. Daya Singh is our youngest Spark. Daya, how's your part of the project going?"

One by one, he asked the Sparks a few questions, ascertaining that everything was going well on each facet of the project. Each time he made a little reassuring off-camera gesture to each of his current Sparks. The past, and now mature, Sparks all smiled and went along with the energy. They knew what he was up to. And, as he had hoped, his presence seemed to defuse some of the tension in the room. By the time he finished his round, the younger Sparks were standing more at ease.

However, he was more concerned by the state the racer was in, or *wasn't*. Barbara looked openly relieved at his arrival. He kept half an eye on her as he chatted with the guests, getting their perspective on the race, and asking them about the reasons they were on the Moon at that time, although he knew the answers already.

"Yes, I'm here on official NASA business," Major Beddingfield said, with a grin. "Checking in on Commander Harbor's telescope project, and a few other things for Canada. I don't mind taking some time to help out my former team. My meetings can wait a little while. We're all excited about the race. I'm glad to lend a hand. I want Team Sparks to win!" Keegan was glad to hear the implied encouragement.

"Me?" Calvin Book said, pushing his glasses up on his forehead. "I'm just hanging around, hoping to persuade Cisca to give me a bunch of free codes for M-Tracker."

"Ha ha!" Keegan chuckled. "Aren't we all? Cisca, what do you say to that?"

Cisca let out a trill of laughter. "Fat chance, Cal! Sorry, Dr. Bright, I can't even tell you. It just wouldn't be fair."

"See that, folks, and she used to work for me!" Keegan smiled into Paul's camera for a close up.

That comment started a lively interchange between the three old-timers. They displayed the camaraderie of former colleagues pulling together. Each of them was able to fulfill his unspoken need to reassure the public and all the other teams that the *Spark Xpress* was an independent effort, not a LFTM project, and all they cared about was putting a real contender out on the course. Leona had picked up some scuttlebutt from the vlogosphere that Dr. Bright was too involved in his interns' project. Keegan needed to dispel any concerns that he was anything but totally nonpartisan about the race.

Three of the helpers were engineers from the SolStar team,

strangers. Keegan was pleased to learn that they had been watching his show for years, and felt honored to pitch in with kids they had heard so much about.

"We learned to work together by watching the Sparks," Alan Stone said, his eyes crinkled with pleasure. Out of the corner of his eye, Keegan saw Jan and Gary look abashed.

Mission accomplished, he thought.

Once he had given each of them a couple of minutes of screen time, he turned to Pam.

"And Pam Yamashita, who was also one of my Bright Sparks," Keegan said, turning to her with his hand out. After a split-second hesitation, she took it. Her grasp was firm, dry, and warm. It would inspire confidence in any business connection. "Pleased to see you back here on the Moon, Pam."

"I am glad to be back," she said. Even though the left corner of her mouth turned up, her eyes looked slightly wary. It seemed she was as uncertain as he was about interaction. Keegan felt a surge of protectiveness, as he did for every Spark, present or former.

"Well, I am happy to see how well you've been doing since you were last on *Live from the Moon*," he assured her. "SolStar has got to think it's about as lucky as it can get."

"Thank you," she said gravely.

"So, this is a curious circumstance. The others aren't racing, but you are. You're the team captain for SolStar. How do you feel about working on a rival's vehicle?" he asked.

Cool-headed as ever, she answered him. "It gives me an insight to the way the chief engineers are thinking about the race."

"This is the first time that you or any of the other teams have seen this buggy. Do you think the designers of the *Spark Xpress* were trying to hide their design from the general public?" Keegan asked.

"No, I believe they were behind in their plans," Pam said. It was an honest assessment, but it earned openmouthed squawks of outrage from Jan and Gary and glares from the others. What humility the engineers had shamed them into went right out the airlock. Pam sure was a lightning rod. "Most understandable under the circumstances," she continued, before any of them could dive in and try to grab the spotlight away from her. "They have been hosts to all the other teams. There are only so many hours in the day. They have been lending assistance and guidance to all of the visitors from Earth. Maneuvering, eating, drinking, even walking in very low gravity is not instinctive. For all the training each of the racers have had before launching to come here, it is no substitute for actually being here. The current Sparks have used a great deal of their time in helping newcomers to cope. It is an admirable display of teamwork. And I have to admit it must have been a major drain on their availability to be here working on their buggy. I'd say we other racers sort of owe them some help here."

It was a gracious answer. Barbara was the first of the Sparks to take her meaning. She smiled at Pam. Dion, as Keegan surmised, was next to accept the olive branch and calm down, followed by Daya, who managed to mix surprise, dismay, annoyance all on one small face. Neil, Jan, and Gary still weren't willing to give her the benefit of the doubt. But Pam's fans from when she had been a Spark would recognize and appreciate her pragmatism. The others would fill the commentary sections of the Sparks' blog one way or another.

"And, what does teamwork mean to you?" Keegan asked.

"It means bringing diverse talents together to get the work done," Pam said. "Some things just require a team to make them happen."

Keegan had to smile. That explained more to him in one sentence than what he had gleaned over all her months as a Spark. He gave her a fatherly pat on the forearm for thanks as he turned away. Pam saw a team as the means to an end and not the big emotional bonding activity that many did. Or, perhaps there were emotional bonds she saw, though she certainly kept them buried deep. Suddenly, Keegan realized more about the young woman than ever. He'd certainly known her family bio and history and knew there was an extreme pressure from her parents and siblings to excel. He now was realizing that her entire life she had been trained to perform and not to bond. She had been raised to achieve and not to "make friends." Keegan was having as much of a growing moment, an enlightenment about her, than anyone else in the room. And he was doing it live on camera in front of, he hoped, millions. Good for TV, and good for him.

"Now, I'd like to bring in Barbara Winton, who's our newest Bright Spark, as you might know, although she's been here for months now."

Behind him, he heard Jackie murmur to Ann to spotlight the Iowa farm girl. Barbara straightened her purple jumpsuit and ran a quick hand over her hair.

"Hi, Dr. Bright," she said.

"Hello, Barbara. You're the project manager on the *Spark Xpress*," he said. "Why don't you give me a quick tour?"

"Um, sure," Barbara said. He realized she was as taken aback as he was over the condition of the racer, but she covered it pretty well.

She had learned so much over the last few months about presenting to camera. Careful to face the lens when she described something, she spoke clearly as she pointed out each feature, from the salvaged seat frames and capsule door to the new design for the bunk area with a clever arrangement of storage compartments.

"That will hold a whole bunch," Keegan said, admiringly. "And how's your team doing on it? All of it?"

"These are the best people in the world," Barbara said, then her face flushed. "On both worlds. I'm really grateful for the way all the Sparks have pulled together, past and present. You know, once a Spark, always a Spark." She shot a thin smile in Pam's direction. Keegan couldn't tell for certain, but he thought he saw Pam slightly raise an eyebrow in response, and that pleased him.

"So, why haven't we seen the *Spark Xpress* in progress?" He kept the interview moving. "I'd have thought that it was natural for you all to post milestones as you reached them."

He knew he was putting her on the spot, but she didn't panic. That was why she was a Spark. Keegan had applicants with all sorts of intelligence and skills. Barbara was just as smart as any of them, but what had stood out to Keegan was how she kept her cool and just kept moving forward during the toughest of life's testing moments.

"We didn't let anyone see it because we wanted to surprise people," she said. She tossed her head as if daring him to contradict her.

"You sure did that," Keegan said, amused. "Now, tell me: Where do you fit in the design team? Who did what?"

Barbara didn't turn a hair. "Well, Dion oversaw life support and ergonomics. . . ." She explained where each of the ideas had come from during their brainstorming sessions, a couple of which Keegan had frankly eavesdropped on. That meant she was fielding questions to which he already knew the answers.

". . . So, my specialty is power systems and overall systems engineering. Jan and Gary consulted me frequently during the initial construction phases. We're basically running on solar with storage batteries under the main cabin. The batteries are also fed by friction from the buckyballs in their sockets."

"Not wasting a thing," Keegan said, approvingly. "I notice that unlike many of your competitors, a lot of your materials . . . aren't new. Why use things like that instead of purpose-made components?"

"I grew up on a farm," Barbara said. "As you said, we don't waste a thing. Our budget isn't as big as most of the teams, but we're resourceful. My family always found a use for pieces of technology that were discarded in a barn or a side field. When something needed fixing, we scrounged for things that were similar to what we needed, and repurposed them. Living on the Moon is sort of like living on a farm. We have to scrounge for and reuse everything. Never discount the items that are right under your nose," she added.

"Or the people," Keegan said, drawing a point. Too bad the other Sparks didn't share Barbara's attitude.

"Or the people," Barbara agreed. "You're going to turn up unexpected gems everywhere."

With that, she turned again with a friendly glance toward Pam. The tall girl had gone back to what she was doing, seeming not to acknowledge the compliment, but Keegan knew enough of her body language to realize Pam was touched, even more than before.

His work there was done. He turned back to the camera.

"Well, thank you, Barbara, and *all* of you Sparks! Now, we're going to check in on the people who run the life-support systems here in Armstrong City, to discuss how they're coping with our temporary increase in population. I think you're going to find that pretty interesting. You wouldn't believe how much dust all these new people have stirred up. It's causing all sorts of issues! Back in a minute. This is Dr. Keegan Bright, and we're *Live from the Moon!*" He sighed with relief as Ann turned off the lights.

"Thank you all," he said, shaking hands with everyone in the room. "That was great! I'll get out of your way now so you can all get back to work."

"Thanks, Dr. Bright," Barbara said. Behind her, Dion gave him a big grin and two thumbs-up.

Keegan led the crew out of the bay. He didn't say a word until they were all back in the main corridor, when the heavy atmosphere doors closed behind them.

"Worse than I feared," he said to Jackie, "but we've got some real cooperation going on in there. Leona, how long until that poor old buggy is ready to roll?"

"From my analysis of the vehicle in its current state, I estimate eighteen hours from completion," Leona said. Keegan shook his head.

"That's squeaking it, but at least they'll make it unless something blows up," he said, wiping sweat off his forehead. Ann, the lighting tech, doubled in makeup. She patted his face with powder. "Man, I feel like I worked as hard as those kids are right now."

"You did," Jackie assured him, steering him toward the city power plant. "You added your own little grease to the wheel. I think it'll help the rest of the process run smoothly. Now, come on! Let's go get some more footage. And you have to get prepped for *your* trip."

It had been a bit uneasy but somehow the team had managed to work with Pam for the better part of three hours. Barbara was impressed by how the former Spark and her teammates had rolled up their sleeves to pitch in. The four extra people were very handy when there were monotonous multiple bolts to be fastened, or wires to be connected, or heavy and cumbersome parts to be held into place. Barbara doubted they would have been able to finish the racer had the other Sparks and Pam's team not shown up to help.

"What goes here?" Alan Stone asked, pointing at several bolt holes and a wire manifold on the side of the habitat cylinder near the back and closer to the top than the middle. "Have we forgotten something or is it not in the blueprints?"

"Yes, that section is not showing on my models either," Pam added, frowning at Ada. "Is the design not complete?"

"That's where the—" Gary started to say but was interrupted by an elbow to the ribcage from Jan. "Um, uh, not sure what goes there. Do you remember, Jan?"

"That was a placeholder for something we never finished. It was going to be a platform for sensors and such. Just leave it. I'll patch those in a minute," Jan said hastily. Jan was a terrible liar. The Nerd-Twins were up to something, *another* something, and that they didn't want Pam to know what it was.

"Very well, then," Pam said, disinterested in subterfuge or secrecy. She looked at her task list. "All that is left are cosmetic additions and final software uploads. There is little more we can do to help."

"Yeah, right," Neil grunted. Barbara shot him an exasperated look. He shrugged. "I'm just saying she's right."

Barbara turned her back on him.

"Thank you all so much for your help, Pam. We'll see you out there. Good luck." Barbara smiled. "May the best team win."

"You are welcome," Pam said shaking Barbara's hand. "The Moon is very dangerous. I hope you all stay safe."

"You, too," Barbara said. "Thanks again, to you all."

Barbara nodded and shook the hands of Pam's team as they filed past her to the door. The door chime sounded and she stood there motionless for a long moment waiting and giving them time to leave. Finally, she turned to Jan and Gary, who were both smiling like cats who'd eaten the canaries.

"I know that bolt pattern," Neil said, accusingly. "That's for the magnetron of the EMdrive propulsion unit on my BrightSats."

"Yes, Neil, we all noticed that," Dion said, grinning. The alumni Sparks looked at each other.

"Well, now you have us curious," Calvin Book said, pushing his glasses up on the bridge of his nose. "What does go there?"

"Dr. Book, you see that conical-shaped copper thingy against the wall over there?" Jan asked.

"Yes, I do, Jan."

"Would you mind giving me a hand with it? That is the frustum for the EMdrive propulsion unit that goes on this side. Barbara, if you don't mind, the one for the other side is under that tarp over there," she said, pointing. "Once we attach these frustums we'll have to then attach Neil's BrightSat parts here and here. Ms. Scruffles, please send the final drawings for the electromagnetic propulsion units to the Sparks in this room *only*."

"Certainly, Jan. Meow."

"What is it, roomie?"

"Why did we keep it a secret from them, Jan?" Barbara asked.

"We don't have to let outsiders like Pam see everything we're putting into the *Xpress*," Jan said.

"It's a surprise," Gary added.

Daya's mouth turned up in a slow smile. "It's our secret weapon."

"And they'll see it soon enough," Dion said over his shoulder, as he continued running adhesive stripping around the seal on the airplane door.

"Am I the last to know about this?" Barbara demanded. The other stared at each other.

"I guess," Gary said. "You and Neil."

"An EMdrive?" Major Beddingfield said, with dawning delight as he and Dr. Book studied the new blueprints. "An EMdrive!"

"So that's why you needed my satellite? You should have just told me," Neil blurted out.

"You can't keep a secret, Neil." Daya laughed. "You never keep secrets."

"Can, too!"

"Neil, we'll need you to patch in the EMdrive control apps from your BrightSat flight computer to the main software desktop of the *Xpress*." Jan slapped him on the shoulder pretty hard. He would have bounced across the room if he hadn't been braced. "Time for you to show off."

"Okay! And, ouch." He smiled and rubbed his shoulder.

"It has been oversized, I see." Dr. Book frowned, doing calculations in his head. "This should be quite the afterburner, I think."

"Fun," was all Barbara could manage to say, as the idea dawned on her with its brilliance. "All right, let's get them installed so we can get some rest."

Chapter Six

"Racers, to your buggies! Fifteen minutes before the starting flag! I repeat," Mayor Petronillo's thin tenor voice announced over the intercom, interrupting the cacophony of voices and threads of music from the hidden TurnTable in the hangar, "fifteen minutes to go!"

Her heart pounding with excitement, Barbara clambered up the ladder on the inner face of the door, and into the cabin of the *Spark Xpress*. The four buckyball wheels glinted bright copper gold, the shiny copper conical frustums on each side glinted and looked unworldly, and the capsule-shaped body shone from being polished a half dozen times.

Barbara Winton plopped down into the right-hand driver's seat and wriggled to get herself deep into the heavy padding. Gary had been right. The tank from which he had cut them made a pair of really comfortable pilot chairs. Even while she was reaching for the impact belts, she kept looking around nervously. The repurposed airplane door rose and sealed tightly against the body of the buggy, blocking her view. A hiss of air meant that the compartment was pressurizing properly. Once the green light illuminated on the control panel, she slipped up her visor, breaking the seal on her helmet. The cabin air rushed in at her. She took in a deep breath then started looking about the cockpit at the various systems and controls. The Sparks had done their level best to think of everything. But nobody, not even Dr. Bright, could think of everything. Other things could go wrong. There were always things that could go wrong. What had they missed? What had *she* missed?

"Atmosphere at Moon normal," she said, glancing at her PerDee's screen. "I didn't have time for a second circuit to make sure everything's all right. Is there anything left on the checklist, Fido?"

"No, Barbara," her PerDee replied. "My analysis of the physical structure confirms that the *Spark Xpress* is intact and operational."

"Hey, lady, don't stress," Dion said with a grin as he plopped into the seat next to her with his visor already up. "We're green to go. It's all done. There's nothing left to do but get out there and win this race."

She gave him a warm look, which he returned with a wink. His easy tone always made Barbara relax. She activated Fido's remote readout in the lower right corner of the front window; it was a misnomer to call it a windshield on the Moon, but a good lunar equivalent didn't exist—yet. When she thought about it a bit more, in a sense there would be a "wind." As cars in front of them stirred up dust and they drove through it, there would be particles flowing into, around, and past the *Xpress*. Even if they were out in front, solar radiation or thermal differences between shadows would cause lunar dust to rise and flow with Brownian motion. As they drove through that dust it would be the same as "wind." Well, it would almost be the same as wind. Every experience here was so new, there wasn't vocabulary for it.

Dion strapped into the left seat, humming some tune that she had heard them searching for earlier. He scanned the pilot controls on his side of the cab. Neither of them had had much time to familiarize themselves with the dashboard. They were going to have to rely on their PerDees to guide them until they got used to the mechanisms. He activated Candy, his PerDee, and her attractive black female avatar appeared in the left lower quadrant of the bubble, where he could glance at the controls without turning his head.

After a four-way game of "Rock, Paper, Scissors" in Sparks Central, they decided Dion would drive the first leg, then transfer the driving controls to the dual identical set on the other side of the cockpit over to Barbara without having to trade seats. The vehicle was "drive by wire," so redundant controls were as simple as making a duplicate version, connecting the wires and wireless functions, then tapping the app when you needed them. They installed a software protocol to give a three-digit code to transfer the controls just to prevent doing it by accidentally hitting the touchpad. The PerDees could also transfer the controls upon voice commands of the pilot or copilot.

In the jump seats immediately behind the drivers, Jan and Gary fidgeted. They had diagnostics control systems and sensor displays on panels in front of each of them. The screens were mostly blank for projection or wireless control from their PerDees. There were also small thirty-centimeter-square side rectangular windows beside each of the seats so they could get actual eyeball views outside. Of course, there were so many camera sensors on the exterior of the vehicle that the PerDees could display any view outside the *Xpress* they wanted, but sometimes actually "seeing" outside was worth more than any video or imagery.

Gary and Jan looked excited, haggard, and both of them had bloodshot eyes. So did Barbara and Dion. Despite the mandatory rest period in the final sleep cycle before the starting gun, they had barely slept. There were still a million diagnostics each of them wanted to run, checking every little thing in the vehicle. The whole crew could hardly sit still. Despite the construction delays, all of them felt the excitement permeating the landing bay.

A blare of music, heavy on horns, filled the small cabin. Barbara nearly jumped out of her restraints.

"Sorry," Gary said, as she turned to glare at him. "I thought Turing had that app set on silent. I'm grabbing a bunch of tracks from the TurnTable while we're sitting here. It's keeping me from jittering all over the place. I'll sort them when we're out on the road."

"That's okay," Barbara said. "I'm just as jittery."

"You ought to get some sleep as soon as you can, brother," Dion said, glancing over his shoulder. "We're gonna run hard for the first fifty or so kilometers, then we'll start to see how the field spreads out. We know it better than anyone else, but I want to discuss strategy with you once you're rested up."

"Sleep? Who can sleep?" Gary squawked. "Let's talk once we hit the Aldrinville road."

Dion chuckled. "I wouldn't be able to rest either," he admitted. "Okay."

"Are you sure everything's in place?" Daya asked over their private channel, a scrambled frequency that Neil had claimed from the bandwidth. "All life signs are normal, but your heart rates are high. Did you get in your final workout?"

"Yes, but it wasn't easy," Barbara said, remembering the crowd in the workout room. "All the other teams were waiting their turn in the gym. I ended up running up and down the residential corridors."

"Very good. You need it to keep your advantage. How are your oxygen levels?"

Barbara glanced at the bracelet on her wrist. She had been fitted with it from the day she had arrived on the Moon, and was never without it, even showering or sleeping. All the lights on the small band were green.

"Everything's a go," she said. Dion confirmed.

"Ready!" Gary and Jan chimed in together.

"Excellent!" Daya said. "Good luck, team!"

"Thanks!" all four drivers called.

Then, the farewell calls began.

"Is this thing on?" Jackie's face popped up on all of the screens. It was a running joke that she always used with the Sparks when filming them. Wild graphics took the place of her face for a moment, then the image came back, but upside down. She tapped at the camera, acting as if she didn't know how it worked, and they played along. It was corny, but Barbara enjoyed it. "Anybody there?"

Dion guffawed. The sleep deprivation, excitement, and the rush to finish put them all on edge. Jackie's hijinks were a perfect tension breaker. The Sparks were so wired that it seemed over-the-top hilarious.

"Hi, Jackie." Barbara grinned. Gary chortled out loud.

"You have to press the red button, Jackie!" Jan laughed. "Maybe you need to get a cameraman to help you out."

"Oh, this red button?"

"That one!" Dion said, poking at the screen. "I put a label on it so you'll know."

Jackie's image flipped right side up again. "Thanks, Sparks! I just wanted to wish you good luck and to remind you to look at some of the cameras every now and then and give us some stuff we can cut into the show. It wouldn't hurt you to film some vlogs while you're out there, too," she added. "This is such a great opportunity, for the show, but for all the rest of our projects up here. Give us some good feedback and visuals. If there are any out there. Remember to drink plenty of liquids, and get enough sleep!"

"Yes, mother." Dion was still laughing.

"Good luck and go get 'em!" Jackie grinned. "Now, if I can just figure out how to turn this thing off . . . hmm . . ." Her face turned sideways and then she whispered as if she were talking into her director's headset. "I need a tech up here!"

The scope went blank. The team laughed.

"Hello, *Spark Xpress*!" Leona's avatar appeared on all the screens. This time, the AI manifested as a Little Gray Person, with buggy black eyes and knobby antennae. The avatar was alien, but most certainly female. Leona never missed the opportunity to express her chosen gender.

"Hello, Leona! How are you?" Barbara always found it fascinating to speak to Dr. Bright's AI. She seemed so "alive" to Barbara.

"Hey, Leona," the others chimed.

"Are you all excited?" she asked them.

"Of course we are!" Gary blurted out. "Are you serious?"

"I am very serious, Gary," the avatar said, bobbing her antennae. "I must say, I have not been so thrilled since your trip to Aldrinville months ago. I know you will all do great. Be safe and best of luck to you all!" Leona winked one of her huge dark eyes at them.

"Thank you, Leona!" Barbara smiled.

"You are all quite welcome. Good luck." Leona vanished from the screen as Dr. Bright's face appeared in its place. He was wearing a spacesuit, and a glare reflected off one side of his bubble helmet.

"Dr. Bright!"

"Didn't think I'd let you race around the Moon without wishing you luck, did you?" he asked. His famous grin never failed to make Barbara's heart turn over.

"We weren't sure you had time to." Dion shrugged.

"You're almost right! I only have a few seconds, but I will always make time for my Sparks. You guys call me if you need anything. If you start getting in trouble, there will be no shame in dropping out of this race. I don't want your egos or some desire to impress me or anyone else to get you hurt or, well, just, there will be nothing wrong with stopping if you get in a bad spot."

"There's no way we're dropping out," Dion said, firmly.

"We will be first across the finish line," Jan insisted.

"By kilometers," Gary added.

"We'll be fine," Barbara assured him. "We'll make you proud."

"I am absolutely certain you will!" Dr. Bright smiled. "Good luck, *Spark Xpress*! Good luck, Sparks. I'll see you at the halfway rest stop on the far side. Bright out."

"We have so got this," Gary said seriously and making eye contact with each of them. Barbara nodded in agreement.

"Racers, stand by for the countdown," the mayor's voice came over the speakers.

Only minutes left. Barbara told the butterflies in her stomach to calm down and let her think. On an ordinary EVA, she would have music blasting, but they needed to concentrate.

"Fido, let's see the competition again, okay?"

"Of course, Barbara," Fido replied.

Her side of the windshield filled with a grid five squares by five. Each contained the image of a vehicle. She let out a low whistle through her teeth.

"They don't even look like they belong to the same species," Jan said, admiring the buggies in spite of the rivalry.

"Taxonomy would be a challenge," Dion agreed. His specialty in biology wasn't going to be as important for the next several days as his skill behind the wheel and his ability to stay awake for long periods of time over boring roads.

Barbara studied the images, ordering Fido to blow each one up in three dimensions and make it turn slowly in the air. The *Spark Xpress* had pole position, right beside the platform where in a few moments Dr. Bright, the mayor, Ms. Reynolds-Ward, and a bunch of important people from Earth would send them off. They had gotten lucky: The race ranks were based on a lap time down the outer city road toward Aldrinville about fifteen kilometers and then back. They knew that stretch of road probably better than any other humans alive. Even sleep-deprived, they had easily been able to get the best qualifying time.

To their right, SolStar's vehicle, *Blue Streak*, all but hovered. Even the Nerd-Twins had to admit that Pam's buggy was not only Moon-worthy, but a real competitor, and beautiful, too. Her team's vehicle had a translucent, pale-blue cabin that looked like a soap bubble mounted on oversized wheels that looked like big rubber tires, but were actually made of a fine metal mesh. Fido's analysis showed the compound was springy and very strong. *Blue Streak* could bound across the landscape like a flea. The suspension had been built to accommodate all that jouncing so the occupants wouldn't get motion sick after a few kilometers. The fore half of the domelike cabin had been made transparent. In the image, Pam sat in the left-hand driver's chair. She glanced to her left, as if knowing that Barbara was studying her. Barb pushed the image away. She hated to buy into any of her colleagues' paranoia about the former Spark, but that just looked like mind-reading.

Next to *Blue Streak* was *Moonracer*, the Paralympians' vehicle. The Para-athletes drove a wedge-shaped car that reminded Barbara of their racing bikes, with the cabin far forward on an extended framework, and big impeller tires in the back. With the narrow prow, they would be more maneuverable than many of the other competitors. Neil had scoped out the track for the Sparks. About ten days ahead was a narrow track that snaked through craters piled one on top of another, as if the Moon had been hammered by asteroids in just that spot for eons. *Moonracer* would have real advantage there, as it would on any clear straightaway.

Team PolymerAce's red buggy *Rover* ran on six big rollers. Theirs was the biggest life-support module, giving them the most comfort, and the most solar panel space on top. Their storage batteries sat at the back. Gary had dismissed the design as so-so. It would run well on a flat road, but it had poor side-to-side maneuverability. Curly-haired Teddy Davis sat in one of the pilot's seats, strapping in. He looked excited enough to explode.

Zhar-Ptitsa, Team Firebird's buggy, and *Cheetah*, Team Solar Wind's brilliant red and yellow car, sat behind the *Spark Xpress* like a couple of glowing jewels. Lois Ingota fussed at the controls of *Cheetah*. One of the gorgeous Russians, her long blonde hair fastened into a severe bun on top of her head, nodded fiercely to a comment from one of her companions. Their two vehicles bore a striking resemblance to one another.

Pam was right: Everyone else seemed to have conferred during the design phase, while the Sparks had isolated themselves. As Barbara glanced at the rest of the competitors, she noticed a feature here and there that echoed on one buggy after another, and wondered what else they had missed out on. She couldn't help but feel a little envious, because all the other buggies were made of new materials. Out of budget concerns, as well as sheer determination to repurpose what they could, theirs had largely been sourced from discarded bits and pieces and, if she was honest, looked like it. She was proud of it anyhow. It was made for this terrain, and no team had more experience coping with it than hers did.

"Twelve minutes!" Mayor Petronillo called. Barbara glanced at the platform. He wasn't up there yet.

"Breathe!" she whispered to herself. "We've got this!"

"Hey," Calvin Book's voice erupted from all four of their PerDees at the same time. His face appeared on the inside of the windshield on both her and Dion's scopes. "I want to wish you all good luck. That was one intense building session! I haven't done an all-nighter like that in years. It was a blast. Thank you!"

"And we can't thank *you* enough," Barbara said warmly. "Hope you have fun watching the race!"

"Wish I could," the tall scientist said, with a grin, "but I'll be out on the range with Dr. Bright. I'm part of the mining and surveying project team that came up from Earth. We're going to build an accelerator around the Moon someday soon, and I'm doing preliminary examination of the site. I'll be checking in on all of you when I have a chance. See you at the finish line! I expect *my team* to come in first."

"We will!" Gary said, punching the air.

"Spoken like a true Spark," Book said. He looked up at the sound of voices coming over the public address system. "I'd better get off and let you all concentrate."

"Bye!" the Sparks chorused as the connection closed.

"He's great," Jan said. She had stars in her eyes.

"Once a Spark, always a Spark," Gary said, with a similarly smitten expression. "I gotta admit, that all-nighter *was* fun."

"I will refrain from saying anything about having to work all night at the last minute," Dion said, with an avuncular look at his younger colleagues, "but, yeah, I agree with you."

"We're sorry," Gary said, hunching his shoulders contritely. "We really thought we could do it."

"Forget it," Barbara said, firmly. "Live in the present, not the past or future. Now, let's win this race."

Jan stuck her hand between the drivers' seats. "Team!"

They piled their hands on top of hers.

"Team!"

"Look!" Barbara said, pointing out the left side of the pilot's compartment. "There's Dr. Bright! We're starting!"

Clad in a full EVA suit and bubble-shaped helmet, Keegan climbed up the metal stairs and turned to offer a hand to Ms. Reynolds-Ward. She wore a red environment suit, custom made with the logo of her consortium on the upper left breast. Behind her was her husband, Joe Ward, in a standard issue spacesuit. Ward was a shy man with a boyish shock of pale hair. He rarely sought out the spotlight, but even he had no intention of missing the start of a groundbreaking event. Keegan remembered that he had been an air-car chauffeur famous for his driving skills when he first met the billionairess, and his gentle, honest character had won her over. Their two children, clad in red like their mother, came up behind their father and immediately grabbed the best positions at the rail. Caitlin, truly her father's daughter with her interest in mechanical engineering and piloting, and an easygoing nature, would be accompanying Joe by shuttle to one of the pit stops out beyond Aldrinville on the Moon's far side. In case of emergency, each of the stopping points was equipped with medical facilities, but a gravely injured driver would have to be flown back to Armstrong City. Peter, Ms. Reynolds-Ward's son, wasn't that happy to be on the podium. Jan had a bad crush on the young man; Keegan felt sorry for her. He didn't like to think ill of people, but the boy was a dilettante. Peter had tried to get into the Sparks program using his mother's influence instead of science academic skills, and had been openly resentful when he was rejected. He had also tried to leverage a position on the Sparks racing team, playing on Jan's infatuation. Unluckily for him, the Sparks had closed ranks and kept all the functions within their own numbers.

Mayor Petronillo and his lovely wife, Eleanor, squeezed in between Keegan and Ms. Reynolds-Ward. Eleanor towered over her husband by a good six centimeters. Her wavy red hair was tied in a braid down her back, showing off her long, slender neck inside the bubble helmet. She had been a professional basketball player in Australia, and promoted sports both on the Moon and on Earth. Keegan had had her as a guest on *Live from the Moon* several times.

"Hiya, Keegan," she said, slapping him on the shoulder. Her voice sounded hollow inside the plastic shield. "Great day, isn't it?"

"I've never seen anything like it," he said, with heartfelt enthusiasm.

"I am proud to be a part of this fantastic event," Mayor Petronillo said. He looked around for the cameras. Keegan pointed him toward Jackie and the crew. Paul was scanning the field of competitors with his lens, but Yvonne had hers pointed up toward the podium. The mayor smiled and waved to her. Keegan had to grin. Jaime wasn't much of a media-hound. He really did prefer to work hard behind the scenes, but the job demanded that he present a prominent public face. Thanks to the in-helmet microphones, he didn't have to project to have his voice recorded. "Armstrong City is proud and happy to host the first ever Moon race."

Cisca, Calvin, and Thomas bounced up the stairs and shook hands with everyone. As the representative of one of the other sponsors of the race, Cisca was invited to be present for the starting flag. She had insisted that her fellow former Sparks be able to join her, and Keegan was delighted to oblige. Dr. Singh, Daya's mother and the city's chief medical officer, brought up the rear.

Overhead, half a dozen of Neil's BrightSats hovered, taking video and buzzing past the pilot compartments of every buggy. If he wasn't careful, a couple of them were going to get smashed by the departing vehicles instead of following them out onto the racecourse.

"Five minutes," Jaime said into the earpiece microphone he wore. "The hangar doors are opening in five minutes. Everyone not in an EVA suit, get out of the hangar now!" Momentarily, his voice overpowered even the overlapping noises from engines, voices, and the musical chaos from the local TurnTable. Keegan knew that the small device that generated the fragments of song and floating notes was hidden close by, but only Cisca knew how to turn it off.

A few dozen people, engineers, reporters, well-wishers and casual bystanders, abandoned what they were doing and took off running for the inner doors.

"Leona, make sure no one is hanging back," he said. "We don't want an emergency."

"All non-suited personnel have cleared the area," Leona confirmed.

"Keegan, this is marvelous!" Ms. Reynolds-Ward squeezed his wrist with her gloved hand. Her narrow face was alight with excitement. "Look at all these buggies! No two are alike, and they're all amazing. I am thrilled with the way this is turning out. You know, this could spark a new auto industry here on the Moon. Eventually, people will want to have Moon buggies of their own and not just city construction vehicles. They'll want to go for leisurely drives about the surface and we can have recharging stations, rest stops, and convenient stores just like on Earth!"

Keegan grinned. He had already been thinking along those lines. "I knew somehow you'd find a way to grow industry here based on this race. But you're right. People will see this and want a Moon racer of their own. Next year, we ought to offer a manufacturing contract as a grand prize."

"Next year!" the tycoon agreed. "We will absolutely have that as a prize. With a contract to build Moon buggies for the city government?"

Her eyes got a faraway look, and the corner of her mouth turned up. Keegan could see she was already putting ideas into motion that would lead to more industry and progress on the Moon. The mayor was paying close attention. He would end up overseeing and regulating any increase in vehicle traffic.

Mayor Petronillo checked his PerDee, and brought his arm up in a sweeping motion. Gigantic extraction fans in the ceiling and walls kicked on, making everything vibrate. The precious atmosphere was sucked out of the enormous chamber, and the vibrations died away. Condensation formed on the inside of every cockpit and helmet as the frigid vacuum struck them. The dryness of the air quickly let the condensation evaporate and clear away. Dry sinuses was one of the things visitors to Armstrong City had to become acclimated to quickly—much as they would in the high-altitude deserts on Earth.

The massive doors rolled aside, revealing the brilliant gray-white terrain of the Moon. The plain within a kilometer or so of Armstrong City had been graded more or less flat, but beyond it rose the edges of craters and lunar peaks silhouetted against the blackness of space. Over his helmet speakers, Keegan heard the collective intake of breath from the onlookers. They felt awe. It *was* awesome.

While the landscape beyond the big doors was inhospitable to life, ingenuity, perseverance, and skill would conquer territory seen by only a few human beings and traversed by even fewer. Every time he flew over the surface of the Moon, he experienced the excitement and curiosity that he hoped these kids would find.

"All right, everybody!" Mayor Petronillo called. "As mayor of Armstrong City, the first city on the Moon, it is my immense pleasure to welcome all of you competitors to this, the first ever race to circumnavigate Earth's largest and oldest satellite. You have all worked hard to get here, so I expect you to compete with fairness and courtesy to your fellow racers. You know the safety requirements. If you run into trouble, ask for help! Don't try to be heroes. That is one hostile environment out there, and any mistake can be fatal. I know," he added, with a grin, "that just makes it all the more exciting. The prizes for success are high, but no higher than having the bragging rights for being in this race and coming home safely. Now, I turn over the microphone to Dr. Keegan Bright, who will start you off. Dr. Bright!"

Keegan cleared his throat, enjoying the thrill of having many pairs of eyes on him, thousands here and millions back on Earth.

"You heard the man, folks!" he said, his eyes fixed on Yvonne Walotski's camera lens. "This is going to be one heck of an adventure! Twelve thousand kilometers, fourteen mandatory rest stops eight hundred kilometers apart, four drivers, and twenty-six of the most awesome Moon buggies ever assembled. Be careful out there and Godspeed everyone!" He reached behind underneath the podium and pulled out a green rectangular flag and held it high above his head. He whirled it around in a circle. "Racers, start your engines . . . get set . . . go!"

He swept the green starting flag down, and a massive hologram of the flag flashed and danced about on the inner wall above the open door. The buggies' engines didn't roar— they were all electric and in a vacuum—but he could feel the vibration through the lunar surface as six rows of cars shot out into the sun. Behind them, six little lights like shooting stars, flew Neil Zimmerman's BrightSats.

Almost instantly, the buggies were obscured by a cloud of regolith kicked up by the tires, treads, buckyballs, rollers, motivators, and whatever else the racers had underneath their buggies. The race was on!

The hangar doors slid shut, cutting off the brilliant sunlight, but not in time to prevent half a ton of regolith being kicked inside by the backwash from twenty-six sets of wheels.

"Oh, well," Ms. Reynolds-Ward said, with a rueful smile, looking down at the mess. The gray stone dust settled in swirls and dunes on the hangar floor. "This is the part that we don't put on the evening news."

"Oh, my, that is going to choke so many intakes in the city's circulation and air handling systems. And I bet the exterior windows will be covered. Should have thought of that," Keegan said.

"Well worth it, Keegan. Don't fret it," Ms. Reynolds-Ward told him with a smile.

"Well done, my friend," Mayor Petronillo said, shaking Keegan's hand. "Would all of you like to come back to our home for a celebratory drink?"

"Wish we could, mayor," Keegan replied. He gestured to Calvin Book. "The two of us have to collect the rest of our party and get on to our project. We're taking Paul Sorensen with us to record some video for the show. It's going to take us a few hours to fly there."

"Then, you go safely, too," the mayor said. He clapped Keegan on the arm. "I need you back here at the finish line when the racers come back."

"We will be," Keegan promised. "We're taking every precaution, too."

"Uh, wait, Keegan," Ms. Reynolds-Ward stopped him, plucking the flag out of Keegan's hands. "Let me have that. I want to make sure it is preserved in the Armstrong City Museum."

"We have a museum?" Keegan asked slyly. The founder met his eyes with a knowing wink.

"We will, Keegan. We will."

Chapter Seven

Despite its last-minute completion, the *Spark Xpress* ran smoothly. It glided out of the hangar and headed toward the open terrain. Even so, Team PolymerAce zoomed past them and took an early lead, followed closely by the *Blue Streak*. The two vehicles could hardly have looked less alike, with the heavy, flat behemoth being pursued by the insubstantial-seeming bubble on translucent mesh tires, but there was no doubting how fast they could move.

"No!" Dion growled, his handsome eyes blazing at the challenge.

He hung onto the controls, staring out at the flattened whiteness as he stepped on the accelerator. The control levers looked like airplane engine throttles being operated by slide bars on the touch panel between the pilot and copilot's seats. There was still an old-fashioned foot pedal or "gas pedal" like in automobiles but it was a throttle for all of the drive motors at once. The individual throttle slide bars were the maximum power settings for each motor individually.

"Catch him!" Gary shouted. "We're not going to take third place!"

"Guys!" Barbara laughed. "We are not even double-digit kilometers into an eleven- thousand-kilometer race. Let them lead for a while. They can run their batteries down by redlining their engines faster than the panels can recharge them. Unless they've created some new physics, solar panels can only do so much. They'll burn out of juice and have to stop to recharge. We'll overtake them then. Just keep the pace we planned. Stay on pace to win the race.

Hey, that rhymed!" She giggled. She felt the same excitement the others did. "How fast can we go and still maintain a steady feed from the collectors?"

"Ms. Scruffles, display the energy usage curve versus speed versus recharge rate on the central screen," Jan said.

"Very well, Jan. Meow."

The curves were projected up in the middle of the main windscreen on a colorful chart. A blue line showed the energy in joules being used by the *Spark Xpress*. It fluctuated up and down based on how heavy Dion's foot got. The line beside it showed the charge on the batteries. Green was optimum. It changed to yellow if it fell even with the usage line, and red if it dropped below. The battery line went down as the speed curve in white and the blue energy line went up. Anytime Dion hit the brakes, friction also regenerated the batteries. The same went for going downhill. For the time being, they were mostly on a flat region of the lunar surface, but the sun was strong above them, and constantly recharged the collectors, as long as they stayed clean. Power went to supply not only the buckyballs, but heating and cooling, plus air recycling. Otherwise, the sun beating down on them could have made it over 100 degrees Celsius in the cabin in full lunar daylight.

The *Spark Xpress* rolled over the lip of the low crater just off the edge of the Armstrong City complex and rumbled through the middle of the depression. It was easy to see the two buggies in the lead. The blinding white cloud of regolith that *Rover* was kicking up could probably be seen from Earth.

"Nice piece of design, coating this bubble with polarizing pigments," Dion said, as the *Spark Xpress* bounded up and out, hitting the main road only a couple hundred meters behind the leaders, and straight into the hovering dust. Scrapers on the front of their windscreen cleared arcs for them to see through. "We're going a lot faster than we ever did running up and back to Aldrinville. I don't need to go blind on the road."

"We thought of everything," Jan said smugly. Barbara's mouth twitched in amusement. Now that the buggy was finished and running, they could brag about its features instead of how long it had taken to put them together, and that the only time any of them had had a chance to drive it had been from the loading dock to the main hangar and then the qualifying run for pole position. "Doesn't it run like a dream?"

"I guess so, so far," Dion said. "Let me open her up a little. I can catch those two. We'll show them what we've got."

"Watch it, Dion. Keep those curves even." Barbara pointed at the display on the window screen. "We've got a long way to go. This is more of the tortoise and the hare than a drag race. And don't forget how things went in Aldrinville. Anything could happen."

"Sheesh, roomie! You are stressing big time," Jan said, poking her in the shoulder with a playful forefinger.

"Not stressing," Barbara said. "I'm looking ahead."

"Let's get some music going in here!" Gary interjected. "Fanfare for the winning team!"

Jan promptly reached for Ms. Scruffles on her EVA suit sleeve. In the cabin, the team wore their spacesuits, minus their helmets, which were stowed in bins under the seats within easy reach, and their gloves, which were tucked back, leaving their hands bare. "I have some fantastic tracks I collected from the M-Tracker! Ms. Scruffles, play Driving Playlist number one!"

"Of course, Jan," the PerDee replied. "Meow!"

A drumbeat like a chugging engine started low, and rose into a hammering pulse, as guitars and trumpets joined in. Barbara automatically began bobbing her head up and down with the rhythm. The others started chair-dancing with her.

"Yeah!" Dion said. He put his foot down, and the *Spark Xpress* sped forward. "We are so going to catch those guys and pass their butts! We rule this road!"

"Hey!" a male voice interrupted their discussion. A quick glance at Fido's screen said that the speaker was coming in over the open communication channel for all the teams to use. "You hear what we heard? There are TurnTables out here!"

"Who's this?" Barbara asked, running her finger down Fido's screen to reply. "I'm Barbara on Team Bright Sparks."

"Hey!" the voice repeated. "Teddy Davis, Team PolymerAce. We're your leaders for today. Awesome to meet you, Barbara!"

"You're moving way out in front of us," Pam's calm voice came on the circuit. Suddenly, Barbara's teammates stopped headbanging. They still behaved as if she was a monster. She had to find out what was going on, but later. "Take it easy. You are bouncing so much you could turn over."

"We're fine!" a deeper male voice retorted. "We designed this baby to take anything."

"Nev DeLeon, is that you?" Dion asked. "Man, the road is deceptive. It looks wider than it is. This isn't like driving on Earth. If you go off the graded track, you could end up in a pit of dust that is deeper than a lake. And you just keep on bouncing or rolling forever in the lower gravity."

"Hey, you just want to get ahead of us," Nev replied, not sounding impressed or concerned, although his voice stuttered from the jostling their vehicle must have been taking. "Anyone playing M-Tracker? Want to have a Battle of the Bands? I'm Crew Rock 'n' Roll!"

"You're on," Gary said. "I'm Crew Spacepunk!" He whipped Turing out of his sleeve, fiddled with the playlist to choose his attack tracks, and poked the center of the display. "Hit it!" Discordant guitar music with a weird, dystopic beat poured out of the PerDee's tiny speaker, and was met by an audible onslaught of heavy drumming and intricate guitar work. Barbara watched the holograms rising from Turing's screen with growing interest. Gary was probably the best combatant of the six Sparks. At the same time, she kept scanning the instruments for problems.

Presently, all the systems were in the green, but they were on the Moon, after all. There was just no telling when, not if, something would happen. She knew that sounded pessimistic, but Barbara knew that it was better to be prepared for an incident and it not happen than the other way around.

With regolith dust and other particulates floating about in the pressurized cab due to Brownian motion, the holographic bars of music rising up from Turing's screen remained visible for a meter or so around Gary with the look of rays of sunlight peeking through window shades. Spacepunk's tunes were rendered in silver, and Rock 'n' Roll's in gold. Nev must have had a powerful track or two, because his first song overpowered Gary's in moments. Gary frowned and queued up his second tune. It had some staying power, but it tapered to silence after just a bar or two.

"All right," he said, his brows drawing down over his thin nose. "This means war!"

He scrabbled at the small screen with all the fingertips on his right hand. Barbara made a face as a harsh male voice began to shriek over electronic music. It had the desired effect, however, as silver notes began to surround and envelop the gold. A gang of notes even surrounded the last tied chords and kicked them until they disappeared. The rictus of a grin on Gary's face told Barbara he knew he was winning. One after another, the third track took down everything that Nev threw at it. At last, Turing's screen cleared, and a big golden disk with a hole in the middle hovered over it.

"Rematch," Nev demanded. "I want a—"

"Holy crud!" Teddy shouted.

The communications link broke off abruptly.

"Brace yourselves!" Dion shouted.

Barbara had been so interested watching the match that she had forgotten to look out the front of the cab. She spun around just in time to see *Rover* plunging nose first off the side of the road. The huge rollers underneath the cab caused it to bounce uphill several tens of meters, and come to a halt half buried in regolith. A huge puff of dust exploded upward, and began to settle, twinkling, on *Rover's* hulk. With expert hands, Dion steered clear of the buggy's broad tail and out onto the open track just behind *Blue Streak*. Triangular *Moonracer* came up close, then veered in behind *Spark Xpress*, narrowly avoiding one of the buckyballs. Barbara clung to her restraining straps. Her heart pounded.

"You totally ate dust!" Gary crowed.

Barbara gave him a look like her mom might have given her. The Nerd-Twins knew how serious being out on the Moon was! "Are you folks all right?"

"Yes," a woman's voice said. "We can back out again. But I am totally taking the wheel away from these two *lugs*!"

"Ow!" Teddy yelped. "Hey!"

"Rule three," Jan said, cocking her head at Dion. "The driver doesn't get to play M-Tracker."

"Driver *or* copilot," Barbara said. "I wasn't paying attention to the road. I shouldn't have been looking at Gary. It's just too distracting."

"Right," Dion said, shaking his head. "That could have been us. Candy, you get that? No M-Tracker while I'm in the front of the cabin."

"Whatever you say, Dion," the throaty voice of his PerDee purred. Barbara laughed.

"Are you guys all right?" Neil's voice came over their private frequency. "I just saw that happen on BrightSat 5. What a mess!"

"Your heart rates are elevated. Were you involved in the accident at all?" Daya asked.

"We're fine," Barbara said, glancing at her fellow drivers. They each nodded. "Check in on Team PolymerAce, will you? Their pilot was playing M-Tracker with Gary. We had no idea."

"I will have my mother call them," Daya promised. "She will have something to say about distracted driving."

"Another first," Gary said, trying to look repentant and failing. "A traffic accident on the Moon."

"No way," Dion said, keeping his eyes on the cloud ahead that concealed the *Blue Streak*. "*We* were first. Don't ever forget that. I earned that title. I'm not letting it be forgotten."

"Let's have some music," Jan said. "No M-Tracker."

"Okay," Gary said, chastened, but he booted up a rocking playlist. Barbara started bobbing her head.

"Let's take a look at the map," Barbara said after an hour or so. "Fido, put the image on the windshield, will you? Flattened, not rotating."

"Yes, Barbara," the PerDee said. Across the bottom, not obscuring Dion's vision, a narrow rectangle of pale green snaked to and fro from the left to the right. The rectangle represented the width of the racers' path so far. To that point in the race, none of the other teams had ventured very far apart from each other, but that was likely because there was an already somewhat improved gravel-packed road to Aldrinville. Once they had gone past Aldrinville, past the second checkpoint, it was likely that many of the teams would spread much farther apart trying to find their own passages and shortcuts around craters and mountains and ravines to the next checkpoint.

A bright spark—Fido's idea of humor, maybe?—showed where they presently were: just leaving the spoked circle of Armstrong City. Despite the grayness of the landscape outside the vehicle, changes in terrain were picked out in deepening shades of green. Brilliant jewels indicated the pit stops. Blue meant a place to check in, eat, sleep, even shower, and do minor repairs. The five red stops had medical facilities, major repair stations, and emergency evacuation shuttles. Ms. Reynolds-Ward had generously donated her personal shuttle for the duration of the race.

We have the edge, Barbara thought to herself, eagerly. *As long as we don't waste it.* She promised herself they wouldn't. No matter how good they were, the other teams couldn't understand how difficult it was to negotiate regolith-covered plains and maintain good control of their energy systems. The one-sixth gravity was both a help and a hindrance. The Sparks could win this!

Once they got past Aldrinville, the marked route went from graded and cleared road to unimproved and very torturous terrain. They were going to have to rely on satellite navigation and positioning data from a constellation of small satellites around the Moon, the lunar equivalent of GPS on Earth.

"In some of those wide-open areas, we've got the opportunity to gain ground on vehicles that can't handle tight maneuvering," Dion said, pointing at wide lunar plains, especially those marked across Mare Ingenii and Mare Imbrium on the far side.

"Yeah, but the judges programmed us their suggested course based on maps made by the shuttle crews," Gary said. "I don't know about deviating from that too much."

"We definitely will have to figure out the most efficient route," Jan said, looking at the same map pulled up in front of her on Ms. Scruffles's screen. "Neil should be of a lot of help there."

"We have several days before we have to figure that out," Barbara reminded them. "Let's see how the *Spark* handles, first."

"Great, compared with *Rover*," Gary said with a wicked smile.

Chapter Eight

"It is this crater here, Calvin, that I think is where we could put the far-side power station," Dr. Keegan Bright explained to his longtime friend and former pupil. Although Calvin Book was in his thirties, had earned two prestigious PhDs, and had grown nearly twenty centimeters since he had been in the Sparks program, Keegan still saw him as one of the kids. The two of them bounced up to a point overlooking the mining site. They were just south of the centerpoint of Mare Ingenii.

"Why this place particularly, Keegan?" Calvin, kneeling, picked up a handful of lunar regolith and let it filter slowly through his gloved fingers. The low horizon "afternoon" sunlight barely clipped the edge of the crater. Only half of the crater was illuminated. It would be days before the sun disappeared over the horizon, and they meant to make the best of their time.

They were being careful to stay in the sunlight and out of the cold while several of the mining team set up ground-penetrating radars. They hoped to locate pockets underneath them that might have exploitable veins of minerals. Dr. Bright could see the reflection of the shuttle on the edge of the crater behind him on Calvin's bubble helmet. They had a few moments to themselves before the mining team would be ready to head down into the entry shaft they had already created. Paul, the lanky LFTM cameraman, moved carefully around them, taking video. Keegan had chosen his vantage point carefully, both for what they could see, and the dramatic image for the folks back home.

"Beneath this plain is a warren of ancient hollow tubes with numerous massive pockets that were formed by gas bubbles. My thoughts are that there are enough natural caves here where the mining company is digging that we could use them for makeshift shelters and storage. That will eliminate the need for a lot of construction and temporary inflatable habitats early on. The main thing, though, is that we are exactly on the opposite side of the Moon from Armstrong City, where we will have a large power supply."

"Ah, yes, so this is the location for the midpoint station of the accelerator?" Calvin stood up. He automatically reached for the glasses on his head but bumped his hand into the suit's helmet instead, and laughed. "Bertie, push my glasses up, will you?"

"Yes, Calvin." From around the scientist's shoulder, a mouse-sized robot climbed up the left side of his face. A tiny claw reached out and pulled the stem of the three-dee glasses until they sat in place on Calvin's nose.

"Thanks. Being on the Moon in space will take some getting used to."

"Nah, you never get used to it." Keegan smiled back at him. "It is just too amazing. I'm sorry you left the program before we got up here. And yes, this could be the midpoint station. Or maybe the endpoint station where we put the particle detector chamber."

"Right," Calvin agreed. He tapped the pocket on his sleeve where his PerDee resided and opened his palm upward. A lunar map shimmered over his gloved hand. Little points of white light were arranged in a rough circle on its surface. "So, while we were flying in, I had Andromeda overlay the concept art for the circumlunar particle accelerator and realized that at each of the major superconductor nodes there is a race checkpoint very nearby. The race midpoint checkpoint is only thirty kilometers east and about ten kilometers south of here. What a coincidence! Or is it?"

"Two birds with one stone," Keegan replied as he turned about with his arms out, gesturing to the lunarscape around them. "We're planning on building a ring around the surface of the Moon that will accelerate particles several orders of magnitude faster than the Extreme Hadron Collider on Earth can and it'll need to be bending magnets roughly every twenty kilometers with larger stations every eight hundred kilometers or so. We'll need roads around the Moon for that. And these racers are charting them for us for free! We've drawn out general guidelines for them to travel, but they'll take the path of least resistance. That'll make it easy to grade roads where it's most effective to have them."

"If anything, sir, you are efficient, and I've never known you to have just one motivation for anything!" Calvin grinned from ear to ear. "And building an accelerator on the Moon where we don't need large expensive vacuum pumps and pressure vessels is nothing short of pure wizardry. I'm glad you invited me to be a part of it."

"Well, don't count your hadrons before they collide, Calvin." Keegan turned to his former pupil. "This could be *the* thing that brings people to the Moon in massive droves. We'll need workers of every kind to begin with: engineers, physicists, metal workers, concrete workers, electricians, truck drivers, tower builders, mathematicians, logistics specialists, foundry workers, computer programmers, and more. All of those people will need housing, places to eat, buy clothes, facilities for entertainment and just plain socializing. And, soon, they will have children with them, and those children will need schools with teachers and administrators and lunch room ladies and the whole deal. This could be the big lunar prize that everybody has been dreaming of. Once people are in the habit of living and working on another planet, we can concentrate on creating a platform for travel to other planets, starting with Mars. The race is just the beginning of making Earth engage with its little sister, and the rest of the solar system."

"But?" Calvin interrupted him.

Keegan blew out a gust through his lips that made a sound like a motorboat. Everything hinged on that "but."

"But, it will cost billions to get started. We'll need grants from governments and investments from private entrepreneurs and investment companies and we'll need a cultural buy-in. I'm thinking on that. How do we get the public excited about it? I'm thinking of getting the Sparks interested in building a linear accelerator in just the right place along the path that might one day be a leg of the circumlunar one, not far from Aldrinville, where we've already got a habitat established. We could at least get their fan base motivated."

"You are always spinning the wheels, aren't you?" Calvin closed his palm, and the display vanished.

"It's what I do." Keegan turned a grin toward the camera. Behind it, Paul grinned back.

"And this is a bit in the future, maybe as much as a decade." Calvin stood and looked at his friend and mentor with a puzzled facial expression. "So, why are we here today?"

"Aha, that."

"Yes, that."

"What did you do before you moved to the EHC upgrade team?" Keegan asked him. Of course he knew the answer, but he always liked to see his students and colleagues figure things out for themselves.

"You know what I did. You helped me get that job." Calvin shrugged. "I did gamma ray spectrum analysis and detection for the U.S. State Department and the United Nations. You know, Doc, I hunted fissile materials, yellowcake uranium, and other such possible weaponizable materials in Africa and the Middle East."

"Of course you did." Keegan laughed out loud. "Leona, show us a gamma ray spectrum live at our present location. Project the image on the ground with large text, please."

"Of course, Dr. Bright." Leona's lilting voice filled their helmets. They both turned and looked to the ground as the PerDee projected the graph there. While there wasn't an atmosphere to support the hologram in the usual way, they had kicked up enough regolith dust to allow the image to populate in three-dee.

"Okay, Dr. Calvin Book. Tell me what you see." Dr. Bright said pointing to the graph. Calvin exhaled in surprise.

"A gamma spectrum between about twenty to two hundred fifty kilo-electron volts." Calvin studied the graph, leaning farther and farther over. He actually reached for his glasses again and bumped his hand against his helmet. Both he and Dr. Bright chuckled. "Automatic reaction. Bertie, just keep them in place, all right?" Calvin pointed at the graph with one long, gloved hand. "Okay, okay, okay, I see. We've got a peak in energy here at about twenty-five keV, that's cadmium probably, one at about sixty-three KeV. That'd be thorium-234. And then all these big energy spikes between eighty-three and a hundred KeV. Hmm, then here at one forty-three, one sixty-three, and one eighty-five! Keegan, is this real?"

"That is a live feed from the local detectors we put out a few months back," Keegan assured him, pointing out over the landscape toward where the devices lay hidden in meters of regolith. "Those are the gamma rays pinging against us right this very minute. So, what do you think?"

Calvin felt his heart pound. "Think? I know! Anybody that had worked for the international atomic energy teams could look at this and tell you they were looking at a uranium oxide spectrum." He looked at the graph, then back at Dr. Bright. "There's uranium here, isn't there?"

"Uranium ores. Lots of it." Keegan nodded at an airlocked inflatable that jutted from the mouth of a cave in the crater wall. The side of the crater had caved in long ago, perhaps millions of years before, forming a sheer cliff that thrust upward for more than fifty meters. "More precisely, right over there is where they have found the bulk of it. That's the first beginnings of a mineshaft. We need help locating where to look, and I thought you might be able to help there. The mining company is willing to pay you a significant consulting fee."

"How significant?" Calvin asked, raising an eyebrow. "I already have a job."

"Yes, yes, I know. You're part of the detector systems redesign team for the renovation and upgrade of the Large Hadron Collider." Keegan paused and collected his thoughts because he wanted to phrase this the right way that would have the greatest probability of convincing Calvin to stay on the Moon. "Calvin, that thing is on the upper side of pushing a century old. It will take billions to renovate it and for what? We've pushed the energy limits with it and still no faster-than-light space travel, antigravity, or even a good understanding of the fundamental four forces of nature. We're setting the groundwork here for the very first particle accelerator that can reach over a quadrillion electron volts. Over ten peta eV could tell us those secrets the universe is still hiding from us, and there is no way you're gonna get to do that on Earth."

"But what does the uranium mining have to do with it, Keegan?" Calvin asked.

"It means infrastructure," Keegan said, half to Calvin, and half to the camera. Jackie would edit out all the parts that were still confidential information, but this would be interesting to his audience, both children and adults. "It means a mining business will be moving in and doing work. It means the Moon will have more than just solar power and reactors dependent on Earth for fuel rods. We have uranium here, Calvin, and plenty other valuable minerals: transuranics, KREEP ores, rare gases like Helium-3—even diamonds."

"Diamonds!"

Keegan saw the sparkle in his former pupil's eyes.

"We'll need to build enrichment facilities and reactor power plants and start spreading power about the Moon. I'm thinking we could put a reactor at each one of the race's major checkpoints, connected by our proposed roadway. The reactors should be designed with the future particle accelerator in mind. Not only should it be able to supply power to the city and infrastructure around it, but also however much the superconducting bending magnets and computational facilities and whatever else the accelerator will need. That means we have to start designing it. Now, not a decade from now. *We* have a lot of work to do."

Keegan paused to see if Calvin understood that he was using the word *we* deliberately. When his former pupil's eyes widened and a smile crossed his face, Dr. Bright could remember that spark of brilliance that he'd seen when Calvin had been just a boy.

"There it is! That's what I was looking for." Keegan nodded, his own grin bursting out.

"What? There what is?" Calvin asked, bemused.

"That look you get when you know that you are going to do something that is going to impress the living daylights out of the rest of the world. You should never play poker, my friend."

Calvin reached for his glasses, remembered at the last minute, and let his hand drop. "Most of the gambling casinos won't let me. Eidetic memory and all. They think I'm counting the cards."

"Ha, ha. I didn't know that about you." Keegan held out his hand to his former pupil. "Whatever the miners can't pay you, I'll add in from the accelerator design project. Ms. Reynolds-Ward has already tossed a few tens of million in on this. That lady is a true visionary."

"Okay." Calvin took Keegan's hand and shook it excitedly. "I'm in. Let's build the biggest atom smasher humanity has ever imagined!"

"Now, you're talking like a Spark." Keegan nodded to Paul, who gave him a thumbs-up. When they made the documentary about this project, a decade from then, they'd have the video of that moment when the team began to come together. "Let's go talk to the mining contractors, and see how they're progressing."

Chapter Nine

Barbara held onto the controls, guiding the *Spark Xpress* over a bump she couldn't see through the twinkling cloud of regolith dust. If it wasn't for the GPS and Neil's constant guidance over the Sparks' channel, she would have no idea where the road lay. According to Candy's neat graph of power versus impedance in the middle of the windscreen, she kept pretty close to the top of the greatest efficiency. One of the things Jan and Gary had kept from the original design that the Sparks had brainstormed was her power storage array. At their present rate of speed, they could run for a solid two days, even when they drove into the night side. Dion reclined beside her, alert but taking it easy after his first shift behind the wheel. Behind them, the Nerd-Twins were tucked into their bunks. Gary was festooned with wrappers from his favorite snacks.

"This is good road!" Tomasz Salenko's resonant voice boomed in over the open channel. "Why so many warnings of danger?"

"The road only goes a short distance past the Aldrinville location," Barbara said. "That's where our pit stop is. After that, we'll be running on unimproved lunar surface, with craters, rocks, and lakes of regolith. Some of the deep dust lakes have beacons floating on the top to warn you away, but not all of them are mapped. It'll be more dangerous once we circle to the limb of the Moon, when we won't have sunlight or Earthlight."

"Our buggy is made to float on those lakes," Lois Ingota put in, from Team Solar Wind's buggy, *Cheetah.* According to Barbara's map,

Solar Wind trailed in sixteenth place, but that could change at any moment. "We'll get ahead of all of you then."

"Not so," added a cool voice from Team Firebird, one of the aloof Russians. "You will see how well prepared we are for such terrain."

"Well, Jar-Pizza," Teddy Davis began. "Wait, how do you say your buggy's name?"

"*Zhar-Ptitsa*," the voice said, sounding friendly for the first time. "You do not speak Russian?"

"*Nyet*. And that's all I know."

A tinkling laugh came from *Firebird*. She repeated the name, and Teddy recited it after her until it began to sound like her pronunciation. "It is a beginning. Which vehicle are you?"

"*Rover*," Teddy replied.

"Oh! You are the one that went nose down in the dust!"

"Hey, that was an accident!"

Other drivers and crew chimed in, laughing.

"It's not so easy to control out here," a warm alto with a lilting Irish accent said. "I wish we'd come up here more with more than a week to practice. The gravity is so light, we're going airborne every time we hit a bump!"

"I'm afraid we're going to fall off the road into one of those craters!" a big basso boomed. "It's too easy to oversteer our controls. Think they'll ever find us?"

"You will be fine," Pam's voice put in. Dion stiffened. Barbara gave him a puzzled glance. She had thought that the joint build phase had helped him deal with his dislike of Pam. It looked like she was wrong. "The road is wider than it looks. Two vehicles can easily pass one another. As long as your buggy maintains life support integrity, nothing will happen. I've reviewed all of your designs, and no one should be trapped by the regolith. Scientifically speaking, there is no evidence that the regolith is more than a few tens of centimeters thick anywhere, but there are theories."

"Just don't crash," the basso said, darkly.

"I believe that goes without saying," Pam agreed. Dion huffed, but kept silent.

"It's beautiful up here," the Irish voice said. "All those soaring ridges, and the wide-open plains in shades of silver."

"I love it!" a fluting soprano put in. "What it must be like to live up here?"

Dion grinned and nudged Barbara's arm with the back of his hand.

"It's great, actually," she said, startled into replying. "I've been here many months now. I mean, it's dangerous, but I love it."

"Who are you?" the soprano asked.

"She is Barbara the Spark!" Tomasz said. "I follow them on the vlog. Don't you?"

"The Bright Sparks!" "We watch Dr. Bright all the time!" "Oh, man, this is great!"

The voices all started talking at once. Barbara waited until the verbal traffic jam cleared. She caught a glimpse of her reflection, a grin warring with mild embarrassment.

"How'd you get to be a Spark?" Teddy asked, sounding just a little resentful.

"You want the truth?" Barbara asked, staring at the bright line on her scope. "I didn't know I was applying. Dr. Bright ran a contest some months ago, I don't know if you remember. I sent in the results of an experiment I did on power sources. The next thing, I got a package with a message pad in it inviting me up here. It was like a fairy tale. I've been a fan of his show since I was a little kid, when it was still called *Science Live with Dr. Bright*. Getting to be up here, getting to be a Spark is better than anything I ever hoped for."

A lot of sighs and cheers came over the speaker, along with a few raspberries.

"How do *I* get into the program?" a woman's voice asked.

"Dr. Bright is the only one who can answer that," Dion said. "He came to do a program with my science class when I was in junior high. Out of all the kids, he asked *me*. Barbara's right. It's the best thing that ever happened to me. I get to work with Dr. Bright, and the rest of the Sparks are my family."

He turned those beautiful dark brown eyes to her with a warm glance. Barbara felt a tingle go through her. She smiled.

"But you're all here on the Moon anyhow!" Barbara said. "This race is like nothing that has ever happened before. Everybody's got their own stories. We want to get some of yours. For the Sparks' vlog." Dion winked at her. She felt herself blush.

"Yes!" Charlton Mbute shouted. "That would be awesome! My family is already jealous I'm up here for the race. I want to be first!"

"Okay," Barbara said, with a grin. "Fido, take down everyone's name who wants to be interviewed."

"Of course, Barbara," the PerDee replied.

"When?" Charlton asked.

Dion raised his shoulders and his eyebrows.

"What's wrong with now?" he asked. "We've got hours to go before the first pit stop."

"Hold on a minute!" Barbara cried, as the fifteenth—or was it sixteenth?—person clamored to start telling her experiences. "I need a drink of water." She scrabbled for the travel cup to her left. Dion picked it up and put it into her palm. Feeling as if she had been eating sand, she gulped the liquid. It had become lukewarm over the long drive, but she didn't care. That reminded her. "Everyone, make sure you drink enough water. And moisturize your skin. There's zero humidity out there. Even in the habitats, it's a struggle for the ventilation systems to keep any moisture in the air. And keep an eye on your monitor bracelets. Anything but green lights, you call for help."

They had been overwhelmed by the flood of stories from the other drivers and crew. The racers hailed from every corner of Earth: big cities, small towns, islands, deserts, mountains, even one from her native Iowa, and every walk of life from students to the owners of corporations. Teddy Davis was the youngest person in the race, just a month younger than Dion, and Drake O'Neill from Australia was the oldest at forty-five. What everyone had in common were their love of science and the excitement of building and racing a buggy on the Moon.

The vehicles had surged out of the starting gate, but over the following hours had jockeyed up and back for position. On a multi-day race, it didn't seem to matter, but everyone wanted to show off what they could do. The Sparks were determined to keep their edge, but kept playing the long game. A couple of other racers were ahead, for now, spraying everyone on their tail with regolith dust.

Out of her side window, Barbara spotted a new set of buggies coming up on their tail, seeing if they could bluff the *Spark Xpress* into the inside lane. Barbara held tight to the controls, riding the center of the road, making the others fall back. She knew it annoyed drivers behind her to hog the road like that, but all was fair in love and war and circumnavigation of the Moon. Hers was going to be the first vehicle to cross the finish line, not anyone else's!

"Oh, no, you don't," she said. The pair behind her dropped back a little, disappearing into the cloud of dust. She let out a crow of triumph.

Suddenly, on her left, the brilliant red and yellow of *Cheetah* burst past them, bounding over the regolith like a beach ball. From the right side of its cockpit, Lois Ingota waved. Barbara jumped in surprise. *Cheetah* slewed onto the roadway ahead of them, its oversized wheels sliding in the cascade of dust left by *Blue Streak*. Barbara held her breath. The brightly colored buggy wobbled alarmingly, then righted itself and sped away. In a moment, it vanished around the edge of a crater that loomed up on the left of the road. Dion opened his lips to say something over the shared signal, then shook his head.

"Nah. This is just the beginning. We're gonna get passed a million times before the end of the race. Okay, who's up next?"

Before giving up the controls to Jan and Gary, Barbara glanced over the list of interview files on Fido's screen.

"Send these to Daya and Neil, Fido," she said.

"As you wish, Barbara," the PerDee replied.

Dion surrendered his place first, making way for Jan. He climbed into the back, taking his self-heating coffee mug with him. Jan sat down and strapped in, then grasped the steering with firm hands.

"Ready? On my mark, passing control in three, two, one," Barbara said. As soon as Jan nodded, Barbara thumbed the switch that passed control over to her. They had made the switch deliberately hard to push so it couldn't be toggled by accident. She unbuckled, and Gary slid past her in the gap between the capsule seats.

"Did you sleep well?" she asked him as he fastened his safety straps.

He grinned. "I don't remember a thing after I laid down, so I guess so."

"Have fun, you two," she said. "We're about four hours from the first stop." She stretched her arms high, feeling every muscle in her back ache. Dion sat on the lower bunk, fishing through the food storage cabinet. He chose a self-heating rice bowl and pulled the tab on the element.

"Want something to eat?" he asked, stirring the food. "I've got some spice packets you can mix into one of these."

"I think I'll wait for dinner," she said. His meal smelled savory, but she didn't feel hungry enough to bother. She climbed up into the top bunk, loosened the collar of her suit, slid off her boots, and put her head on the pillow.

The next thing she knew, Jan was gently shaking her shoulder. The Asian-American girl had her suit fastened up to the neck. She held her helmet and gloves in the crook of her arm.

"Hey, roomie, we're here!"

Barbara sat up. She felt energized by her nap. It felt odd not to be swaying or bouncing any more.

The four of them suited up and waited impatiently for the air to cycle down in the compartment, then clambered down the built-in ladder one at a time. Barbara threw herself backward and landed, bouncing, in a puff of dust beside the right rear buckyball. It felt as though it ought to be sunset, but hard sunlight still beamed down on them. *It won't be night for days*, Barbara thought with a grin.

Outside, brilliant spotlights on a stalk about fifteen meters high shone down on what had become an exotic parking lot. Beside them stood Team Podracer's long wedge-shaped vehicle, its cabin already darkened and empty. *Rover* came to a halt at their other side.

"We came in twelfth!" Nev DeLeon announced, bounding over to join them. "Hey, let's get to the food before the others all come piling in!"

"What were we?" Barbara asked.

"Sixth," Gary said, looking a little disgusted. "*Blue Streak* was first."

"That's because *Firebird* caused a traffic jam at that choke point on the road," Jan added. "You missed all the excitement, roomie."

"Hey, that was a fancy swerve you pulled off back there at that spire!" A tall, slim redheaded person with a heart-shaped face stuck out a gloved hand for Gary to shake. "It's a miracle we got ahead of you, but there you are. Tracy McGuinn, *Tuatha Dé Danann*," he said with an Irish lilt. "We got here fifth, but I've been fixing a wobble in our rear axle."

"Gary Camden."

"Jan Nguyen," Jan added. "It was nothing. We've been up this road before, you know."

Tracy laughed. "That I do know. I read your blog every day. I'm such a fan, you have no idea."

"Come have dinner with us," Gary said, his eyes shining. Barbara had to admit that Tracy was cute.

"I'd like that," Tracy said, giving them a gap-toothed grin. "Let me check in with my team, then I'm all yours."

"Sweet," said Jan, with a wicked grin.

The lanky Tracy bounded ahead of them into the rectangular recess marked ENTRANCE, and was swallowed up by the sliding airlock doorway. Barbara looked around them.

The pit stop lay downhill from the roadway, in a broad, shallow crater over a kilometer in diameter. Heaps of regolith had been piled up by a dozer, similar to the one that she and the Sparks had used to clear the telescope crater at Aldrinville. Four round, inflatable habitats had been bonded together to make one big building. Upslope, next to the road, stood a massive tank, the water supply for the building. The roof had been lined with solar collectors and topped with an antenna array.

"They did a lot here!" she said. "And this is one of fourteen around the planet? This is more than we put in place in Aldrinville."

"And all just for the race?" Jan added, frowning. "Seems sort of ostentatious."

"No, they're making them permanent after the race is over," Dion reminded her, as the airlock opened again. "Remember the news article on the city blog about expanding shelters?"

"Oh, that's right," Jan said, pretending to slap her own forehead. "Right. We've just been inside our own heads so much, building the Xpress."

"Lack of blood sugar," Gary said, swinging her into the doorway. He jumped inside with her, and the door closed behind them, but Barbara could still hear them over the in-suit speaker. "This is your brain on empty."

When it was Barbara's turn to go through the airlock, she and

Dion crowded in together. She grinned up at him as the floor shook under them, then she felt rather than heard the vacuum system sucking the regolith dust from their suits.

"We've got to install something like this at Aldrinville," he said, with a nod of approval for the design. "That little floor vac we left when we finally finished the telescope isn't enough to keep the place clean. It keeps sending me distress calls."

"You just can't completely escape the dust anywhere up here," Barbara said, with a laugh. "Just think what we could have accomplished there if we *hadn't* had a radiation storm."

The hatch slid aside, and a little holograph issuing from the door frame showed a space-suited figure removing its helmet.

"The air is breathable, Barbara," Fido told her.

Even before she unfastened her headgear, she was aware of the noise and the smell. Coupled with the usual system odors of stone dust, lubricant, and disinfectant were the musky stink of several dozen human beings who hadn't had a shower since early morning, or maybe even before, and the savory aromas of cooking.

"Food!" Gary cheered. He had an incredible appetite. Even constant snacking never seemed to fill him up.

"Wait a minute!" A tall African-American woman came over with a medical scanner in her hands. Dr. Lena Johnson was the colony medical director's second-in-command. Her high cheekbones and lush lips highlighted the narrowness of her light brown face. "Let me get a reading. I want to compare it with your baseline."

"But I'm hungry!" Gary complained, sticking out his lower lip. Jan laughed.

"It will only take a minute," Dr. Johnson assured him. The device blipped, and she nodded approval. "There. You're fine. Next?"

Barbara stood with her arms out.

"You don't have to do that," the doctor told her. "Your blood pressure is a little low. Are you dehydrated?"

"Probably," Barbara said. "I just woke up from a nap."

"Well, I want you to drink at least a liter of water right away. Next!"

"Hey, welcome!" Joe Ward came over to shake their hands. His daughter Caitlin smiled at them from beside him. "Let me check you in. Who've we got here?"

Mr. Ward called up a roster on his own PerDee, a fancier though not more powerful version of the Sparks' devices. As the infrared detection scanner read each of their faces, a tiny matching icon lit up, followed by a big red checkmark.

"Great!" Joe said, waving the group forward. "Go get yourselves cleaned up and have a meal."

"Thanks!" Dion said. Caitlin took his arm and pointed him toward the rear.

"There are eight shower cubicles in the back, and a rack of microfiber towels. You're early enough you might not have to wait for your turn. Do you have your own kits? We have some chargeable shavers if you need them, and toiletries in dispensers. The capsule bunks are small, but they're new, with clean linens and data hookups. Choose whatever ones are empty, and code-lock the hatch with your name. One to a customer, please."

"This is amazing," Jan said, looking around with delight. "When did you have time to build these? Are they up all around the track?"

Joe grinned. "Everything's modular. The sleeping cubicles, plumbing/dispenser walls, and cooking facilities were completed and flown up from Earth, to be installed in these inflatable habitats. The first four are ready for you. The others are still being completed, three or four at a time. I don't know if numbers thirteen or fourteen are more than cleared spaces in a crater yet, but I promise they'll be set up and prepared for customers when the peloton reaches it. After this is all over, my wife and the mayor have uses planned for the shells. Meantime, have a good evening. We'll check you off in the morning when you leave."

"What's it like?" Daya asked, her voice wistful, as Barbara and Jan went into the sleeping area to choose their bedrooms.

"It's really well designed," Barbara said, turning Fido this way and that so the two Sparks left behind in Armstrong City could see everything. She edged between two small café tables where eight of the racers were eating and laughing with one another, and passed through a broad double door with safety shutters and a cabinet containing the usual emergency EVA suits. The raucous music and flitting holograms told her a TurnTable had been hidden there somewhere. "They've put together several of the kinds of habitats we used at Aldrinville."

"Bigger, though," Jan said. "At least five meters diameter larger. Then they fitted them out like the Armstrong City Hotel. It's pretty nice!"

"They knocked out the interior wall between two of them to make a dining hall, and the third one is mostly kitchen, storage, and the power and plumbing plant. We'll be going back to the dining area in a minute," Barbara continued. "Look at this!"

The left quarter of the dome had been made into a big, bright bathroom. Soothing steam rolled in the air, but dissipated almost as soon as it hit the edge of the white floor at Barbara's feet. A half dozen unisex toilet cubicles lay on one side, facing a line of shallow sinks and mirrors. Ahead of them were the individual shower stalls and a broad bench, where two women wrapped in pale blue microfiber towels were sitting, drying their hair. One of them was Pam. Jan grabbed her arm and pulled Barbara onward, before the former Spark spotted them.

The rest of the dome had four rows of portholes about a meter across with metal cleats above each opening. More cleats were fixed into the walls beside them to act as ladders for the users.

"How about here?" Jan asked, clambering up the wall on the side opposite the bathroom. "It'll be the quietest over here." She tapped her name into the lock on the topmost cube.

"Great!" Barbara said. She claimed the bunk at the bottom, and peered through the porthole at the interior. It looked like a capsule hotel at an airport, with a narrow bed alongside a shelf that ran the full length of the bunk, a wall-mounted control center, and a screen at the far end. The habitat was warm enough that she wouldn't need more than the thin white microfiber blanket folded on the bunk on top of the pillow. From outside, she could just see the edge of the interior curtain she could pull across for privacy. She opened the door, grasped the cleat, and slid in on her back. "What do you think of that, Daya?"

"Efficient," Daya said, approvingly. "Easy to clean. Everything you might want or need. Most tourists would not care for the cramped conditions, but it's enough for a night's rest."

"I'd be happy with *anything* if I could be out there," Neil said, fretfully. Jan hopped down, and continued to bounce lightly on the smooth floor.

"Next year," Jan promised him. "Do you have enough images to post on the vlog?"

"Yep!" Neil said, cheering up at once. "And thanks for all the interviews. I'm—I mean, *we're*—conducting more of them tomorrow with the support staff. Oh, a couple of reporters are out there, following the hospitality people from pit stop to pit stop. They want to talk to you."

"After we get some food," Barbara said, grinning down at her PerDee's screen. "Shutting down for now. I need to get out of my suit."

It took some wiggling in the cramped quarters to undo her EVA suit and get into a clean purple jumpsuit, but she managed. She joined Jan on the floor, where the two of them fastened on their canvas deck shoes over bare feet. Barbara wrinkled her nose, suddenly aware how she smelled after a long day.

"Definitely a shower later," Jan said, with a nod.

"Excuse me," a woman's voice called. Barbara and Jan jumped up. The voice's owner rolled up to them in a canvas-sling chair with wide, spoked wheels, a woman with warm, tawny skin, dark curls, broad, blunt nose, and bright green eyes. "Hey, you're the Sparks!" Her somewhat nasal pronunciation flattened out her vowels in a manner Barbara associated with Australia. She put out a hand clad in a fingerless black glove. "I'm Francine Kellan, Team Podracer."

"Hi!" Jan said. "We were admiring your wheels." Her cheeks reddened. "I mean, *Moonracer*! Great design. How's it handle?"

"Excellent," Francine said. She held up a bag. "I just came to drop off something. You two want to come and eat with us? I have to warn you, we're all mega-fans."

"That'd be great!" Barbara said. The admiration still made her feel shy, but she pushed it away.

Francine rolled up to one of the cubicles. Barbara noticed that a number in the bottom row were double height with doors instead of hatches, and nodded. Those gave easy access for wheelchair users. The designers had pretty much thought of everything.

"Great!" the Paralympian said, slamming her capsule hatch closed and wheeling around to face them. "Let's eat."

"The food's not up to your standards," Barbara told Dion,

spooning up her last bite of biryani. The rice and protein—which protein she wasn't quite sure—just wasn't spicy enough.

"Well, they're cooking for a hundred or more," the tall youth said, pushing his bowl aside. His grandmother was a noted chef who wrote cookbooks, and sent her eldest grandson herbs, spices and liquid extracts on shuttle runs from Earth. "I give them credit for trying."

"Tastes good to me," Francine's teammate Alicia de la Paz said. Team Podracer came from Paralympian teams all over Earth. Alicia hailed from Bolivia. "I expect nothing up here to be excellent. The experience is what counts."

"And the win!" Francine said. They all laughed. "Don't forget the prizes."

"My favorite thing is the low gravity," added Hale Bowdoin, from Canada. He pushed his chair back from the table, and began bouncing it up and down a few centimeters. He glanced from side to side, making sure no one else was close by, then locked the wheels. "Watch this!"

He bounded higher and higher, then, on the next rise, flipped over backwards, chair and all. The others applauded.

"That's great!" Barbara said.

"We need to get that for the vlog," Gary said, whipping Turing out of his sleeve pocket.

Grinning widely, Hale started his chair bouncing again, yanked upward, and turned over backward.

"You need to set that to music," Svetlana Karokskaya, one of the Russian women said, holding out her own device. "*Igrat'v khard-rok pesnyu!*" A driving beat, accompanied by horns and guitars, burst from the small speaker. Hale started bobbing his head, then bounced his chair up and down. Francine zipped over beside him.

"And over!" Hale shouted. In unison, the chairs flipped.

By now, the rest of the racers were on their feet, stamping and cheering. Tomasz took Francine's hands and whirled her in a circle. She laughed. That made everyone join in, dancing and laughing. Dion and Barbara leaped up. This was the kind of headbanging beat both of them liked to dance to.

"I challenge you to a Battle of the Bands!" Nev DeLeon said, pointing at the Russian woman.

"Accepted!" Svetlana cried.

The dining hall erupted into a kind of chaotic disco. All of the tables and chairs got pushed into the kitchen area out of the way. After the first song, Barbara was claimed by Hale for a country swing, then moved on to Joe Ward, who waltzed her around to a smooth R&B tune. Off on one side, both Gary and Jan danced with Tracy McGuinn. Dion boogied with Svetlana. Two of her colleagues stayed partnered with one another, but the fourth bounced around and stepped with anyone free.

At last, Barbara ran out of breath. She remembered Dr. Johnson's warning, and edged into the kitchen to find a glass of water. She took it to one of the empty tables and plopped down in a chair. Jan and Gary sat at a table several meters away with a man with thinning, black curly hair who had a recording device hovering in the air between them: one of the promised reporters. They waved to her to join them, but she just waved back.

"That was fun," a soft voice said. Barbara looked up to see Pam. "I will go away, if you wish."

"No, please," Barbara said, pulling one of the loose chairs over with her foot. "Sit down."

"Thank you." Pam sat. Her expression didn't change, but her body language showed she was hesitant. "I enjoyed your direction of the over-air chat today. I . . . couldn't have done that."

"Well, I appreciated you putting in your experiences," Barbara said.

"We've all got a different take on how being on the Moon affects us," Pam said. "It makes sense to share that information."

Barbara was dying to ask her what bothered the other Sparks so much about the former Spark, but too many people were close enough to hear them, even over the noise and music.

"I'm curious," she said, forcing herself to take another tack. "How did you make the transition so fast from the Sparks to a corporate job? You're a lot younger than the people I think of as executives in major corporations."

"Not in technology," Pam corrected her. "Most of my colleagues are no more than five to seven years older than I am. It's not that different from having been up here. University was far different with professors and counselors. It was nice to get into a peer situation again."

"You got a college degree since leaving?" Barbara asked, agog. "Already?"

"Oh, yes. I tested out of several classes, like advanced physics, based upon knowledge I gained up here. Dr. Bright is an excellent mentor. And I got credit for an independent physics practicum. That brought me down to four required courses. I took them all in a single semester, and graduated with a BS. I am studying for my first master's degree now. The company is paying for it." Pam cocked her head. "You should be thinking ahead to your career once you leave the Sparks. Your time here will go by very fast. Someone with potential like yours needs to make the most of it."

"I'm enjoying what I'm doing too much right now to think that far in the future," Barbara said. She noticed Pam's pained expression, and instantly regretted how she had phrased that. "I'm sorry."

"Don't be," Pam said. "I love my life now. It will mean a lot to my company and to me to win this race."

"Except that we're going to win it," Barbara said, cheerfully. "I wish you luck, though."

"Thank you. I wish . . . Never mind. May the best team win."

Barbara wondered what she had been going to say. It sounded as though Pam had made the best of her situation. Once more, Barbara had it on the tip of her tongue to ask what had estranged her from the other Sparks. To her relief, Tomasz came over and held out a hand.

"We arrived in here last. You can make me feel better if you will kindly dance with me."

"I . . ." She glanced past him at the open space still heaving with people sliding, whirling, and hopping, bounding high in the low gravity. "It looks like fun. Yes, I'd like to." She glanced at Pam. "Do you mind?"

Pam gave one of her wintry smiles.

"Go ahead. We will talk again another time. Here comes one of my crew, Tomiko. I can tell she has a question." A young Asian woman in a blue jumpsuit the same shade as the *Blue Streak*'s bubble hurried over, her PerDee in hand. "Thank you," Pam said to Barbara, and turned away.

Barbara watched her go, overwhelmed with mixed feelings.

She and Tomasz spun on the floor to sounds played by Charlton, who was DJing from his own PDE. The TurnTable kept sending out bounding segments of tracks, adding weird squawks and trills to the noise, but Barbara was having too much fun to chase them.

She was in the minority, though, as her fellow racers dived and bounded after the music icons and the wisps of sound like cats chasing a laser pointer, showing amazing energy for people who had had a long and grueling drive from Armstrong City. *Funny how human beings adapted so fast to alien conditions*, Barbara thought. If she had thought for a moment there was something special about her and the other Sparks, and the first colonists of Armstrong City, that thought was washed away. Everyone there was capable of coping under extreme circumstances, and even enjoying it a bunch. She was proud of everyone who had joined up to make the race. It wasn't just a competition; the racers were becoming a community.

Barbara enjoyed the party a while longer, then suddenly felt overwhelmed. The crowd seemed to close in on her, appearing to suffocate her.

"Excuse me," she told her latest dance partner with an apologetic smile. "I've got to go."

She crept away to her capsule bedroom, keying in her name code. The hatch unlocked, and Barbara hauled it open.

Jan peered down from the porthole of her own bunk.

"Is the party over?" she asked.

"No, I just couldn't . . . I felt crowded."

Jan chuckled. "You, too, huh? We're just not used to this many people any more. What will it be like when we go back to Earth for a visit?"

Barbara felt dread rise in her belly. "I'd love to see my family, but maybe that's it. This is too much for me."

Jan shook her head. "You know, by the time this race is over, I bet we'll like it. I bet we'll miss the crowds when they go home."

"Maybe," Barbara said. "But, right now, it doesn't feel like that could ever happen."

"Good night," Pam called softly from the entrance to the corridor. With a withering look at the tall girl, Jan slammed her capsule hatch shut.

"'Night," Barbara called back.

Chapter Ten

Daya smiled at Yvonne's camera and gestured to the handsome man in the dark blue coverall at her right.

"Welcome back to the Bright Sparks vlog," she said. "We are happy to be talking with Dr. Paulus Stefanotis representing the Thessaloniki Science Center and Technology Museum, and a part-sponsor of Team Helios. Your buggy, *Apollo's Chariot*, came in eighteenth last night to the pit stop, but the judges have said that its design favors it to outstrip many of the other vehicles when the race reaches the plains beyond Aldrinville. Welcome, Dr. Stefanotis. How did the museum become involved in the race?"

"Don't you have a major outreach program for science to involve not only kids in Greece, but in other countries on the Mediterranean?" Neil asked, leaning forward, before the scientist could open his mouth. Her expression never changing, Daya put her bony little elbow on his outspread hand and pressed downward. Neil bit back an "Ouch!" Because they were live online, he had to keep smiling, but that hurt! He had promised her he wouldn't interrupt *this* interview, and he had already broken that promise. That was the third time that morning already. She had every right to be ticked off at him. He sat back in his chair, his mouth clamped shut. Daya let go of his hand.

Stefanotis smiled, fixing a charming gaze on Daya. Neil thought he probably had seen what just happened, though the camera couldn't. Some of the viewers seemed to have guessed. On the small monitor tilted toward him on the floor, he could see an excited flurry of comments from the bloggers.

"Well, Daya and Neil, we are very excited to be a part of this amazing enterprise. As you may guess from the name of our team and our vehicle, we draw from our long history of aspiring to fly across the spheres of Heaven. . . ."

For once, the vlog had a live audience. The two youngest Sparks sat at the news desk in the *Live from the Moon* studio. Dr. Bright was due to video a remote segment from his post on the far side in two hours. In the meantime, he and Daya had the place to themselves to collect as many interviews and race updates as they could. Visitors and terrestrial reporters hung out in the rows of chairs that the crew had set up near the rear door of the studio. Up close to the set, two rows were reserved for subjects that the two of them and Jackie, the producer, had invited to come and talk live online. Dr. Stefanotis made a joke, and the listeners broke into a low titter. He was a bit longwinded, but overall a good guest.

"Where is *Apollo's Chariot* now? Dr. Stefanotis wants to know," Daya asked, repeating the question for Neil.

"Einstein, open the feeds from the BrightSats on the big screen, please," Neil said, happy to show off his creation. "We had six following the action to start with. Two of them are back to recharge, and I sent out number four again this morning," he added.

"Here they are, Neil," the old-man voice of his PerDee announced. The three of them turned their seats to face the trio of wide screens on the back wall of the set.

"Thanks, Einstein," Neil said, picking up the device. "Laser pointer on."

"Laser activated."

"We're partway into Day Two of the race. The first teams to reach the pit stop yesterday were Team Podracer, Team Cheetah, and, uh, Team SolStar." Neil hesitated in spite of himself. He knew the design engineer for Pam's buggy, Charles Murayama, was sitting in the front row watching. He had seemed like a nice guy. Neil had started out with no intention of interviewing him, but Murayama had pretty much volunteered, in front of witnesses and Jackie, so he and Daya had agreed to include him, despite their feelings about anything promoting Pam and her team.

Neil drove the small red pinpoint over the main map. The buggies showed up in satellite imagery as undistinguished gray dots with contrails of more gray. They didn't look very interesting, but telemetric data rolled up over each one. He circled the front-runner. "The last to arrive was Team Doppler, driving *Výdra*. They left first today, hoping to make up some ground. Team Excelsior is still at the pit stop." He circled the flashing data. "It's got some kind of technical glitch.

"In the lead right now, we've got *Výdra*, followed by *Rover*. Way back from that, *Firebird* and *Cheetah* are trying to pass each other. They're still on the way to Aldrinville, so the graded road is wide enough for two to drive side by side, but nobody wants to do that. And right behind them, *Apollo's Chariot!*"

The Greek scientist cheered, holding his hands clasped over his head. Neil grinned at him.

"This is most exciting for us," Stefanotis said, his blue eyes flashing. "We look forward to winning."

"Tell us about the drive system in *Apollo's Chariot*," Daya urged him. She signed to Neil, who brought up the schematics of the buggy. It looked like a really old-fashioned carriage, with oversized skeletal wheels front and back.

"Ah, well, it is highly efficient. We kept the whole chassis light and very flexible. The system for suspension is interleaved fiberboards, which become stronger and tighter in subzero conditions."

"The cabin looks kind of small," Neil observed, seeing the dimensions come up. "A three-meter cube of living space for four people for two weeks?"

"We ask our drivers to recall what an overland trip of many centuries back would have been like, crossing hostile terrain in the gravest difficulty," the scientist said. "And like the days of old, it is a stagecoach of sorts, with only basic needs. Comfort will be obtained at each stop. In the meanwhile, speed is the most necessary, and our motivators are made for speed."

"Thank you so much for talking to us," Daya said, standing up to shake hands with Stefanotis. "Next, we have the Chinese ambassador to the United Nations, Chin Le-Dao."

Stefanotis made way for a small, stocky woman in a trim white suit. Madame Chin set her PerDee hovering a few centimeters above the desk. She spoke Mandarin in a musical fashion, and a similar sounding voice came in translation from the device.

"Thank you for your welcome," it said in English.

Daya got her to answer a few puff questions. They had been warned by the mayor's public affairs office that the ambassador would not take kindly to being asked about possible failure in the race. Neil had to admit that Daya handled it well.

"I hear your team's name is the Young Stars," Neil added. "The Niánqīng De Xīngxīng." He had practiced the name a dozen times, but his pronunciation made the ambassador's back stiffen. "*Jade Dragon* is a beautiful buggy."

"Yes," she said, her expression still pleasant but noncommittal. "Our nation's team carries our pride with it."

Throughout the following two interviews, Neil kept pressing his index fingernail into the palm of his other hand to remind him not to overstep Daya. He did what she asked: putting up the race progress, spinning schematics, and displaying profiles of each team's racers, but it was hard not to take over the interview. At least she wasn't gloating about it.

"And our next guest is Charles Murayama, chief of mechanical engineering for SolStar," Daya announced, as the last interviewee vacated the seat. The narrow-faced man rose from the chair and stalked toward the table. "Welcome, Mr. Murayama."

"It's Doctor, Ms. Singh," Murayama said. Daya's expression told Neil that the slight had been deliberate, and he suspected the visitor knew it.

"Yes, Dr. Murayama. SolStar has been a rival of the company run by Armstrong City's founder. Has that been a problem for you?"

"Not at all," Dr. Murayama said, waving both arms energetically. His rangy limbs reminded Neil of Calvin Book. "Science should not operate behind barriers, Ms. Singh. Ms. Reynolds-Ward has made use of our products and services over the years. It seemed only natural that we should support such a venture. And," his long brown eyes shone avidly, "we would not have missed such an opportunity as this. No, never."

"What do you think is the most novel feature of the *Blue Streak*?" Daya asked, as she had inquired of every designer.

"The suspension, I believe," Murayama replied. Neil put the

schematic up so the audience could view it. "This was a classified design up until the race began, of course. Now it can be revealed. Not only do the shock absorbers keep the cabin from becoming unstable and making the occupants motion sick, but the kinetic energy is absorbed into the batteries using Faraday's law. The longer it runs, and more precisely, the more it bounces, the more power is stored from its motion."

Neil got interested in spite of himself. He studied the design, admiring the way not only the pistons fed the dynamic engine, but the gyroscopes did, too. "You mean, like a perpetual motion machine?"

Murayama's grin made him look like an eager child. Neil realized he couldn't be that much older than Dion, maybe twenty-five at the most. "Exactly! It will not run perpetually, of course, but it helps to feed the engine even when the sun will disappear near the end of the race."

"That is very clever," Daya said, with a genuine smile. "I can see many uses for this in atmospheric design."

"Even more, because friction can be increased without fear of the mechanism seizing up from a lack of standard lubricants. We at SolStar lead the world in non-polluting, self-generating or self-assisting, non-internal combustion engines."

The design really intrigued Neil, but the scientist's superior attitude bugged him. "So, what's it like working with a former member of the Bright Sparks?"

"Pam?" Murayama asked. "She fits well into our corporate ethos. We work on independent projects, then come together to refine the designs and troubleshoot one another's ideas. One of her major creations will go into full manufacture early next year."

"So, you don't work in a team with her?"

"We do not have teams, per se," Murayama replied, easily, sticking his long legs under the desk and crossing his ankles. "We are a culture of individualists. It has proved to work well for us. I think from my reading of your blogs that the Sparks are more of a gestalt. Different strokes, as my grandfather would have said."

"I guess that's true," Neil said, thoughtfully.

"It has been a real pleasure speaking with you," Daya said, sincerely, folding the engineer's hand into both of hers.

"Thank you," Murayama said, with a charming smile. "I, too, am a fan of the Bright Sparks. I would love to see your headquarters. It is featured on so many of your vlog entries. And I am much a fan of you, Ms. Daya."

"I . . ." Daya began, looking totally disarmed, to Neil's disgust. "I would be delighted to show you around Sparks Central."

"I would love that! A guided tour!"

Neil started to protest, then realized he had an audience.

"Some of the stuff there is confidential."

"Hide what you like," Murayama said, with a wave of his hand. "I want only to stand in the home of my idols."

Neil and Daya exchanged glances. She looked hopeful. Maybe there was something in what the engineer had said about cooperation in the sciences. It was going to take some thinking in private. Her eyes pleaded with him. What would be the real harm?

"Okay," Neil said. "Yeah. I'll move a few things, then she can show you around."

"I am very grateful," Murayama said. "Thank you."

"Let us see how everyone is doing out on the course," Daya said, as the engineer rose. "Neil?"

Neil cleared his throat. "Well, *Apollo's Chariot* and *Rover* are the clear front-runners today," he said. "Right behind them is *Firebird* and . . ." He scanned the field, and frowned, reading each of the data crawls.

"Where is *Spark Xpress*?" Daya asked.

"Way back here," Neil said, brandishing Einstein's laser pointer, to the twelfth gray nub. It was moving back and forth in an erratic fashion. "BrightSat Three, drop back to *Spark Xpress*. Dion? Barbara? What's going on?"

Chapter Eleven

"What do you mean sluggish?" Barbara wiped at her eyes with her bare fingers. Her gloves were peeled back and fastened to her forearms. While she wasn't really sleepy, she was getting tired of staring at the windshield. The race along the road to Aldrinville had brought back memories of her first trip out this far from Armstrong City. That trip, while having ended up successfully, was a bit frightening and unnerving at times. It had also been one heck of an adventure that she'd never have had back on the farm in Iowa.

After seven hours of staring at a monochrome landscape mostly obscured by dust clouds, she was beginning to rethink how they had scheduled the driving shifts. She and Dion had swapped the controls back and forth a couple of times since they had left the pit stop. Gary and Jan had manned the cockpit for a two-hour stint in between so the first two could take a break and eat some lunch, but they were all still exhausted from not having slept much in the last couple of days. Barbara wanted to give the Nerd-Twins some time to catch up on their sleep during the first two legs, but it was hard on her and Dion. The overnight rest they had taken wasn't enough to make up for the hard work or the excitement of starting the race. The late-night party had just added to her weariness, although it had been a lot of fun.

She took a swig of coffee from her travel mug, and discovered it had gone cold.

"Fido, warm up my cup, will you? Sipping temperature, please."

"Of course, Barbara."

The automatic heating controls made the mug start to warm in her hands as it raised the liquid on the inside to a more desirable temperature. A wisp of fragrant steam escaped from the drinking spout. She gulped a mouthful and sighed.

"What's the problem?" she asked Dion.

"I mean, it's driving funny," Dion said. His fingers were clenched on the steering wheel. The steering operated on a drive by wire with a feedback loop that ran an electromagnetic field coil that added resistance to the wheel based on sensor data from the suspension and buckyballs. It had digital responsiveness, but it felt like a mechanical steering system. "Sluggish."

"Sluggish how?"

"Up until now, the *Spark* was driving like a dream. I could feel every bump in the steering being compensated out and it drove like a luxury car. Now, though, I, uh, don't know how to describe it other than rough, and funny and, well, sluggish. When I turn the wheel, the response is slower than before. It's vibrating, too. Watch."

Barbara watched as he yanked the wheel to the left. It wobbled back and forth before stabilizing, then rocked again as Dion corrected the steering once more. Barbara frowned. The autotractors back home on the farm acted like that if the control system was underdamped. If the control circuit ever went, well, off, odd, wonky—she wasn't sure what to call it—then the tractor couldn't cut a straight row to save its life. The *Spark* was doing the same thing, but so far not as badly. In this case, there was a human driver in the loop to help compensate for the errors of the failing system, but it shouldn't be behaving like that at all.

"That's not right." She shoved the coffee mug back into its holder. "Fido, show me a full diagnostic readout of the control and steering systems."

"Certainly, Barbara."

"Let me take it for a few seconds, Dion," she said, gripping the wheel in front of her and tapping the controls for transfer to her seat.

"Okay, no problem. Transferring control in three, two, one." Dion hit the toggle.

"I have it." Barbara held the wheel straight for a bit and didn't like how she had to fight it to stay in the road. Then she tilted the wheel a hair, and it started to oscillate back and forth between her hands. "Yep. Not good."

"See what I mean?" Dion asked. "Want me to take it back now?"

"Yes. Transferring in three, two, one." Barbara hit the toggle and let go of her wheel. She turned her attention to the display of the vehicle her PerDee was now projecting for her. She spun it about in various directions, not sure where to start.

According to the scope, the power flow was good, but the capacity was pushing near the limit between yellow and red. It shouldn't have been doing that. The communications system in blue and life support in cyan were all connected properly, and all the power, fluids, air, and levels were in the green. The control systems in orange were all in the right places, but on the rear right buckyball suspension, she spotted what appeared to be a drain in power. The electromagnet motor system was using twice the level of power it was supposed to be, and the thermal management system showed a tremendous hotspot on that motor—more than twice as hot as it was supposed to be. Excess heat meant power that wasn't being used efficiently. That didn't bode well for a two-week trip.

"Dion, back off the throttle," Barbara said urgently. "This doesn't look good."

"What do you see, Barb?" Dion eased back a bit on all four buckyballs. "Okay, down to eighty percent."

"Hold it at that for a moment." Barbara watched the diagnostics view hoping that the overheating system would start to cool down. "Fido, zoom in on the rear right buckyball drive motor components."

"Certainly, Barbara," Fido responded as the three-dimensional view zoomed inward on the rear of the racer.

"Hey, have we slowed down?" Jan asked sleepily from the back right seat. "Is there a problem?" Barbara could hear her tapping at her console and her PDE screen.

"We've got an overheating drive motor on the rear right buckyball. It's using way too much power." Barbara paused a moment, listening. "Dion, slow down to fifty percent, please."

The drop in speed was almost like hitting the brakes. The electromagnetic field generated by the slowing motors backwards fed energy into the system and began to add stored power to their batteries, but it also increased the wobbly feeling underneath the buggy. Outside her right-hand window, *Rover* passed them. Cantia Frerent gave her a look of concern.

"Are you all right, *Spark Xpress*?" Cantia asked, over the intrabuggy frequency.

"No problem! We're fine," Barbara said, automatically. "Fido, cut open signal for the moment."

"Yes, Barbara."

And, almost instantly, Neil began pinging them over their PerDees. Barbara didn't answer immediately. She needed to focus on what was happening and didn't want to start speculating for the team back at Sparks Central.

"Roomie, I'm seeing it. The motor is almost at three times the heat load it is supposed to be. That's not good," Jan told her. "Maybe something is stuck between the ball and the hub."

"That might explain why the motor is having to work extra hard." Barbara unsnapped her safety harness and rose from her seat. She snapped Fido into the transparent pouch on her left wrist just above her suit diagnostic band. "I'm going out there to look at it," she said, pulling her gloves out of the sleeve ends and fastening them. "Can't tell what is going on out there from in here. Dion, drop to twenty-five percent throttle. It's not cooling down like it should. And if something is stuck in there, let's dig it out. It shouldn't be a technical failure. It's too early for problems like that. We'd better find out."

"At twenty-five percent," Dion said, his left hand flicking over the controls. "You want me to just pull over? We're going twenty kilometers per hour."

"Not yet. I'd prefer to see the vehicle in action, so I'm going to go out the observation bubble hatch. Jan, wake up Gary. Everyone put your visors down and pressurize. Fido, prepare the cabin for an EVA."

"Okay, Barbara," Fido replied. Lights on the console turned amber. Gary scrambled up, reaching for his helmet.

"Do you need my help out there?" he asked. "I designed those wheels."

"Yes, but I installed them. Please monitor life support for me."

"Remember, a fall could damage your suit!"

"I don't plan to fall," Barbara replied with a confidence she didn't completely feel, sealing her helmet. "I'll take a snap-tether with me. Besides, these ruggedized compression suits are almost bulletproof!"

"I'll help you get the bubble open," Jan said. "Ms. Scruffles, tie in to Fido and monitor Barb's life signs."

"Yes, Jan. Meow!"

"I don't like this," Dion said. The power system monitor was flirting with the region on the meter between yellow and red. "I hate to stop for a major repair out here. We're only about two and a half hours out from the second checkpoint."

"Neither do I," Gary added, now fully awake and looking at diagnostics himself. "There's nothing in our design that should have set off the alarms like this. Should we call it in?"

"Go ahead if you'd like." Barbara grinned. On her wrist, the hails from Sparks Central scrolled insistently down Fido's screen. "You can do it for us. I'm sure Neil and Daya are having fits about us slowing down and not answering their calls."

"Way to pass the buck, Barb!" Gary chuckled. Then he turned to Turing and let one of the calls come through. "Hello, Neil. Yeah, sorry, we were looking over a problem . . ."

"Everybody all buttoned up?" Barbara asked, her voice sounding hollow inside her helmet, and received three thumbs-ups in affirmation. She climbed up the internal ladder to the observation bubble, with Jan close by to help support her through it. "Okay, Fido, cycle the air."

"Yes, Barbara." Once the vacuum began, she couldn't hear the pumps reverse, sucking the precious oxygen into the reserve tanks under the floor, but she felt the vibration of the buggy change under her hands. "Neil, are you monitoring us?"

"You bet I am! I'm using the internal acoustic sensors to analyze if there are any background vibrations you can't hear. I'll cross-reference that with the accelerometers on motor four." Neil sounded all business, until he added, "And take some video while you're out there for the vlog."

Barbara groaned. He was incorrigible, but he was right. This would make good material for the website. "Fido, transmit all your video and the video from the external cameras back to Spark Central."

"Yes, Barbara."

The pressure gauge on her wristband dropped to lunar normal over the next couple of seconds, then showed equal pressures on either side of the hatch. Barbara and Jan worked the mechanical hand-crank release for the bubble and slid it out of the way. The step up to the bubble put her shoulders just through the opening. She paused for a second to attach the long tether into a snaffle on the outer surface of the buggy, and to look out at the open view of the Moon. Barbara watched the Internet repeater towers along the roadway to Aldrinville that she had first seen on her mission with the Sparks several months back loping past them at what seemed to be a rapid pace, but was really a crawl. That mission seemed like ages ago now. Behind them, she saw puffs of dust gleaming in the brilliant sunlight that were the buggies about to catch up and pass them. She resented whatever was slowing down the *Xpress*'s drive.

She placed her gloved hands on either side of the exit rim, and jumped while pushing herself upward. Jan held onto her ankles. Barbara landed in a sitting position on the edge of the exit. Jan's expert grip kept Barbara from falling out and over backwards, almost as if she had practiced it before. Maybe she and Gary had.

"I'm good, Jan. You can let go now." She waited until she felt unencumbered, then, all in one motion, she swung her legs and feet up and out of the hole and slid down to the buckyball strut. She landed straddled on the angled upright brace with a foot on either side of it on the main horizontal strut jutting out from the main body of the racer, panting with nerves. She never thought of herself as a daredevil, but this was taking her life into her hands!

"We've got you on the camera in here, Barb. Looking good so far," Gary said through the suit radio.

"I love this!" Neil exclaimed, sounding as if he was in her helmet with her instead of hundreds of kilometers away. "That was awesome! The viewers are going to love it!"

"Neil!" Daya said, exasperated. "Barbara, your heart rate is elevated, and your respiration has jumped. Be careful."

"I know!" Barbara replied. "Fido, infrared temperature app on. And overlay the diagnostic blueprints over my view in my visor."

"The app is operating, Barbara. Overlay mode engaged," Fido replied.

Barbara pointed the sensor at the motor housing. To her alarm, the temperature read 200°C, though the surrounding structure was only about one hundred twenty. Both temperatures were too hot to touch even through insulated gloves.

"It's not cooling down even at twenty-five percent," she told the others. "There's no way for it to radiate off that heat fast enough with more power still being pumped into it. The strut is acting like a heat sink. It'll start buckling if we can't stop this."

"Yeah, we're seeing that in here," Jan said, sounding just as concerned. "The power is still redlining. What's wrong with it?"

"I don't know! I'd better take a look at it from underneath," Barbara said, hanging on tight with her legs and feeling around the sides of the strut. "Gary, I don't see any handholds on the superstructure."

The young engineer sounded abashed. "We didn't install any. We never anticipated having to examine the buggy *in motion*."

"Hmmm." Clinging hard to the strut, she studied the frame. How could she get a look at the motor without grabbing something that would burn her through her gloves? The protruding arm she sat on was the only part cool enough. Well, she'd have to use it.

"Don't try this at home, kids!" She laughed, knowing that Neil was going to use that on the vlog.

Barbara wrapped her right leg around the long strut and swung herself upside down like a kid on a jungle gym.

"Aaah!" Her fall was slow, thanks to lunar gravity, but she was still on a moving vehicle. She wrapped her arms around the strut and hung on. The tether pulled tight, but if she lost her grip, it would slam her against the buggy's side. Her helmet could crack, and she'd suffocate before the team could pull her back inside.

"Are you all right?" Jan asked.

"Yes, I'm fine." Barbara gulped, making sure that was true. Using all four limbs like a sloth hanging from a tree, she inched herself closer to the moving copper-colored ball. One brief glance over her shoulder made her realize that her head was only about a half of a meter from the sandy surface. Hastily, she looked back up.

Wiping her visor over and over to clear it of the regolith dust the buckyball kicked up in her face, Barbara searched the connection between the ball and its housing. There was *nothing* lodged in there that would cause the problem. All was clear. She groaned.

"Oh, no!"

"What's wrong, Barb? You okay?" Gary asked.

"*Nothing's* wrong. And that's what's wrong." Barbara grunted as she pulled herself back up and around to the top side of the buckyball strut. She sat on it, shaking the strain out of her arms. "I'm coming back in."

"There's nothing *in* the housing for the ball, is there?" Jan asked, her voice flat.

"No, there isn't," Barbara replied, crawling back up to the top of the buggy, past three sets of concerned eyes looking at her through the right side window. "I don't see anything we can do to fix it. As hot as it is, the thing is going to seize up soon."

"If it seizes, we'll be in trouble," Gary warned. "We wouldn't even be able to roll in neutral on that ball."

"Hey! That's a good idea, Twin!" Barbara could see Jan actually slap him on the shoulder as she dropped back through the observation bubble opening. "*Great* idea, even! Dion, drop the throttle to the bad motor and put it in neutral. That should at least stop it from overheating and seizing up."

"What?" Gary seemed dumbfounded at first. Barbara only half listened as she dogged the bubble back into place and sealed it off.

"Done," Dion said.

"Fido, repressurize the cabin."

"Yes, Barbara."

"So, we are down to three motors," Barbara said glumly, settling back in her seat. "That one must have faulty wiring. Maybe it got some dust in there."

"It couldn't be," Gary protested. "We paid specifically for those motors to be hermetically sealed for that reason."

"Must have been a manufacturing fault, then. But I'd bet a dime to a donut that the windings are burned out." Barbara returned to her front seat, stuffed her helmet underneath it, and swiveled sideways.

"No, it couldn't have been a manufacturing problem, because we had each of the motors tested for many hours of runtime before they were shipped to the Moon." Gary screwed up his face in frustration.

"Tested on Earth?" Barbara asked.

"Yes." He eyed her. "Does it matter where if they were sealed?"

"Maybe." Barbara thought for a second and rolled her neck side to side. "Okay, more than maybe, perhaps. Think of it. The motors were built on Earth and hopefully were built in a very clean environment. But there could have been a metal shaving, a tiny piece of wire, even a pencil mark on the inside that would have been jostled on launch and then could float about freely during the microgravity of the trip to the Moon."

"Of course!" Gary slapped his forehead with his palm. "I see it now."

"Right," Dion agreed. "Something got loose in there and now it is in a place that allowed an arc inside the motor windings and boom! We have a motor burning itself out."

"You're probably right, roomie." Jan looked frustrated as she tapped at her controls. "The worst part of it is we don't have a spare. I know having extras for vital pieces was number eleven on our checklist! Those windings were one thing we didn't plan on having to change. Those motors were warrantied and guaranteed to function for a hundred thousand hours. I'm not sure what the rules are if we wanted to get one rapid-shipped by shuttle to one of the checkpoints."

"Even if the rules let us." Gary shook his head. "I don't think they could deliver us one before the race is finished."

"Probably not," Barbara agreed with them. "I hate to do this, but I have to. Fido, pull up the map of the racecourse."

"Of course, Barbara." A lunar sphere appeared on her half of the windscreen, and rotated. Blue and red jewels indicated each of the pit stops. The *Spark Xpress*, a dot of white, rolled slowly in between the first two. Their location was a tiny distance from Armstrong City, and a long, long way from the end of the race. Her heart sank.

"Why do you need that?" Jan asked. "From here, we follow the road up to the telescope habitat and the second pit stop."

Barbara shook her head, feeling as if she had aged sixty years. "This fault could lead to a catastrophic failure of the whole buggy, Jan. I don't know whether we can safely continue on. We probably should consider turning back."

"What do you mean?" Gary asked, aghast. "Go back? Scratch the race? We can't do that! We have to win this race!"

"There's no sense in continuing if we're going to break down completely that much farther away from safety," Barbara said, holding out her hands to him. "I don't mean to criticize your design—"

"It's a great design!" Jan said.

"Which you didn't have time to finish, little sister," Dion pointed out. "If it wasn't for all the others helping us, we wouldn't be out here."

"Are you going to bring that up forever?" Gary asked. He and Jan wore twin expressions of mulishness.

"If we knew about what you were doing from the get-go, maybe we would have found the problem earlier!"

"We ran into delays!" Jan protested. "It would have worked out, but shipments came later than we expected . . ."

"And the three-dee printer wasn't always available," Gary added.

"You've been up here long enough to know fabrication times," Dion pointed out.

"Hold on!" Barbara said, raising her voice. "Throwing up the past isn't going to help. You want to finish the race. So do I! We have to figure out something else." She was torn. She knew what she wanted—what they *all* wanted—but common sense pointed in the opposite direction. At last, Barbara turned back toward the windscreen. She didn't want to give up, either. They were the Bright Sparks. They would find a way to manage. "Let's punch it, Dion, and see what kind of speed we can get now."

Dion raised the throttle. Even inside the capsule, Barbara could feel the vibration thrown up from the bad buckyball. It seemed to be getting worse.

"We've got to disconnect that somehow," Barbara said.

"Not physically," Jan said. "We just don't have the tools. Maybe at the next pit stop. We'd need a hoist and some other gear."

"It's pretty bad," Dion said, looking beaten. "We might not make the next pit stop. Can we improvise a hoist out here?"

"Barb, you don't need any of that," Neil interrupted, his face appearing on all their scopes, with Daya beside him. "The software was designed to optimize all-wheel drive for four balls. I didn't design any code in there for three."

"Oh." Barbara felt her heart sink to her boots.

"But I *can*."

"Really?"

"Sure!" Neil looked ready to crow. Barbara couldn't begrudge him his moment if he could solve their problem.

"How long until you could write a patch and upload it to us?" Jan asked, eagerly.

"An hour?"

"Wow, okay, that would be great! But, you'll need to add the capability to run on one, two, three, or four motors based on user control inputs," Barbara said.

"Why?" both of the Nerd-Twins asked in unison.

"We don't know for certain why that motor overheated," she said. "I'm only saying it *could* be a particle inside the housing. And it could happen again."

"What, do you think someone damaged it?" Jan asked, narrowing her eyes. "No one would do that!"

"Pam," Neil said, darkly. "She and her people helped assemble the *Spark Xpress.*"

"No!" Daya said, looking at her companion with horror in her eyes. "Don't even think a thing like that. She's not out to sabotage us. Come on, Neil!"

"Just because you bonded with their engineer and took him on a tour doesn't mean anything," Neil said. Daya looked hurt.

"What does that mean?" Jan demanded. Neil's nose turned red. Daya's eyes were bright as if she wanted to cry.

"Neil, can you get right on that piece of programming?" Barbara asked, wondering what was eating him. "Taking motor number four out of the rotation will put extra strain on the three remaining engines, and we don't know if the others have a flaw that will make them burn out either. Set it up so that we can start cycling the motors in and out to preserve their integrity. We need to avoid using motor number four unless we are on the final stretch or if it's all that we have left. It's all we can do. Or we have to turn back."

"I don't want to turn back," Gary said.

"Neither do I," said Jan.

"Or me," Dion added.

"Neil, you're our only hope," Barbara said, staring him straight in the eye.

"I can do it, Barb," Neil said, distracted from his argument with Daya. His voice seemed to soften when he addressed Barbara. "I bet the batteries will last longer with a patch like that. It might be possible to drive them at lower speeds and keep traveling longer once you hit the night side."

"Maybe then we'll be able to make up time, but until then, we are going to start dropping behind." Gary frowned.

"Let's just stay as positive about this as we can," Barbara said firmly. "We're not even to the second checkpoint yet. Maybe we can make lemonade from the lemons."

"We're on it!" Daya said, grasping Neil by the shoulder. "Come on, Neil." The screen image blinked off.

"Are you all right, Team Sparks?" Pam's voice came in over the open frequency. "I see you have dropped velocity."

Jan's expression became flat.

"We're fine!" she snapped.

"We're all right," Barbara added, patting the air to try and calm Jan down. "We had a little problem, but we handled it."

"Yeah," Dion said, nodding defiantly. "We got this."

Chapter Twelve

"Now, that's thinking like a Bright Spark!" Barbara said approvingly, as she and Jan sat hunched over her PerDee's projection of Neil's new software upgrade for the *Spark Xpress* in the second row of seats. "The user interface looks simple enough."

"Well, it is," Neil said, torn between pride and honesty. "Your PerDees can control it, but it will take the full power of one of them to do the motor optimization calculations while you're moving. If there is just a bad winding, the microcomputer can use the temperature and power inputs required as feedback coefficients and then it can change the pulse modulation signal to the motor. In other words, we are going to run that motor like a stepper motor and move it tiny fractions at a time and then turn it off for tiny fractions at a time. The algorithm I came up with should allow your device to close in on a pulse shape and frequency that minimizes the heat generated and optimizes power usage."

"Neil, you did all that in two hours?" Jan was astounded and so was Barbara. She was pretty sure she couldn't have generated that algorithm and the code in that short a period of time. It was college-level electrical engineering or beyond from a fifteen-year-old.

"Well . . . Daya helped some, and I did pull some of the code from another stepper motor control project we did a while back, but yeah," he replied sheepishly. "I'm not sure how well it will work in real life, but the simulation I did here looked promising. We might get fifty percent or more out of that motor."

"That would be better than what it's doing turned off!" Gary said in the *Spark Xpress*'s pilot seat. "Right now, it's working at a whopping zero percent."

"I hate to ask, Neil, but have you got eyes on the rest of the racers?" Dion asked.

"I've been, uh, busy, big brother."

"*I* will look," Daya said. She turned away from the camera for the moment. "Here is the latest from the BrightSats." The view on each PerDee's screen changed to satellite images. Tiny light gray dots clustered on a darker gray surface beside a huge round object. "They have all made it to the second checkpoint in Aldrinville. The *Blue Streak* got there first. I'm estimating you are still another hour out at your best speed available to you. So sorry."

"Hey, don't worry, little sister!" Dion assured her, although he shot a worried glance at Barbara. "This is just day two. We have a long way to go. The plans have to change, but we've still got this."

"That's right!" Gary added. "We are *not* giving up so quickly."

"No, we're not," Barbara said. "Great job, Neil!"

"Thanks! We're with you," Neil said, gazing at her a little too intently. Barbara began to worry that he was starting to crush on her, the way he had on Jan when Barbara had first arrived on the Moon. The last thing she needed out in the middle of nowhere was a bad case of unrequited love. It was cute, but distracting. "At least, I wish I was there to help, but you're at least four hours behind the last-place car. That's going to delay you leaving the pit stop tomorrow morning."

"Four hours, hmmm." Barbara drummed her fingers on the chair arm. "Four hours? Neil, could you look through the rules right now and tell us the *minimum* time we have to spend at the checkpoints?"

"Oh, he doesn't have to look that up." Daya looked into the video camera over Neil's shoulder. She looked peeved, as if she had noticed Neil's mushy expression. Barbara had seen how Daya often looked at him when he wasn't paying her any attention. There was another crush, utterly unnoticed by its subject. More teenage woes. "I was there when my mother forced the race committee to put the rule in place."

"So, Daya? What was it?" Neil asked, annoyed that she was impinging on his reputation as the Spark with all the answers.

"The racers are required to be checked into their sleep quarters for *four hours* minimum at each checkpoint. This is to insure that they get some sleep, and so the race medical officer, Dr. Johnson, can check over their vitals to make certain there are no safety or health risks popping up," Daya explained.

"Four hours!" Barbara exclaimed. "I thought so. But, that is the minimum, right?"

"So what?" Gary asked.

"I get it." Dion nodded approvingly. "While all the other racers are still in bed in the morning, we are going to slip out and get on our way."

"Absolutely! You saw what it was like at the first pit stop. Everyone was so wiped out from partying that we were half asleep piling back into our buggies," Barbara said. "They'll never notice if we leave early, after that four-hour minimum."

"So, as soon as you reach the checkpoint, you must take your health check, eat, then go straight to bed," Daya said. "When your minimum sleep time is over, Neil and I will wake you up and get you moving." Daya poked him hard in the shoulder with a forefinger. "Won't we?"

"Hey," he said rubbing at his shoulder. "Why do we have to get up, too?"

"We're mission control, silly."

Barbara couldn't help but laugh at Daya's idea of flirting.

"Right," Neil said, with a nod to try to make them believe it had been his idea in the first place. "We'll get you on your way."

"Great! We have a plan. That is exactly what we'll do." Barbara fastened her seatbelt back into place and then set her PerDee in place on the console in front of her. It might not win the race for them, but it would get them back in the pack. "Fido, start running Neil's motor optimization program and take control of the right rear motor as defined therein."

"Affirmative, Barbara," Fido replied.

"You know, roomie, your PerDee could really use some personality." Jan laughed.

Almost as if on cue, Leona's voice sounded over the com system.

"Hello, Sparks. Dr. Bright noticed you are moving slower than planned and asked me to check in on you. Is everything okay?"

The team looked at one another, with almost guilty expressions on their faces.

"Well," Barbara began, resignedly. "Here's what's been going on. . . ."

Chapter Thirteen

"Wake up, Barb!" Daya's voice tore through the sleepy haze that Barbara was fighting. She'd programmed Fido to alarm twenty minutes prior and had told him to snooze three times. "Your four-hour required sleep cycle time is now complete."

"Oh, my . . ." Barbara rubbed at her eyes and blew a sigh out between her lips almost making Dr. Spark's signature motorboat sound. "There's not enough coffee in the world . . . !"

"Brighten up, Sparks!" Neil trumpeted over the speaker of her PerDee. "See what I did there, Barb? Ouch!" Barbara could only assume Daya had poked him again.

"Barbara, it is time to get up. Would you like to snooze again?" Fido announced.

"No! I'm up." She raised up, almost hitting her head on the second pit stop's sleep chamber ceiling. "No, Fido. Alarm off."

"Very well, Barbara."

"Did you wake the others?" she asked.

"You were last up since you were last down," Neil answered. "The others are already suited up and in the racer."

Barbara threw off the thin cover.

"Okay then. To the *Spark Xpress*."

"Dion says to tell you not to worry, that your mug is filled and in the copilot's cup holder spot with the warmer set to high." Daya told her. "He has also taken pastries and egg sandwiches. How do you feel, Barb?"

"Like I got only four hours of sleep, that's how." She quickly changed out of her pajamas and into her spacesuit undergarment, followed by the compression layer. The boots quickly adjusted to her feet and lower legs and sealed off as she slipped them on, too. Picking up her helmet, she cycled the door of her sleeping tube and quietly eased out, doing her best not to wake any of the other racers.

Just as Barbara eased the hatch closed, the one across the corridor slid slightly open. Pam, in her pajamas, peered out, looking quite sleepy herself. She checked her PerDee for the time and then looked back up at Barbara with one eyebrow raised. Barbara tiptoed over to her.

"The 'problem' was worse than you let on, I take it?" Pam said quietly. "You didn't wake me. The others were noisier than you."

"I . . ." Barbara felt like a deer in headlights or a kid caught with her hand in the cookie jar. She didn't know how to respond. "I don't think I should talk about it."

"Don't worry," Pam smiled and waved a casual hand. "One Spark to another, I never saw you."

"Thanks." Barbara smiled back at her uncertain if she should say anything more. "I, uh . . ."

"You better go," Pam said, nodding toward the airlock. "The others are waiting. You should tell them to be quieter next time. And you know, your secret will be out once everyone else is up. I hope you determine a better solution to your problem."

"Right." Barbara started to thank Pam again, but she had already closed her hatch and pulled the privacy curtain.

"Everything okay, Barb?" Daya's voice came over Fido's speaker.

"Yes," she whispered. "Fido, quiet mode."

"Yes, Barbara," Fido whispered back.

"Full charge on the batteries and we are good to go," Dion slapped the emergency brake release and eased the throttle forward. As the *Spark Xpress* passed the pole position, the light blinked red three times, yellow twice, and then green once and it then stayed green continuously, indicating they were free to go. "And, we are off and racing."

"Go, *Spark Xpress*!" Daya and Neil both cheered over the PerDee channel.

"All systems look A-okay, guys," Jan said. Looking up from her console she yawned slightly. "Four hours is tough."

"All right, you two," Dion said, peering over his shoulder at the Nerd-Twins. "Both of you go to sleep now. We swap out in two hours just as we planned."

"No argument from me," Gary replied. Barbara looked back. He was already reclined in his seat with his eyes closed.

"I know I have to go to sleep, but I'm just so awake right now." Jan looked at the controls projected in front of her and then back at Barbara and Dion. "Barb, we could trade spots."

"No, Jan, I think Dion is right. Let's stick to the plan for now. Count sheep or something." Barbara almost laughed out loud at the old cliché and she wondered if anyone had ever actually fallen to sleep while pretending to count imaginary sheep.

"I have just the thing." Jan put her earbuds in her ears and whispered something inaudibly to Ms. Scruffles. In no time, she was asleep, too.

"Good," Barbara said softly and turned back in her chair. "Fido, show me the map, flat."

"Yes, Barbara."

"Neil, can you give us the latest up-to-date imagery and terrain data for today's journey?"

"Already thought about that last night and I picked out what I think is your best bet." Neil's face on the windshield nodded and then looked as if he were tapping at his computer. "I'm sending it now."

The map popped up in front of them and then a direction arrow appeared on the windshield in green. Barbara noted that as Dion tilted the steering controls from side to side that an arrow would pop up in yellow or red, directing him back to the path.

"When did you write this new code, little brother?" Dion asked.

"I finished it last night, but I've been working on it for a few days," Neil said.

"And it's based on the best predicted path from the BrightSat's data?" Barbara was impressed.

Neil was almost puffed up with pride. "That's right, Barb. It should keep you on the most optimal path, but there are possibilities that the sats didn't see everything and there are hazards that were undetected."

"We get it, little brother," Dion assured him. "Good work."

"So, zooming out," Barbara used her fingers to squish the view so she could then zoom much farther out. "The road from Aldrinville ends in about another five kilometers over here past the crater dish on the southeast side, then goes for about another kilometer near this volcanic dome thing that Dr. Bright likes so much. After that, we are trailblazing for the next twelve days. We need to keep a sharp eye out for obstacles when we drive off the improved road in a few minutes."

"I agree," Dion nodded. "Maybe we'll need to slow down at first until we are used to the terrain."

"Not a bad idea." Barbara agreed with the elder Spark. "Thanks, Neil."

"It is good work," Daya said. "Come on, we have an interview with the mayor in thirty minutes. We can use your expanded map to get his impression of how the race is going."

"Great idea!" Neil said, then looked a little jealous that Daya had thought of something that used his work before he did. Barbara laughed and turned off the feed from Sparks Central.

"Hey, Barb and Dion!" Dr. Bright's face appeared on the viewscreen. Behind him, Barbara recognized the inner wall of a shuttle. A few people, all unfamiliar to Barbara except Calvin Book, were leaning over a big table. She couldn't identify the projected images they were looking at, but it seemed to be some kind of terrain.

"Morning, Doc," Dion said, with a big grin.

"Hi!" Barbara said, giving Dr. Bright a warm smile.

"You're all off pretty early, aren't you? Leona's been keeping me informed on things, and said the *Spark Xpress* fell behind yesterday, but there was nothing in the blog. What's going on?"

Dion and Barbara exchanged guilty glances.

"We had some trouble with the right rear buckyball," Barbara said. She realized with a shock that they had never informed their mentor about the problem. "It was redlining on power usage, so we disabled it and had Neil write some new programming for the drives that bypassed it."

"I see, I see," Bright said, sticking out his lower lip thoughtfully.

"We got the buggy going again, although not as fast as we want," Dion said. "We're not going to be able to keep up with the rest of the racers, so we took the minimum rest period possible to gain ground while we can. It's going to be tough, but we think it'll work. I guess we should have let you know, but we got it handled."

"I know! And I'm proud of you for doing it. But here's the real question: You're only a fraction of the way around the Moon and running on three wheels. Should you have turned back? That would have been the safe thing to do."

"We're not giving up, sir," Barbara said, firmly. She hadn't thought so before, but she had made up her mind. "We're the Sparks. We've got this. We will make it. And we will win."

Bright laughed, his handsome face lighting up.

"I believe in you," he said. "Well, keep me posted. I'm working on some interesting stuff here. I'm looking forward to seeing what you think of it. Watch yourselves, Sparks!"

"We will, Dr. Bright," Dion said.

"I know it," the scientist said. "Bright out."

"Whew!" Barbara said, as his image disappeared. "We'd better make it now."

The next hour or so had pretty much been uneventful. Dion had handed the wheel over to Barbara. She blazed a new trail across the lunar surface for the better part of forty-five minutes or more, feeling privileged to be seeing a part of the Moon that few eyes had ever seen before her. Barbara used the *Spark Xpress* as a "front wheel drive" vehicle with both rear wheels in neutral. For the next couple of hours, Neil's chosen path led them over fairly easy terrain. There were the occasional boulders and soft patches but nothing extraordinarily difficult or dangerous.

"One hour twenty-eight minutes in," Daya alerted them. She was looking a little sleepy herself, Barbara thought. "You sure you are awake enough to drive, Barb?"

"I'm fine for now, Daya. Thank you for keeping such a good watch on us. And Neil's suggested track seems to be working out just fine."

"That's what mission control does," Neil interrupted before Daya could respond.

"Yes," the youngest female Spark added, looking sourly at her companion. "That's what we're here for, Barb."

Barbara opened her mouth to intercede, but decided she didn't want to get involved. Suddenly, a burst of sound came out of the speakers on the frequency common to all the speakers.

". . . Stuck in the middle with you!" a singer wailed, followed by guitar riffs and horns.

"What's that?" Gary yelped, coming awake all of a sudden.

Dion glanced down at the face of his PerDee.

"You're not gonna believe this, but there's a TurnTable ahead about two klicks."

Neil's eyes dropped to his computer screen, then his brows went up.

"That's a rare track!" he wailed. "What's it doing out there?"

"Cisca said they were placing TurnTables out along our route," Barbara said. "Nice job, Neil. You figured out the way that the judges thought we would travel."

"Get closer," Gary said, grabbing Turing out of his sleeve. "I want that!"

"Me, too," Jan said, bringing up the game on Ms. Scruffles. "What a coup!"

"We don't have to turn at all," Barbara said, looking at the map. "It's almost straight ahead."

"Can you use my account to snag it for me, too?" Neil wheedled.

"Sorry, little bro," Dion said, with real regret on his face. "Violates the terms of service. We could both lose our accounts."

"I wonder if I can load Einstein onto one of the BrightSats and send it out there," Neil said, a speculative look knitting his brows.

"And what would you do if it fell off somewhere out on the surface of the Moon?" Daya asked.

Neil set his jaw.

"I can't wait until I can get out there with you four," he said. "This isn't fair."

At the end of the first four hours, Gary and Jan took the pilots' seats, letting Barbara and Dion stagger back toward the bunks. Jan spun through the radio frequencies, checking for emergency messages and beacon transmissions. Voices came over the speaker. Jan hastily muted it and listened to it on her earpiece.

"It's started," Jan said, muting her microphone with a finger touch on Ms. Scruffles's screen. "The rest of the teams are setting out from the pit stop. They've noticed we're gone. They're asking each other if anyone knows *when* we left. I don't think anyone saw us." Barbara didn't say a word.

"Well, we have a good head start," Gary said, projecting confidence Barbara was sure he didn't feel. "It'll take them a long time to catch up with us." He scanned the plain ahead. "Hey, Neil, there's a massive ridge up there. Which way are we supposed to go from here?"

Neil's face popped up, split-screened with an image of the topography.

"The arrow says to go right, south of it," the young man said.

"But we can't go right, probably for a long way. Look!" Gary held his PerDee up and pointed the camera ahead. A ridge at least ten meters tall covered with shiny black volcanic rock mixed with pulverized gray lunar regolith stretched south for kilometers. The long line of boulders looked like the back of a long-dead super-giant dinosaur sprawled across the silvery gray surface. "Don't you see those in your satellite imagery?"

"No! We must have done a low-resolution scan of this area." Neil sounded hurt. "I'm not sure how that could have happened. Hold on and I'll get up-to-date high resolution imagery from BrightSat Two. It's just ahead of you now."

"Do we stop and wait on that or keep going, Jan?" Gary turned to his Nerd-Twin.

Jan reached out to the map on the windshield and scrunched it in with her fingers. The map zoomed out. "We have to go west anyway. I will be really upset if we have to double back. I say just keep going west until Neil gets our path straight, but don't come to a full stop unless we just have to. If we stay on this course it looks like we'll reach the end of this crater ridge here in about fifteen kilometers. But what is this dark spot here?" She pointed.

"I dunno. Maybe it's another one of those weird volcano domes Dr. Bright mentioned." Gary shrugged.

"Maybe. We should get Neil to take some detailed images of it for us just in case." Jan leaned back in her seat with her arms crossed. Gary couldn't decide if she was frustrated, tired, or just taking a break. The two of them were usually so in tune with each other that they knew what the other was thinking, but he was so tired and hungry that he didn't feel he was reading her.

"Good idea. Can you hand me that bag of jerky from the console behind me?" he asked, plaintively. "My stomach is starting to rumble."

"Are you ever not hungry?" Jan grinned at him as she unbuckled. She had already been on the move before he asked. Gary could hear as she rummaged about the console compartment to find the beef jerky as quietly as she could hoping not to wake up Dion and Barbara. She still made a lot of noise in the process.

"Uh, I don't know about that either. Probably not." Gary looked over at Jan as she slid back into her seat. She looked as gloomy as he felt. "This is gonna get grueling if we have to do this every day for the next twelve days."

"Nah, we just aren't used to it yet and our sleep cycles are all wonky. In a day or two we'll be fine." Jan smiled back at him reassuringly. Gary knew she was being sincere and not just saying what he wanted to hear. Neither of them wanted to talk about what they were really thinking. They still felt guilty about keeping the design so secret they ran into trouble finishing. It was going to cost them, soon.

"Hey, thanks for the route markers!" Teddy Davis called as *Rover* hurtled past the *Spark Xpress*, followed by *Zhar-Ptitsa* and *Cheetah*. "We were worried about traveling over all this unknown territory this morning, but you saved us the trouble!"

"Aye!" Tracy McGuinn called. "And that TurnTable was just another benefit! I finished a fine rare track right there."

Dion growled into the steering wheel. One after another of the competitors passed them and vanished ahead in a massive cloud of regolith.

"We knew it was going to happen sooner or later." Barbara gave them a weak smile. No matter that they were all expecting it to happen, it still hurt. "We're six hours and eleven minutes in. We made it quite a good ways before they all passed us."

"That still doesn't make that pill any easier to swallow." Dion had a grimace on his face.

"Hey, don't lose faith, Dion. It is a very long race."

Team SolStar in *Blue Streak* was the last to pass. Pam sent a sympathetic look their way. Jan sniffed and turned a cold shoulder. Dion's hands tightened on the controls.

"*That* hurts," he said.

"Hang in there," Barbara said, stoically. "The pit stop is only a couple of hours ahead."

Chapter Fourteen

Four days into the race, and Neil felt idle. He sat at the control console in Sparks Central, jumping from feed to feed of his BrightSats and drinking cola after cola. None of the tiny satellites needed charging at the moment, or any other kind of attention. The buckyball optimization program couldn't really be tweaked any further until he had more data, and no interviews were scheduled for *Live from the Moon* until later. Even Daya had deserted him, to go off for coffee with Dr. Murayama. Giggling! But why should that bother him? He pushed the thought aside.

"Einstein, full map showing all the racers," he ordered.

"Of course, my boy."

More than a quarter of the way around, the teams had spread out across the landscape. *Rover* was moving flat out, with Team Podracer's *Moonracer* close behind. According to the data scrolling up underneath, Teddy Davis was at the controls of *Rover*. Teddy was a great guy. Maybe he would check in with him and get a live feed from the lead buggy in a while. But what would Teddy say that was different from the day before? No, wait, *Blue Streak* was coming up on *Moonracer*'s right. Neil made a face as Pam Yamashita's buggy passed both of the leaders and shot off ahead. He would rather have had his fingernails pulled out with needle-nose pliers than interview her.

Spark Xpress was kilometers behind, and his friends were trying to make it sound like they didn't mind coming in dead last day after day. He was frustrated for them. He knew it was too early to worry about how they could make it over the finish line first. Two weeks was going to feel like a galactic eon.

He wished, for about the millionth time, that he could be out there on the track with them. Even though the others complained about how boring it was just running over lunar terrain, he knew he wouldn't be bored! It was frustrating not to be legally old enough to be out there without adult supervision.

Speaking of adult supervision, there it was. Dr. Bright's face popped up in an inset in the corner of the lunar map.

"Hey, there, Neil! How's my man in mission control?" The scientist's voice sounded hollow inside the bubble helmet he was wearing.

Neil cheered up and sat straighter in his padded swivel chair.

"Great! Where are you, sir?" he asked. Only Dr. Bright's face was illuminated against a dark background. The glimmer of distant lights came and went on the edges of Leona's image.

"Halfway down mine shaft number two," Dr. Bright said. "We're getting some very promising samples here, Neil. I can't wait to show you when I get back. I can't talk about it on open channel. Leona tells me there have been a couple of attempts to hack the secure frequencies and our confidential files. She's running around putting out fires. I've got half an idea as to where those are coming from, but no proof yet. How's the race going?"

Neil promptly sent Leona the current telemetry, although he knew she had access to all the Bright Sparks' databases already.

"The *Spark Xpress* ran around that fifth dome there," Neil said, having Einstein highlight the rounded feature on the map with a bright yellow circle. "They got almost all the way to the edge of the chained crater system before the rest of the pack caught up with them."

Dr. Bright nodded approvingly. "Your BrightSats are doing good work!" he said. "How are you doing on that side project with the laser radar? Have you done the 'uncooperative target' test yet?"

"Nothing in the last couple of days," Neil admitted. "We had that emergency, you know."

"Right! The extra programming for the *Xpress*. I was really impressed by how fast you were able to program a work-around, Neil. You're going to go far with those skills."

Neil sat up just a little straighter.

"Thanks, sir, but it's just part of being a Spark."

Bright laughed, his eyes crinkling in the corners.

"Well, when you get a chance to finish those tests, I'd be interested in seeing your data."

"Yes, sir!" Neil said, grateful to have a project. "I can do it this morning. Do you need me to take care of anything before today's broadcast?"

"I think Jackie got everything else set up," Dr. Bright said.

"Dr. Bright?" Calvin Book's voice came over the scientist's headset. "You're going to want to take a look at this."

"Got to go, Neil. Keep me up to date, won't you?"

"Of course, sir!"

"I knew I could count on you, Neil. Bright out."

The transmission ended. Neil let out a gusty breath. Well, that sounded like permission to him.

"Einstein, which BrightSat is close to the front-runners?"

"BrightSat Two is nearest."

Neil glanced around to make sure Daya wasn't on her way back. He told himself he didn't really feel guilty about what he was doing. After all, it was just an experiment to see how well his laser radar system worked. He had tested it in the lab, and even from an altitude on the satellite onto the large window on Sparks Central, but he had yet to test it on an actual "uncooperative target." Certainly *Blue Streak*, currently leading the race, could be considered "uncooperative." At least, as far as Neil was concerned.

Originally, the BrightSats were designed to be in stationary orbits over certain points of the Moon. Orbital mechanics made that a tough endeavor unless the satellites had propulsion onboard that would last a long time. The perfection of the electromagnetic or EMdrive propulsion system had made that possible as long as there was electrical power available. Neil had designed the little satellites to stay far enough out from the Moon that they could always be in the sunlight and therefore harvest solar power to recharge the onboard batteries.

Unfortunately, like their initial use overseeing the build of the Aldrinville radio/radar telescope, his latest satellite's mission required him to get closer to the lunar surface. Dr. Bright wanted him to gather extremely high resolution lidar imagery data as well as to map out a solid racecourse for the Sparks. In order to get that close to the surface, he had to put the little spacecraft in standard low-altitude orbits around the Moon. That meant they had to zoom out frequently or return to base to recharge.

"Bring up BrightSat Two's control panel, please, Einstein," he said.

"Right there, Neil," the PerDee replied. In the lower right corner of the big map, the telemetry screen appeared. It had plenty of power, and all its functions were on green.

Neil leaned over his console, calculating angles in his mind. BrightSat 2's orbit was very close to the lunar equator and at an altitude of about one hundred kilometers. The latitude of the orbit had been modified by the EMdrive propulsion unit onboard so that it would make a long pass over the current path that the Sparks were planning to take. Neil had enough data to generate what on paper ought to be the perfect pathway for the *Spark Xpress* to circumnavigate the Moon. He hadn't told Dr. Bright that the laser vibrometer package on the satellite would work perfectly for eavesdropping. He tweaked the propulsion system to slightly adjust its position. It ought to spend a good deal of time in range over *Blue Streak*.

Calculating the right propulsion adjustments and guessing the path Pam's team would take had taken some doing. Dr. Bright had said the astrophysics calculations alone were graduate level, but Neil was proud of learning more than just the ins and outs of satellite orbital mechanics when he had taken on building the very first BrightSat many months prior. From the reading he had done in physics journals, his level of knowledge on the topic put him on a level with other experts in the field of astrodynamics. He was dying to see his name on articles in those digests next to them, and dying to hear what was going on in *Blue Streak*. This was going to work, he told himself.

"Okay, Einstein, as soon as the footprint of the laser vibrometry system is over the racer, we turn it on," Neil said. In his mind, it was just an experiment. He wasn't cheating in any fashion.

"The laser imaging and range-finding field of view will be incident on the designated target in thirteen seconds, Neil," the little micro supercomputer's AI responded.

"Great, cycle the laser heads. Go ahead and start firing the system on zero."

"Activating in seven, six, five, four, three, two, one . . ."

"Give me any return live on audio now." The speakers crackled on, blaring with static.

"Very good, Neil," Einstein replied.

Neil listened patiently for a few more seconds until the algorithms in the filters started working. The voices became more and more clear, until the system locked onto the audio signals. Suddenly, it sounded as if the speakers were sitting in the room with him, rather than in some lunar racer buggy several thousand kilometers away on the other side of the Moon being eavesdropped on by a laser beam from a satellite.

A male voice came through loud and clear.

". . . *Karera wa akiraka ni, sharyō no shuyōna shisutemu ga godōsa shite iru. . . ."*

"Yes! We did it, Einey!" Neil beamed with pride at his technical triumph. "Translator on, please."

". . . They clearly have a major system malfunctioning on their vehicle. . . ."

". . . We cannot know that. . . ."

"That's Pam's voice! I'd know it anywhere, the evil . . ." Neil said, letting his voice trail off in disgust.

". . . Come on, Pam, you know something, don't you? . . . Spill it. . . ."

". . . If I knew something that would give us an unfair advantage, it would be unethical of me to make use of it. And I would not share such information to potentially compromise the integrity of our team . . . and, they are my friends . . . I owe them some, uh, privacy on some things. . . ."

"Friends?! Ha! Friends?" Neil couldn't restrain his outburst.

". . . Friends? The way they've treated you? Friends?" another of the team exclaimed. Neil started. No way could they hear him! In a panic, he fumbled to make sure his microphone was disabled. It was. His heart stopped pounding.

". . . Some of them may have treated me unfairly, to some point of view. They are mostly very young and may get over it or may not, but, yes, friends. And I owe them some privacy. . . ."

"... Then you *do* know something ...!"

Pam sounded coldly annoyed, an emotion that Neil was all too familiar with. "... I will no longer discuss this ... now let's bring up the path coordinates against the high-resolution imagery that the Japanese Space Agency furnished us, and make certain we are still on the optimal path...."

"... Whatever, you're the boss. Friends, really?"

"... *The imagery data ...!*" Pam said, with pointed emphasis.

"... All right, all right ... It was brilliant to convince the Japanese government not to release this data to the public until after the race. ..."

"... I didn't really convince any government ... my colleague at the JAXA office in...."

The voices vanished in a burst of static. Neil stared at the speaker.

"I'm sorry, Neil, but the signal has been lost. The orbit is no longer over the racer's position," Einstein informed him.

"She's cheating," Neil whispered to himself. He slapped the side of his fist against the console. "She's cheating! Some friend."

You're cheating, too, his conscience told him, but he ignored it.

Chapter Fifteen

"You don't know that she is cheating, Neil. How would you know that?" Barbara didn't care what the rest of the Sparks thought about Pam at this point. "Pam is a perfectionist, Neil, an alpha type. She wouldn't cheat to win. It is in her personality to make herself better than the competition."

"Yeah, by cheating," Neil replied, darkly.

"I wouldn't put it past her," Gary agreed from his seat behind Dion. Barbara turned and looked at Jan, but couldn't decide what she was thinking.

"Okay, little brother," Dion interrupted. "Then if you have evidence that she's cheating, what is it?"

"Um, well, I know that she got the high-resolution imagery data of the lunar surface from the Japanese Lunar Mapper Probe and is keeping it from being released to the public until after the race," Neil said triumphantly.

"I'm not sure that's cheating," Barbara said. "You aren't giving the mapping data from the BrightSats to anyone but the Sparks."

"I never thought of it like that." Jan frowned. "Are *we* cheating?"

"No, of course not," Neil said. "The BrightSats are ours and we can use them however we want and do with the data whatever we want."

"I suspect the Japanese research team could say the same," Barbara replied. "No difference, in my opinion."

"Wait a minute." Dion still had a puzzled look on his face that Barbara hadn't quite understood yet. "Neil, you haven't answered my question."

"What question?"

"How would you know this?"

"Well, I, uh, I just do."

Barbara was almost startled out of her suit when a crackling and squealing sound came over the speakers and then it cleared to voices. Pam's voice and one of her teammates were in conversation.

". . . Now, let's bring up the path coordinates. . . ."

Neil looked horrified.

"Einstein, I didn't tell you to play that."

"No, you didn't," Daya's face appeared in Barbara's monitor. "Guys, you should hear this. All of it."

"Daya, you don't have the right to do that . . ."

"Oh, shut up, Neil. You aren't telling them the entire story either!" Daya sounded more like her mother did when she scolded Barbara for not getting her exercise done as often as she was supposed to.

"Daya!" Neil protested.

"I said shut up, Neil, and let them listen. Achi, tell Einstein to play it all the way through."

Neil looked sulky and angry and maybe a bit frightened. She'd never heard Daya talk so sternly to him. Barbara was hopeful that the youngest of the female Sparks was finally overcoming her crush and would no longer blindly follow Neil in his wild schemes.

The six Sparks quietly listened to the audio. Dion's face twisted with frustration and anger. He clenched his hands on the controls. Barbara was pretty sure from the look on his face that the eldest Spark would strangle the youngest were they in the same room together.

"Where! Did! You! Get! This! Neil?" Dion spat out one word at a time through a clenched jaw.

"Does it matter that much?" Neil asked, in a tiny voice.

"Answer him, Neil!" Daya added. "Answer them."

"I, uh, well, I used the laser system on the BrightSat Two and listened to them," Neil finally answered sheepishly.

"After we told you not to?" Barbara asked, hearing her own voice rising in tone. She tamped down her temper.

"Dr. Bright wanted me to test the laser system on an uncooperative target," Neil protested. "And who's more uncooperative than Pam?"

"And that didn't seem creepy or maybe wrong to you at all?" Dion grunted almost as a statement rather than a question.

"Well, no. . . ."

"Neil, you can't just violate people's privacy like this," Jan finally spoke up. "I don't know, but it might even be illegal. I mean, don't cops have to have a warrant or something to do this?"

"Neil, this is bad, bud," Gary said. "I don't like Pam any more than you do but, Jan is right. You aren't supposed to do this kind of thing without people knowing."

"But does that matter if we can prove Pam is cheating?" Neil pleaded.

"How is she cheating, Neil? She isn't doing any more or less than us or probably any of the other teams." Barbara didn't want to make a mountain out of a micrometeorite crater. To her the most telling part of the audio was Pam not ratting them out that they were having major technical problems.

"She said she was our friend." Jan sounded puzzled.

"And it sounded like she knows something about the *Spark Xpress* that she's not sharing with her team." Gary was puzzled as well. They'd never considered Pam as an ally. Barbara could see them beginning to question their preconceived ideas about their former colleague.

"It is curious, as if she knows something." Dion turned and looked at Barbara. That made her squirm. She must look guilty. "What does she know? Barb, any ideas on that?"

Barbara folded her arms.

"I didn't tell her a thing. If she's smart enough to be a Bright Spark, she's smart enough to figure out something is really wrong with us. Right? Anyone can see we've been falling behind day after day."

"I don't like it," Gary said. "But you're right."

"She didn't tell them," Jan said. "I wonder why?"

"Once a Spark, always a Spark," Barbara offered.

"Yeah, well, she didn't let *you* down," Dion said. They all looked at each other. Barbara wondered if the stress of going on only four hours' sleep a night was going to precipitate them all into an argument, right out there in the middle of lunar nowhere.

"Let's talk about this when we're all safe back at home," Barbara pleaded. "Please. We're still hours out of the next pit stop, and we've got days more to run. Neil, as if you couldn't figure out what we're telling you: stop eavesdropping on our competition. We're going to beat them fairly, or not at all."

"Well?" Daya demanded, glaring fiercely at her companion.

"All right," Neil said. He hung his head. "Sorry, guys."

Dion nodded, obviously having made up his mind.

"Candy, crank up playlist number three."

"Right, Dion," the PerDee said, in her sultry voice.

Barbara settled into the copilot's chair, stiff with tension. Pam wasn't her problem at that moment. It looked as though her own team was.

Chapter Sixteen

"And would you believe it, we're out of the race, just like that," Tracy McGuinn said, thrusting long legs under the table at the pit stop on the seventh night. Jan and Gary listened sympathetically. The peloton had moved into deepening twilight, and something—no one on the Tuatha Dé Danann team had been able to figure out what—had gone wrong with the power storage system. "We're not generating enough friction to produce motive force. Marooned. It's over." The redhead looked glum.

"You can't give up," Gary said with a sympathetic look at his new friend. "I mean, the rescue shuttle will take you back if you want, but your team has come all this way!"

"We're not giving it up so easily," said Georgina McNair, a fair-haired woman in her thirties who was one of Tracy's teammates. "We're going to stay out here and work on it, but it looks bad. At least we weren't the first to go."

Everyone in the dining area grimaced. *Výdra*, driven by Barbara's admirer, Tomasz Salenko, had scratched the day before. The handsome green vehicle had steered wide on what looked like a safe lane to avoid *Firebird*, and crashed into a sharp-edged boulder hidden in a dune of regolith. The team had been flown back to Armstrong City. The two drivers sustained only minor injuries, but the buggy itself was undriveable. By the time *Spark Xpress* passed the abandoned car, it had acquired a dusting of regolith, like a long-discarded toy.

"We could end up like that," Dion had said as they rode by. "Why didn't we turn back?"

"We don't quit," Gary insisted. "No matter what." Jan and Barbara had nodded vigorous agreement. They had steeled themselves. Whatever they had to do to win, they would do. Anything fair, that was.

They had already had to say goodbye to the teams driving *Apollo's Chariot*, *Silver Surfer*, *Pete's Jalopy*, and two other buggies. The pit-stop habitats started to feel empty instead of crowded. If it wasn't for the irrepressible good humor of Team Podracer and Charlton Mbute's DJing skills, the big dining area might have felt funereal, in spite of the M-Tracker TurnTable that seemed to be planted right in the middle of the room. Holograms and musical notes rose from it like smoke from a campfire, tempting Barbara to pull out Fido and build songs. She knew it was generating rare tracks, but she did not dare take the time to do anything but eat, bathe, and sleep. As on the previous few days, Barbara regretted deeply having to forego the nighttime party with the other drivers. She had to get what rest she could before the team had to set out again.

"Stay!" Charlton called out to her as she rose from her table with her empty tray. "Don't go to bed! I have new music you will love that I put together just today! Play the game! Look at all the new tracks you can catch."

"Thanks, Charlton," Barbara said, deliberately keeping Fido in her sleeve pouch. "I wish we could. Good night!"

"Good night, and good luck, Barbara Winton!" Lois Ingota said.

"Thanks," Barbara said, feeling a wrench of shame. "Good luck to all of you, too!"

It stung having everyone notice that they were running with a damaged vehicle, but no one ever referred directly to it. The *Spark Xpress's* bad right rear ball was the biggest open secret on the Moon. Everyone knew they were taking the minimum required rest period and leaving hours before the others just to come in last every night. She couldn't believe they had been so blind as to believe they could hide the problem from everyone else.

In a weird way, it hurt more that nobody else was shorting their nights to get out on the road ahead of the *Spark Xpress*. Anyone could have done what the Sparks were doing. It seemed that the rest of the racers had already dismissed them as serious contenders to win the race. Barbara refused to let herself think that way, instead putting it down to a show of good sportsmanship. She kept encouraging the other Sparks to keep heart. Every day, Neil came up with more adjustments to the program to improve their mobility and speed. In a matter of days, they might be able to run at a normal speed and be able to stay up for the party. Maybe they could still win the race.

Maybe.

"Wasn't this supposed to be fun?" she asked, heading toward the sleeping area.

"Come on," Jan said, sympathetically. "Let's get to sleep."

"I don't really feel like sleeping," Dion said.

"You're dead on your feet," Gary said, yawning. He gathered the last four cookies off his tray. "So am I."

Pam and Team SolStar sat at the table at the rear of the food service area, speaking quietly among themselves. As Barbara came closer, Pam looked up from her conversation. Barbara gave her a small smile. Pam nodded without changing expression.

Jan turned her nose up as she passed. She and the boys still regarded Pam with suspicion, which Neil's snooping had not helped to dispel. For her part, the Japanese-American girl could have cared less.

"Have you thought of running on your front two wheels and allowing the left rear to drag for more friction?" Pam asked, in an even voice. "As we pass into the night side, your power requirements may not be satisfied by what is in your storage batteries."

"We don't need your help to calculate energy supply," Gary said.

"As you wish," Pam said. She turned her back on them and resumed her conversation.

That had been a friendly suggestion, meant to help. Much as she didn't want to open old wounds in the middle of the race, Barbara made up her mind to confront the others about their problem with Pam the very next day. Enough was enough.

Chapter Seventeen

"No, I get it, Keegan. I mean the business end of it anyway." Calvin Book adjusted his glasses with a forefinger. In the mine with the outer door to the shaft sealed, the caves and mineshafts were pressurized so they could remove their visors. Just in case, safety protocols required them to keep the helmets on. "The geophysics just doesn't make a lot of sense to me. Uranium ores in the wall of craters on the Moon. On Earth, they're never where they can just be plucked out like that."

"The Moon was more highly volcanic for longer, and with less atmosphere during its formation, meaning there is a good deal of radiation inherent in the rocks," Keegan said, turning toward Paul the cameraman as he fell into lecture mode. "We exposed this place to neutrons and looked for decay products. We were able to find strong pockets of returned gamma rays and stuff." Dr. Bright grinned at the informal vernacular.

"'Stuff' being the key technical term, I take it, Keegan?" Calvin grinned.

"Precisely."

"But there's no water or oxygen on the surface to allow for the uranium to form compounds that typically are then flowed about and through various rocks and soils that cause the U-235 to form in any real useable quantity like on Earth." Calvin still sounded perplexed.

Keegan and Calvin had looked around up top for a while but the other four members of the mine team had already headed farther down into shaft number four. The pilot, copilot, and engineer of the shuttle stayed onboard, keeping the craft ready for a departure in case they had to make an emergency return or rescue one of the racers. That hadn't happened yet, but Keegan kept an ear on both the open race channel and the Sparks' private frequency just in case.

He was concerned for the kids. They were resourceful enough to stay in the race, but their pride had to be hurting a little. No way could they have foreseen a technical glitch like that. They had recovered well, but he hoped it would be good enough. Although he was supposed to be neutral, he wanted the Sparks to take first prize. He couldn't wait to see what kind of buggy they would design if they had all the money they really needed.

He dragged his attention back to the project at hand, and steered Calvin toward the metal cage of the mine elevator. He and Calvin had spent the first few days on the upper level of the mine where equipment and future quarters for the particle accelerator scientists would be, letting the younger scientist get to know the rest of the crew and the structure of the underlying terrain, while Paul recorded data for *Live from the Moon* and future documentaries on the mining operation. Keegan and Calvin had spent a solid two days discussing the best location for the new collider, and noted five potential candidates, each with its own attractions. Together, they also investigated the first few exploratory mining pits, which had been left mostly in their primary states because their deposits weren't as exciting as in this one.

"The transuranics will be our bread and butter, but this site is interesting for other reasons. Something else much more amazing happened here. I'll give you a hint. Remember, I mentioned diamonds," Keegan said with a raised eyebrow.

"Many of them?" Calvin asked, eagerly.

"Enough to make mining them also beneficial and maybe even lucrative." Keegan couldn't help but grin from ear to ear with his well-known smile. "Impact diamonds."

"The crater. Of course, that part is now obvious." Calvin nodded his head in understanding. "The impact of the meteor or comet—"

"Comet," Keegan interrupted.

"Comet? Really? You know that for sure?"

"Yes."

"Okay then, the comet's impact energy formed diamonds in the surface just like the crater diamond mines in Russia on Earth."

"You got it." Dr. Bright smiled at his pupil-turned-peer and pulled the elevator gate to. "I know Paul wants to get lots of video of masses of diamonds." The cameraman grinned behind his rig. "Now is when the fun begins. We're going down another forty meters. It took the boring bots almost a month to get there but all of our tests pointed us to the main deposit vein." Keegan steadied his balance as the elevator clanged to a stop at the lower level of the mine. "Here we are. This way."

Although there were bright white cold-lamps hanging along the walls of the lava tube next to the elevator, Calvin had to let his eyes adjust to the darkness.

"Here we are . . . where?"

"Well, as we turn this corner, you can see." Keegan held out his hands gesturing at the cavernous room before them. There were several shafts and openings running off in multiple directions and the walls were mostly smooth. Tests the geologists had run said they were granite. Light trees had been set up about the room and fastened into various wall mounts. The cavern was large enough to play a full-court basketball game in and still have room on the sides for bleachers. Across the big chamber, by one of the openings, several of the robot diggers sat idle. Rumbling issued from somewhere as though one was operating nearby. To the left of the bots was a pile of a fine, yellowish gravel. Calvin estimated that it was about thirty meters in diameter and at least ten meters in height, or several tens of tons of material.

"What the . . . ?" Calvin gasped. "A cave? This one is different than the others. How did such a big chamber develop?"

"There's a lot of residual water ice in this cave. Most of it has melted as we've heated things up down here some, but further down it's still there. Right here, we are underneath the southeasternmost edge of the crater just under the shuttle pad. Seismographic surveys suggest there are more of these spread out about this crater," Keegan explained as he tossed his PDE up allowing it to hover in front of them. Thanks to the trapped atmosphere, its functions were almost as complete as they would have been in Armstrong City. "Project our findings on the ground, Leona."

"Yes, Dr. Bright."

A three-dimensional view of the crater and the mine appeared on the ground at their feet. Keegan reached out and picked it upward and spun it about until he pointed out where they were currently standing. The image showed many dark spots that were representative of underground caverns across the crater.

"The geophysics here is something that may be rare or it may be common in the universe; we don't know yet. This impact crater was created by a fairly large comet. The water ices then were vaporized some, and liquefied some, and a lot of it was forced into the surface during the impact. Tubes and caverns were created by something flowing like lava." Keegan laughed. "I'm just kidding about the lava. It was clearly water. There are geophysical signs of liquid water flowing, freezing, melting, and erupting in geyser fashion through the surface at times. How any of that happened is beyond me at this point. I predict there will be many dissertations written on this crater in the future."

"Amazing." Calvin whistled through pursed lips as he stood looking anew at the cavern he was in. "How solid are the walls, floors, and ceiling?"

"We're not completely certain yet." Keegan spun the three-dimensional image once again and pointed at a clustering of shafts that ran upward toward the surface. "These tubes here I personally think were geysers millions of years ago whenever this happened. That makes this site unusual on the Moon, though not unique."

"Did they burst through to the surface, you think?"

"Maybe, likely, dunno." Keegan rubbed at stubble on his chin and pointed at another structure under the crater. "This pocket here looks like it was once a cavern but caved in. Or maybe it blew out then fell back in. Again, I dunno."

"Do you think there are other craters like this one on the Moon?"

"Search me." Keegan shrugged. "But we know this one is here. So we're going to dig in and exploit its riches. It will probably take decades to excavate this place completely. Mining on the Moon is still a very new idea, and all of the technologies and procedures are still in their infancy. Who knows what we'll find here?"

"Where are the mining engineers? Aren't they down here?" Calvin looked about still with a look of wonder on his face that in turn made Keegan smile. "Can we see what they're doing?"

"Not sure, hold on." Keegan reached up and grabbed his PDE and touched a couple of icons and then the map was overlaid with ten blue dots. "Blue Force Tracker program."

"I see." Calvin nodded. They had used it several times in the last few days to check on the rest of the group. He pushed his glasses up and pointed at the map. "So, we three are *here*. Up there is the shuttle crew. These four over here. . . ."

"Yep, there they are. That would be, um, let me get my bearings—this way. This is the newest vein they're working." Keegan pointed at one of the passageways leading west and slightly upward. The rumble of a mining robot was slightly vibrating the ground. Keegan could feel the ground shaking underneath his boots as they got closer to the entrance to the passage. "Leona, put me through to the mining engineers. Tulip? Hey, Larry, it's Keegan. We're headed in your direction." No answer. Keegan shrugged. "Let's go see what they're up to. I also mentioned gas, like helium-3. It's worth a mint per cubic centimeter, and almost impossible to obtain on Earth, but it's trapped in the rocks down here. We can dig it loose and trap it. Just money waiting to be gathered up."

Keegan turned and tramped across the stone floor. Calvin obediently followed, with Paul taking up the rear. Although regolith got almost everywhere on the Moon, surprisingly little of it was down in the mine shaft, no more than a few centimeters deep. As he walked, it seemed to dance slightly.

"Do you feel that vibration in your feet too?" Calvin asked.

"Yes. The mining robots really shake the ground, don't they?" Keegan asked, with a chuckle.

"I'm not sure that's the robots. Seems too, uh, well, I don't know, low frequency." Calvin knelt down and touched the floor of the cavern with his hand. As he did, the floor rumbled even deeper, like a train was rolling by them. "Keegan!"

His old teacher picked up on the change in vibration at the same time he had.

"To the passage entrance, Calvin! Move!" Keegan turned and hopped in the low gravity several meters and then bounded again until he landed near the entrance to the passage. He held up his wrist. The lights on the band around it had turned yellow. Air and dust rushed past them in a whirlwind. "Pressure alarm, Calvin! Shut your helmet! Paul, you, too!"

Calvin slapped his faceplate down just as Keegan closed his. The three helmets sealed off quickly, but dust continued to slam against them, sandblasting their visors. Calvin spat out the regolith that coated his mouth and nose. He could barely see his hand in front of his face.

The rumbling turned to a roar. Rubble began to slowly descend from the ceiling of the cavern. Rocks and debris fell into the floor throwing more dust upward, causing visibility to fall to almost zero.

"Keegan!"

The loose stones fell more slowly in the Moon's gravity, but fall they did. Calvin let out a cry as a boulder the size of a desk dropped on one of the light-trees, crushing it to the floor. The cables tied to that one pulled over the rest in a cascade. The lamps were knocked over, down, or simply crushed under falling debris, leaving them in darkness.

"Bertie, flashlight!" he shouted.

"On, Calvin," the calm voice of his PerDee said. A white beam of light issued from the small device.

"Keegan, where are you?"

"Over here, Calvin," Keegan said, sounding astonishingly unruffled under the circumstances. "I'm by the elevator. Don't be frightened. Come on, Paul. This way. Follow Leona's beacon."

Instantly, Bertie's screen showed a red arrow, pointing off to the right of the direction Calvin was facing. The younger scientist fumbled his way toward his mentor, and tripped as another rumble rose underfoot.

"This wasn't on your agenda, Doc," Paul said, wryly.

"No, it wasn't, Paul," Keegan replied. "Makes good video, though, doesn't it?"

"What is that?" Calvin landed beside him. He scrambled to his feet, holding onto Keegan's arm for balance. The fierce rush of dust and air felt like a terrestrial sandstorm. It knocked him off his feet again, tumbling both of them into a passageway that sloped upward toward the surface. Air and dust rushed past them like a desert dust-storm front.

"What in the world?" Keegan pushed himself up to a knee. The ground heaved beneath them like a bronco. Suddenly, the airflow was too great to stand against. Calvin felt them being sucked upward and off their feet up the passageway. The lanky cameraman was swept away before their eyes. "Try to hold on to something!" Keegan shouted.

"Keegan! What's happening?"

"A blowout! Grab something if you can! Anything! Otherwise, just roll with it!"

Chapter Eighteen

Daya sat in the café in the atrium of Armstrong City, sipping from a large mug of cappuccino. Charles Murayama set down his cup of green tea on the small round table and smiled warmly at her. She hoped she looked nice. She'd worn her best scarlet blouse and blue dress trousers instead of her usual jumpsuit, adorned with the loan of her mother's favorite gold necklace, and she had done her hair in a complicated braid pulled around over one shoulder.

"You Sparks are much too modest about your accomplishments," he said. "The earthquake an hour ago alarmed me and my SolStar friends a good deal."

"They happen more frequently than people on Earth realize," Daya said, matter-of-factly, though secretly she was pleased by his praise. "That was a moderately strong one, but not too bad."

"We didn't have everything battened down as you do in our habitat," Charles said, with a self-deprecating grimace. "My calibrator vibrated off the table in our quarters. Luckily, the low gravity meant it fell in slow motion. That amused me, but it also gave me time to grab it."

"There wasn't much damage," Daya said. "We do lose small things, and cracks develop in the floors in a bad quake. Neil was tracking the epicenter when I left Sparks Central. It wasn't near here, though the aftershocks affected us. We will incorporate the information as part of *Live from the Moon* later today once we have more data."

Charles's eyes gleamed. "I'm such a fan! I am delighted to spend so much time with you, Daya. It's very kind of you to take away from your busy schedule for me."

"Oh, I'm enjoying it, too!" Daya assured him, beaming. He was such good company, as well as being a brilliant engineer, and very handsome, too.

She knew she shouldn't be interested in him. Charles was almost nine years older than she was, but he treated her like a peer, with respect and admiration, unlike Neil. She often felt that her fellow Spark considered her a nuisance to be tolerated. Why she cared so much, she just couldn't say, but it hurt! Perhaps, she thought, peeping up shyly at Charles through her long eyelashes, she ought to be looking for positive interaction elsewhere.

Achi, lying on the table beside Charles's PDE, buzzed. Neil's face rose up from the screen. Daya groaned.

"Daya, listen to this!" Neil exclaimed.

She put her hand over the screen, cutting off the hologram.

"Neil, not now!" She glanced up at Charles. He stared off into the middle distance, doing his best not to appear to be eavesdropping on a private call.

"No! This is important!"

Wasn't it just like Neil to interfere with something she was enjoying? Daya summoned up her patience and kept her voice level.

"Neil, I am certain whatever it is, it can wait . . ."

"No, it can't! Dr. Bright is missing!"

"Missing?" Daya sprang up with such force that her feet momentarily left the ground. She seized Achi and stared at Neil. "What happened?"

Her fellow Spark's hair stood out in all directions as if he had been hit with an electric shock. "It sounds like there was a massive blowout at the mine site about the same time as the earthquake! Wait, here comes the broadcast!"

Daya heard an echo from Achi's speaker at the same time as all the video screens around the café turned to the same frequency. Carroll Wu, Armstrong City's local news anchor, appeared flustered and upset.

". . . The effects of the moonquake on Armstrong City were negligible, but the midpoint station for the race suffered some minor damage and repairs had to be made. Presently, there are no known casualties. However, a scientific expedition into the region has yet to be heard from. Among the expedition were several mining engineers, a shuttle crew, and the acclaimed science spokesperson Dr. Keegan Bright and his former pupil Dr. Calvin Book. The expedition has not been heard from since the quake. A rescue shuttle has been dispatched, but it is a nine-hour flight to the location. Stay tuned to Armstrong City News Channel for latest updates."

Daya gawked at the screen. It felt as though her heart had stopped beating. Dr. Bright! Then she turned to Charles.

"I have to go," she said. "I am sorry."

"Don't be sorry," he said, rising from his seat. "I hope everything is all right."

Daya was already running toward Sparks Central.

"So do I!"

"And there's no word from Dr. Bright at all?" Barbara asked Jackie over the Sparks' open channel. The producer was on the rescue shuttle piloted by Major Beddingfield headed out to Dr. Bright's last known location. Another shuttle, flown by Armstrong City's emergency response team, was on its way as well.

On the other frequencies, the rest of the teams were clamoring for more news than the official broadcast. The vlogosphere had blown up completely. Neil and Daya couldn't keep up with the frightened well-wishers and commenters posting on the Sparks' site. Their faces, broadcasting from Sparks Central, were side by side with the producer's.

Jackie looked as worried as Barbara felt. Her thick, dark hair tangled under her headset, and dark circles surrounded her eyes, showing just how frantic she must be.

"No," Jackie said. "Even Leona was cut off from the PerDee link with Dr. Bright. That could just mean the device was damaged, or the repeater at the surface of the mine facility was knocked out. The quake was only a three-point-one on the Richter scale. Not that big as far as moonquakes go, but the epicenter was only a few tens of kilometers from the mine's location. Keegan could be in trouble and we have no way to know."

"We're only an hour or so from that part of the course," Barbara said. She saw the resolve on the faces of her teammates, and knew she spoke for all of them. The race would have to wait. Dr. Bright's life could be at stake! "We're going to get there and see what we can do."

"Barbara, no, you can't do that! It could be dangerous. None of you are trained or certified for below-surface rescue." Jackie's eyes were stern.

"Jackie, save your breath," Dion said gruffly. "We're going. Nothing you can do to stop us."

"I had to say it," Jackie admitted, with a resigned shrug. "I knew that would be your response. But don't do anything to get yourselves into danger. We don't need to add a second rescue to this."

"We won't," Gary said. "We'll be careful, but we have to find Dr. Bright! Who knows what happened to him and Calvin?"

"Neil, get your satellite over that mine as quickly as possible!" Barbara told him. "Get images, sound, data, anything you can give us."

"I'm on it, Barb. BrightSat Five is just past there. I was, uh, following the leader," Neil replied.

Barbara didn't ask. She was too worried about Dr. Bright.

"Turn all your resources on getting us data ASAP," she said, her voice trembling. "We need to know what we're heading into."

"Right, Barb," Daya said. Her eyes were swollen with tears. "Good luck. Let us know as soon as you find him."

"Sending you coordinates for the fastest route," Neil said, his hands flying across his console. "Einstein, keep *Spark Xpress* up to date on any more tremors. Be careful, Sparks!"

"We will," Barbara said. The screen lit up with the revised route.

"We're altering our course now," Dion said, with resolve on his face. "On it. We got this. We'll find him."

"What are you doing, Pam?" Riku Ishida asked, from the copilot's seat of *Blue Streak*, watching his captain's actions with concern.

"I'm stopping," Pam replied, pulling to the side of the track. *Rover*, *Cheetah* and *Moonracer*, who had all been fighting to get around the leader, hurtled by her. Charlton Mbute gave them a puzzled look as *Cheetah* passed. She removed her wireless earbud. "You all need to hear this."

"What is it?" Tomiko asked.

"The open channel that the Bright Sparks use," Pam said. "I was once one of their number. I am entitled to listen to it."

Pam set Ada to play the broadcast back over the internal speakers. The rest of her team listened with dismay and disbelief.

"A moonquake? I didn't even feel it," Shiro said, his broad face blank with disbelief.

"Me either," said Tomiko.

"The shock absorption system probably damped it out, thinking it was standard motion. After all, this is a pretty bumpy part of the road," Riku suggested, drawing down his winged eyebrows.

"You're probably right about that." Pam pulled up the high-resolution data maps from the Japanese mission and scrolled it to their current location. "We are here. Neil said he was following us, and that we were closer than they were. We might get to them quicker. Every moment might be precious."

"Wait, we're pulling out of the race?" Tomiko asked, aghast.

"No, we are detouring to see if someone needs help," Pam explained. "That doesn't mean we don't pick up where we left off after we check on them."

"This could cost us the race!" Riku exclaimed.

"This could cost them their lives. This man was my mentor, and he is important to the Moon's future. Emergency services are en route, but they will take hours to arrive. We're going. The discussion is over."

"Of course," Tomiko said, in a small voice. "I apologize. Naturally, life is more important."

The others looked ashamed of themselves. Pam was unconcerned with their feelings. Life took priority over pride.

She tapped at the historical imagery map they had stored in *Blue Streak*'s memory until she found a larger crater with a square shuttle landing pad near it. Rectangular excavators and disruption of the land adjacent to the crater wall marked it as a location where active work was taking place. "This has to be it."

It took the little BrightSat 5 about seven tense minutes to get into position over the mining crater, then another two or so to gather data with the high-resolution laser imager and return that data over the high bandwidth digital link between the other BrightSats and Sparks

Central. As the three-dimensional mosaic of the mine location was built up in front of Neil, a larger lump formed in his throat and he felt his stomach twist in a knot.

"Oh, my gosh! Look at this!"

"Uh oh!" Jan exclaimed as she and the other Sparks examined the three-dimensional image of Dr. Bright's last known location. "Look where the landing pad used to be! There's nothing but a sink hole!"

"Is that the tail of a shuttle sticking out of the rubble here?" Gary asked pointing and then grabbing at the image to stretch it. "Why isn't this clearer, Neil? It's practically eight-bit imaging!"

"It's not that bad! I only did ten-centimeter resolution to cut down on the data transmission time, and I'm cleaning it up. That's a really big file. The important thing was to get you current video and telemetry," Neil said. "But look here."

Neil took over the image and expanded an area about thirty meters west of the caved-in shuttle pad. A hole had opened out from underneath the lunar surface, and from debris scattered about its periphery, it looked as if something underneath the surface had exploded, blowing the hole outward and upward.

"Whoa!" Dion gasped.

"Right there!" Barbara pointed and quickly took over the image. "Look at this object."

"What is it, roomie?" Jan did her best to lean over Barbara's shoulder for a better view of the three-dimensional image projected about the pilot's cabin of the *Spark Xpress*. To their horror, it appeared to be a human shape.

"That's a spacesuit!" Dion nodded in affirmation with Barbara.

"Yes. It looks like it is just lying there on the surface. Neil, what's the time this image was taken?" Barbara was genuinely scared now. Before, she was expecting simple technical failures, but this looked like a very severe accident. There were at least unconscious bodies, lying motionless on the surface of the Moon, or . . . no, she didn't want to think the worst.

"Uh, let me see, it looks like fourteen minutes and thirty-six seconds, give or take a few," Neil replied. "That is a long time to be lying still."

"Could that be Dr. Bright?" Jan asked.

"I don't know! I can't see any detail."

"No assumptions!" Barbara cut them off, quelling her own fears. "We make no assumptions of survivor's status until we *know*. Dion, what's our ETA?"

"At our top rate right now, another thirty minutes."

"Too long!" Jan wailed. "We need speed!"

Gary sat up straight. "What if we use the EMdrives?"

Barbara had almost forgotten the cone-shaped pods attached to the sides of their limping craft.

"Will those work with the damaged buckyball?"

"Yeah, that would get you all there much quicker," Neil said, his face brightening with hope. "Maybe in half that time."

"Okay, fire them up, Dion," Barbara said. "Everyone stay buckled."

"All right, we'll do it." Dion leaned forward and toggled the EMdrive control menu on and then put it through the startup cycle. A crackle of energy brightened the cabin lights, and the *Xpress* seemed to hum under their feet. "She's ready to go when everyone else is."

Gary and Jan tensed in their seats.

"Punch it, Dion," Barbara said.

The microwave magnetrons began firing up as the metal frustums on either side of the *Spark Xpress* filled with electromagnetic energy. The asymmetric cavities interacted with the very inertia of the universe, creating a high-level propulsion. Dion only had a moment to nod before the force shoved the buggy forward as if it had been kicked in the rear. With more than one gee of acceleration, a full Earth's gravity, the *Xpress* propelled forward like a bullet. Barbara gasped. Her body felt incredibly heavy. She wasn't used to that level of continuous force since she had come to the Moon months ago. While it wasn't actually difficult to breathe, it did take extra effort. Though her ribs were pushing toward her backbone, she concentrated on drawing in enough oxygen.

"Barbara," Daya's face popped up on the windscreen in front of her. "All of your heart rates have increased significantly and your core temperatures are changing."

"We're all right," Barbara said, though it came out as a gasp.

"We're working out just sitting here, Daya. We're pulling at least a gee," Gary added, trying to make it sound light.

"I think maybe more than one gee," Dion added, holding tight to the controls, his eyes intent on the terrain ahead. The buckyballs ate up the klicks. Barbara wished she had time to appreciate how good the design the Nerd-Twins had come up with really was, but she was too worried. "We are *moving* right now. Good thing this is a fairly flat stretch."

"How fast are we going, Dion?" Jan asked from the back seat.

"One hundred fifty kilometers per hour."

"Wow."

"Hold tight!" Barbara shouted. "Dion, we're coming to a dip!"

"Got it," Dion said. The *Spark Xpress* hit the lip of the depression and bounded up out of it in a shower of regolith. The team was thrown hard against their straps and back in their seats. Barbara was grateful the restraints were so strong, but her ribs were going to be bruised. She didn't care, as long as Dr. Bright and the others were all right when she got to the mine.

Moving almost five times as fast as the other racers, they passed the last few at the back of the pack before diverting off the main route.

"We all heard about Dr. Bright," Lois said. "We're praying everyone is safe."

"Our hearts are with you," added Svetlana.

"Good luck!" called Teddy.

"Thanks," Barbara replied, her voice coming in staccato bursts from the jostling and bouncing.

"Hang on," Dion said. "We're going to jump another trench!"

"Neil?"

"Leona?" Neil was startled awake. He had dozed off on his console for a moment while waiting on the image enhancement algorithm to get more detail of the collapsed mine site. He hadn't slept normally since the race had started over a week ago, and it was beginning to catch up with him. "What can I do for you?"

"Neil, I cannot reach Dr. Bright and I'm concerned. I haven't really been out of direct contact with him as long as I can remember existing," Leona told him.

"It will be okay, Leona. We're all worried." Neil didn't want to tell her *how* worried. It sounded even worse if *Leona* couldn't reach him.

He kept telling himself Dr. Bright was amazingly resourceful. If there was a problem, he'd solve it. He'd find a way out of whatever tight spot he might be in.

"I want to take over the communications transceiver of the BrightSats and try to communicate with him at maximum output power," Leona said. "Since you are directly overhead with number five, his mobile unit might be able to pick up the signal through the debris from the cave-in."

"That makes sense. I could even bring the satellite lower to the ground if we need to." Neil pulled up the ground station control menus for the satellite. "All you need to do is be authorized for the software-defined radios and use the encryption key for the flight computer, and you can do what you want. I can give those to you."

"I already have them, but I didn't want to take control of your satellite without permission," Leona said. Neil frowned.

"You already have them? How did you know them?"

"Well, I am a supercomputer, Neil, and you are somewhat predictable, no offense."

"Really? I'm predictable?"

"So, do I have your permission?"

"Yeah, of course. But keep me posted on your progress real-time on one of the menus here. We want to know if you get through to him!"

"Very well."

Chapter Nineteen

"Bringing the drive off-line. Coasting in the last quarter kilometer or so." Dion tapped at the menu icons. Barbara could feel the acceleration on her body stop. She suddenly felt almost as light as a feather, but a little tired and out of breath to boot. They had been eating a lot to make up for the exertion. Gary was surrounded by wrappers. Once he could lean forward, he gathered them up in a ball and stowed them in the waste basket.

"Jan, grab the emergency kit from the stowage bin," Barbara ordered as she recovered. "First thing is to get to that survivor on the surface and assess him."

"Do you think that's Dr. Bright?" Gary asked.

"We won't know until we look," Barbara said. She kept her voice as even as she could, but her heart was in her throat.

Barbara unbuckled her safety restraints and made her way to the back of the racer. From it, she helped to unload medical gear, including a stretcher. Dion set the parking brake, took Candy from the console and slid it onto his suit's sleeve. All of them checked to make sure their PerDees were in place.

"Helmets on," Barbara said, pulling her gloves onto her hands and reaching for the bubble under her seat. They automatically checked each another out, as safety protocol dictated. "Fasten up. Fido, cycle the unlock sequence." They waited impatiently until the buggy's life-support system sucked the air out of the cabin. A very, very faint squishing vibration translated through the floor as the seal of the door broke free, and they stood atop the stairs looking out at the Moon.

Dr. Bright and the company with which he was working had chosen a crater in the vicinity of Mare Ingenii, one of the few "seas" on the far side of the Moon. He knew from briefings that the area was known for multiple pockets of radiation, probably owing to transuranic ores in the lunar rock. Apart from the lip of the crater, the area looked fairly flat and almost uniformly gray, except for the black hole where the mineshaft used to be.

An astronaut lay motionless about ten meters away from them. They climbed down the ladder, helping one another with the equipment.

"Gary and I will take him first!" Jan said over their suit channel as she leaped upward into a slow arc bringing her down only a step from the fallen man. "His PDE is cracked wide open and hasn't been on for some time. There's a trace of condensation on it."

Gary was right behind her with a stretcher board and an emergency medical bag.

"Keep the channel on open mic, Jan." Barbara nodded to Dion to follow her. "Dion and I are going toward the mouth of that blowout."

Gary and Jan hauled their equipment over to the prone body. With her heart in her throat, Barbara waited until Jan gently turned the spacesuit over. A stranger, a man in his thirties with dark skin and short, dark brown hair in twists, stared blankly at the sky. She took a closer look at his spacesuit, and took note of the insignia on his shoulder and chest.

"It's not him!" Jan called out. "It's one of the flight crew."

"Thank goodness," Barbara said. Her knees went weak with relief. "Ms. Scruffles, see if you can take over his suit."

"Yes, Jan. Meow."

"He's alive!" Jan shouted. "His suit went into low power–low oxygen survival mode. Ms. Scruffles is repressurizing him to half an atmosphere."

"That's great news!" Dion replied. "Can you tell if he has any major injuries?"

"Hard to tell out here. We could use the mobile millimeter wave scanner," Gary suggested. "Should we scan him before we move him?"

"Strap him to a stretcher and get him inside," Dion told them.

"I agree with Dion. Get him inside and close up the *Xpress*," Barbara added.

"That still doesn't help us," Dion said, his voice hoarse with emotion.

"No," Barbara said, feeling overwhelmed. The area was so bleak, and the damage so extensive that she didn't know where to start. "We need to get to wherever Dr. Bright is, but the problem is that we have no way of knowing where that is."

"Barbara, perhaps I can help you with that." Leona's avatar popped up on the windscreen.

"Leona? Any luck communicating with him?" Gary asked. Barbara wondered for a moment how often Leona was watching them. She realized, even though now wasn't the time to worry about it, that Dr. Bright probably had her watching them all the time.

"No, Gary. However, I do have the last-minute data up until the quake and cave-in. Dr. Bright and the others were all using Blue Force Tracker apps that used all the internal and external network routers and multipath signals to triangulate their whereabouts. Here is a three-dimensional map with their last known locations marked." The image appeared on each of their PerDees with blue dots indicating personnel.

"That's helpful, Leona." Barbara blew up the detailed map and started to study it. The intersecting tunnels and caves made the underground system look like a massive bowl of spaghetti and meatballs. By the scale noted in the lower corner, Dr. Bright and Dr. Book and several others had been about forty meters below the surface. The map showed them at the mouth of a winding tube that angled upward and almost to the surface, but not quite. "*Oh*. Fido, can you overlay Neil's three-dimensional data with this map and correct them to be on the same scale?"

"What are you thinking, Barb?" Gary was watching her intently.

"What have you got, lady?" Dion asked.

The surface map that Neil had created rendered atop the subsurface map that Leona had given them, and the two adjusted themselves to appropriate scale and then became one image. Barbara grabbed the image and zoomed in on Dr. Bright's blue dot. Two other dots were close by.

"Look at this location here. See this tube or corridor or shaft, whatever they were in, here? It tilts upward and stops here about fifteen meters beneath the surface. Look here at the blowout hole. It's just beyond that and to the west a bit. It looks to me like the shaft blew out at the top. Our survivor here was probably in that shaft. Looks like we need to go down inside there, Dion."

"We should tie off to the *Xpress* or something," Dion said as he looked about for some place to tie a tether to. There was nothing since the blowout hole was at least seventy meters from any manmade structures.

"We planned for everything, but not this," Barbara said, trying to hide her frustration.

"Actually, we did, kind of," Gary admitted, sounding sheepish. "We did bring some auger stakes in case we needed to winch out the racer from soft regolith."

"That's right!" Barbara said. She had seen those on the list of supplies. She had to pull herself together, or she would be no good to anyone. "We can put one in right there at the edge of the hole and tie off to that."

"Roger that! I'll be right back." Dion didn't hesitate and had bounced more than fifteen meters before Barbara could respond. Barbara always liked watching him move, but she pushed those feelings back down. Now was not the time.

"Um, okay, Dion. I'll wait here." Barbara looked down. If only it had been daytime on this side! Her light could only reach a fraction of the distance into the hole. She strained her eyes hoping to see into the dark shadows and that there would be some sign of Dr. Bright.

She carefully paced around the opening, looking for what she hoped to be the best point of entry, until she found the shallowest edge. The tunnel must have been about ten meters below the surface. The blowout was almost straight down all the way around. The angled mineshaft at the bottom was covered in rocks and debris ranging from gravel all the way up to chunks as big as a beach ball. Some shiny bits lay strewed about and mixed in with the dull rubble as well.

"Here." Dion landed next to her panting for breath and holding out a meter-long metal rod with auger blades spiraling up to a triangle-shaped loop handle at the top. Barbara snapped the torque rod from its slot in the handle and thrust it through the loop, forming a huge letter T. She slammed the auger bit into the soil as hard as she could manage, then twisted it like a giant corkscrew into the Moon's surface. She and Dion got on either side of the torque bar and twisted.

"Slowly now," Dion warned her. "We don't want to get tossed over or hurt a wrist or something."

"Yeah, I seem to recall one of the Apollo 12 astronauts nearly got hurt trying to do the same thing we're doing, but they were trying to take soil samples." Barbara grunted as they forced the bit into the packed surface. "How deep do you think this thing needs to be?"

"Up to this mark, here, to be safe."

She glanced over her shoulder.

"I wonder if we should have parked the racer closer to the blowout," she said.

"I wouldn't do that, Barb. We don't know how the quake messed things up around here. There could be openings underneath here that could cave in on us or even blow out if there is still pressure in there."

"Um, right. Didn't think of that." She frowned.

"Hey, two heads are better than one." Despite his own worries, Dion gave her an encouraging smile.

"Four," Gary interrupted through the radio.

"Six," Neil added.

"All right, all right, I get it." Barbara would have smiled if she wasn't so concerned about Dr. Bright. "That's deep enough, you think?"

"Yeah, I think it's good." Dion rested his hands on his knees and looked over at Barbara as he took a big inhale. Barbara was doing the same. "Whew! That was too much like work! I'm winded."

"Me too." She grasped the end of her suit cable and smacked the carabiner against the triangle loop atop the auger bit. The spring-loaded metal catch locked tight. She tugged at the cable to make certain the stake wasn't going to pull free from the ground. She waited for Dion to snap on and then raised up and took a long, slow breath. "You ready?"

"Hold on." Dion reached into a pouch on his chest and slid out a small box with a whip antenna on it. He toggled a button and then let it go. It apparently had a magnetic base which attached itself to the top of the metal auger bit. "Wireless range antenna. I've got two more with me. Maybe we'll be able to keep communication with the surface this way. Now let's go."

"Ready."

Barbara took a deep breath, and stepped off the edge.

The three-story drop to the bottom wasn't so bad in lunar gravity, and the winching action of the cable reels on their harnesses made the landing even softer. Barbara was glad because there was so much debris blown against the outermost wall of the hole that footing was difficult. She shined her lights down the shaft and it appeared to be bottomless, but she knew it couldn't be. According to the map, it was only about forty meters long. And Dr. Bright had last been only a few tens of meters beyond that where the shaft met the larger chamber.

Dion landed behind her and windmilled his arms to regain his balance. She caught him by the arm to steady him.

"Thanks, lady," he said.

"Fido, keep the map up on my suit visor with the blue dots on it. Give me a direction arrow and distance line marked off as we go."

"Yes, Barbara."

"Fido, broadcast on the Sparks channel and on the *Live from the Moon* frequencies."

"Yes, Barbara. Channels open."

"Good. Dr. Bright, can you hear me? We're in the mine. We're coming for you. Calvin? Are you there? Anybody?" Her voice rose to a nervous squeak.

There was no answer. Dion picked his way down the heap of debris and held out a hand to Barbara.

"Careful, Barb, it's getting a little steep here."

"Yeah, but at least the debris blew past here and the floor is clean . . . ish."

"Yeah, clean . . . ish, is a good way to put it," Dion agreed.

"Wow, look at that!" Barbara stopped. Her lights finally shone onto something just shiny enough to tell that it was manmade. The two of them sped up their pace with caution until they got close enough to see what they were looking at.

"This looks like the back end of a boring device. The blowout must have tossed it up through the tunnel and then it got stuck here. I bet there's debris packed in from the other side." Dion whistled. "We need to get past this thing somehow."

"A boring machine?" Barbara said thoughtfully. "A 'bot tunnel boring machine?"

Dion studied what part of the machine he could see. "I think so. Why?"

"Fido, can you handshake with this bot?"

"I don't know Barbara. I'll try."

"What are you thinking, Barb?" Dion asked.

"Let's turn it on and see if we can get it to shake loose an opening for us."

"Is that safe?"

"I think so. It doesn't matter. We don't have a lot of options." She scanned all around the tunnel with her light. Geology hadn't been a specialty of hers before she came to the Moon, but Dr. Bright had given her videos and texts to study. "Look at the walls. This tunnel looks solid."

"Barbara, I can turn on the machine and give you virtual control," Fido told her.

"Can you drive one of these?" Dion asked, a little skeptically. "It doesn't look like any vehicle I've ever run."

"They're just like my tractors back home, Dion." Barbara smiled. *Thank goodness for something familiar!* "Okay, Fido, put the display on my visor and let's crank her up!"

"Yes, Barbara."

The excavator's panel appeared on the inside of her helmet. The controls were all marked with their functions. She chose the ones that approximated to her robot tractors back at home in Iowa, and hoped they would do the job. First, she needed to get the machine oriented and back on its tracks.

"Activate!"

Instantly, the ground vibrated under their feet. The rubble that was piled up and wedged all around the machine that was blocking the tunnel began to shake and slide. The boring machine seemed no less worse for wear other than just being almost completely sideways in the tunnel. Barbara studied the control panel display on her visor for a moment, then reached out to the virtual buttons and slidebars and put the machine in gear. It rocked forward about three centimeters and stuck itself into the side of the tunnel.

"Can you turn on the teeth?" Dion asked.

"Not yet. We should step back about ten meters in case it throws stuff." Barbara backpedaled up the tunnel; Dion was right beside her, carefully watching her footing. "Now."

"Okay, do it, Barb."

"Right."

Barbara slid the virtual control that started the forward-boring teeth spinning. The vibration under their feet increased tenfold. They could see a cloud of dust and small chunks of lunar rock being chewed up and rolled through the machine and then spat out on the side. Barbara worked the machine back and forth until she had created enough space that she could start turning the wheels. The tunnel maker squirmed like an earthworm digging through a flower garden until she managed to break it free enough that she could back it up toward them. Barbara let out the breath she didn't realize she had been holding. The machine was much larger than she thought, and the silver digger wheels on the front were terrifyingly sharp. She hoped she wouldn't run into one of the survivors with those. She hoped there *were* survivors.

"Does this thing have a forward view camera, Fido?"

"Yes, it does, Barbara."

"Turn it on and give me the view in a window on my upper right screen. I'm going to see if I can push it through."

"Okay, but go slowly just in case there is someone on the other side!" Dion exclaimed.

"Right. Slowly, now."

Through the image projected inside her visor, Barbara saw the flurry of chips and rocks flying past the camera like a snowstorm of stone. The machine inched forward, and rubble piled up on both sides of it. It felt like hours, but it couldn't have been more than another three or four minutes until the boring machine broke through into empty space.

"Safe mode, Fido. Turn the borer off."

"Yes, Barbara."

"But leave the headlights on. They're much brighter than our suit lights."

"As you wish, Barbara."

"I think I can get through here." Dion worked his way around the machine and into the chamber on the other side. "Barb! There's another person down in here! It's Paul!"

Chapter Twenty

"Is he alive?" Barbara held her breath briefly, praying hard. All the Sparks knew him well. She scrambled for the heap of stone beside the digger and climbed up.

"Yes. His suit is in survival mode, too," Dion replied. "Hey, Gary, get down here with another stretcher. We need to haul him up."

"Roger that, Dion," Gary replied. "On my way."

"Hey, don't forget to tether off to the stake at the mouth of the tunnel," Dion told him. "We could get another aftershock."

"Okay."

"Any sign of Dr. Bright?" Jan asked. Her signal wavered. Barbara worried that they were going to lose contact with the surface.

"Not yet," Dion said.

Barbara squeezed past the borer and into the next chamber. It was small, less than a quarter the size of the one they had rappelled down into, on a distinct downward slope. Dion knelt next to the cameraman's long body. Paul was too tall for the open floor, so his feet were propped up on a nearby rock. His faceplate had impact marks and scratches, and his suit was well powdered with regolith. Lights inside Paul's helmet were on amber, showing that the suit had retreated into minimum power output.

"Daya, can you read his vitals?" Dion asked.

"No," the youngest Spark said, her voice trembling. "His PerDee is off-line, and your signal is poor. Let me know when you can examine him. I hope he is all right."

"You and me, baby sister," Dion said, soothingly. "Hang in there. We've got him, and he's alive. We'll find the others."

Barbara appreciated Dion's brave words, but she was worried. She saw no sign of another living being. Where was Dr. Bright? Across the cavern, she caught the glint of a round, shiny object. Its familiar shape sparked a memory.

"Look, there's his camera," Barbara said. Very carefully, she bounced down the slope of the chamber to a mixed heap of rocks and crystals. Paul's shoulder-mounted apparatus was visible only by the lens sticking out of the pile of dust. Barbara brushed away the dirt surrounding it. The device was heavier than she expected because of the battery pack and transmission pod. It could upload wirelessly to a satellite or other source.

"Fido, is the camera still working?" she asked.

"It is, Barbara."

"Is it connected to anything? Jackie? Sparks Central?"

"Yes, Barbara. It was connected to Leona, Tombaugh, and PDE 9567e, for the purposes of recording voices from helmet microphones."

"What's that last one?" she asked, puzzled.

"Paul's personal digital engine," Fido replied. "It is not as sophisticated an AI as those in the Sparks program."

"Tombaugh? Is that Calvin's PerDee?"

"Yes, Barbara."

Hope rose in her heart. "Can you contact Leona and Tombaugh and patch me in?"

For answer, a voice came from the speaker in Barbara's helmet.

"Barb, thank goodness!"

"Calvin!" Barbara's knees went weak with relief. She shot a thumbs-up to a beaming Dion. "What happened to you? Where are you? Where's Dr. Bright?"

The scientist's voice sounded breathless.

"I'm okay. We had a blowout. It was a monster! I think that the mining engineers accidentally freed some trapped gas, and the friction in the sealed chamber caused an explosion."

"Where's Dr. Bright? Is he okay? Leona didn't reply when Fido pinged her just now."

"His PerDee is, um, nonfunctional," Calvin said. "It was damaged in the cave-in. I can talk to him with our helmets touching, but that's all. We will need medical attention."

He sounded just a little too casual.

"How bad is he?" Dion demanded. "Critical?"

"No! Well, I can't really tell. I'm not that kind of a doctor! He's trapped in a rockfall. He's been coming in and out of consciousness. I can't pull him free by myself."

"Dion? Barb?" Gary's voice came through their helmet speakers. "Where are you?"

"Follow the lights, Gary," Dion said. "You've got to squeak past the excavator. It's a tight fit."

Gary scrambled into the chamber, pulling the stretcher behind him. "Where's Dr. Bright?"

"We're just trying to find that out," Barbara said, holding onto the camera unit. "Get Paul out of here and see if you can bring him around."

"Roger," Gary said at once. He dropped the backboard on the ground in a puff of dust and crossed Paul's arms on his chest. "Dion, can you give me a hand?"

"No prob," Dion said. Together they eased the unconscious cameraman onto the backboard and strapped him in. "Are you okay being in here alone, lady?"

"I'm fine," Barbara said. "I'll try to get more information." She watched as the two young men gently maneuvered the rescue board up and over the body of the borer. She was left alone in the glare of the machine's headlights.

"Calvin, we are at the base of the western tunnel. Can you tell me where you are?"

The former Spark groaned.

"Not really. We're using the Blue Force Tracker application, but I can't seem to raise anyone else on it."

"I'll bring that up," Barbara said immediately "Fido, do you have Blue Force Tracker loaded?"

"Yes, Barbara, but it needs three transmitters to function."

"Ugh! And I just let the guys go up. Wait a minute," Barbara said, as a thought struck her. "Calvin, are you playing M-Tracker?"

"No offense, Barb, but this is a bad time to think about games!"

"No! It's got a GPS function, to make sure two players doing a

Battle of the Bands are in close enough range. It only needs *two*, and a low-level location scanner that any satellite can supply. We've installed one repeater already. Challenge me. We can talk over in-game chat. Going over to game mode. Fido, open M-Tracker."

"Initiating," Fido said. In a moment, a blare of cheerful music and dancing graphics issued from the PerDee. From the center issued a pair of tied eighth notes.

Words rose above the screen, with the figure of a male in tight black trousers and a ripped white shirt with a shock of blue hair caught in a headband and a bright yellow guitar slung across his chest.

"DJDeathStar47 challenges you to a Battle of the Bands!"

Despite the seriousness of the situation, Barbara had to giggle. She touched the eighth notes.

"BlazeOfGlory915 accepts your challenge!" the graphics read, as a copper-haired female in a tight red dress and thigh-high boots slammed her hands down on a floating keyboard. The two characters squared off against each other. "Hit it!" Notes began to pour upward from the PerDee's screen. In the upper right corner, an arrow pointed off to Barbara's right, indicating Calvin's direction.

"Now, mute it and suppress the graphics, Fido. We need the coordinates. Bring up the map."

"Working, Barbara," the PerDee said.

To her relief, the colorful chart beneath the characters' feet showed the relative location of the two players. Calvin was within only five or six meters of her, though whether above or below she couldn't tell, but it was in the same orientation as the tunnel she was in.

"You're not far from me, Calvin. I'm going to try to bring the borer through to you," she said.

"Be careful," he said. "Dr. Bright's location is almost up against one end of the tube we're in. I'm so disoriented, I don't know where you're coming from."

"It looks like I'm uphill. Get as far downhill as you can. Fido, fire up the borer," Barbara said. "Forward camera in my helmet. On my mark, slow crawl!"

"Yes, Barbara."

The floor vibrated under her feet as the excavator moved toward the rubble heap at the far end of the chamber. The teeth chewed into the rocks and began to throw debris back toward Barbara. She retreated into the tunnel it had just made to avoid being struck by the flying stones and clasped her hands together anxiously.

"Can you see any movement yet, Calvin?" she asked.

"No. Are you sure we're on the same level?"

"No! I hope so. I can't tell!" Barbara said.

"Barbara, Blue Force Tracker has identified an approaching source," Fido said.

"Great! Who's there? Jan, are you up there?"

The voice that answered surprised her.

"Barbara, this is Pam. I am on the lip of the crater blast. Do you need help?"

"Pam! Uh, yes. Please come straight down the shaft until you get to me. Can my PerDee handshake with yours and give you the maps and information we have?" Barbara turned and looked back up the tunnel but could only see a silhouette against the bright headlights of the machine.

"Certainly, Barbara," Pam replied.

"Fido, connect to Ada and upload the maps and tracking app, and patch her through to Tombaugh."

"Very well, Barbara."

"I have them," Pam said, a moment later. "Rappelling down to you now."

With the Blue Force app operational, Barbara pushed M-Tracker to one side. She saw a blue dot exactly where the game had pinpointed Calvin. To her relief, he and Dr. Bright were just downslope of the borer on the same level. She pushed the borer into half speed. The vibration increased enough to make her teeth chatter. The piles of debris grew bigger and bigger on each side of the machine.

Another blue dot appeared on the level, meters behind Barbara. She glanced back to see Pam unwind a rope from around her waist and bounce lightly down toward her.

"Thanks for stopping," Barbara said. "*Blue Streak* was in the lead. I . . . I didn't expect you to come."

Pam's face was expressionless. Barbara suspected she had already been interrogated, and not that gently, by Jan and the others up top.

"I'm a Spark and a human being. You needed us, and we were close. My team is helping with the wounded and working on how to rescue the shuttle crew. I am here to help you."

"Thank you."

"Don't mention it. I see your data," Pam said. Her face twisted with concern. "Why can I see Calvin's indicator, but not Dr. Bright's?"

"Calvin says Leona is busted. Calvin says he's with him. They are having to use old school helmet-to-helmet communications."

"Why can Dr. Book's PerDee not interface to Dr. Bright's helmet microphone?" Pam asked.

"Uh, Pam? I can answer that, but, I don't want to alarm you. Dr. Bright is fine, but the interface is out of commission," Calvin said.

"Is his suit integrity compromised?"

"No!" Calvin said. "I'm pretty sure it's fine. He's breathing normally. Most of the time."

"Hold tight, Calvin," Barbara said, with determination. "We'll be there in no time."

Another eternity of waiting until the borer did its job. At last, Barbara saw a faint light in the excavator's camera.

"Fido, slow down the teeth," she said.

"Slowing."

The vibration dropped from a heavy pulse to a purr. The teeth had run out of things to chew. And Barbara could see Calvin's helmet visor turned toward her.

"Shut it down!" she crowed. "Come on, Pam!"

Barbara climbed up and over the machine's track, disregarding all the stone dust and pebbles she picked up along the way. Pam followed more cautiously. The two young women bounded over to Calvin, who grasped their hands gratefully.

"I sure am glad to see you," he said. "I have only a couple more hours' worth of power in this suit."

"Where's Dr. Bright?" Pam asked.

Calvin pointed. "This way."

Except for the mess that the borer had just made, the floor of the tube Calvin was in had very little regolith dust.

"It all got swept up by the blowout," he explained. "We got whirled around in gale force winds like a tornado. I'm surprised we didn't end up in Oz. But Dr. Bright got the house dropped on him."

He fell to his knees beside a scree of rocks of every size at the bottom of the long chamber. Barbara scanned it with her suit light. She didn't see anything unusual, until a tiny movement between a couple of good-sized boulders told her the gray mass there wasn't a rock—it was a spacesuit, face down and half-buried in gravel. The scratched and gouged bubble helmet was covered with dust. Calvin had been doing his best to remove rubble from around Dr. Bright and to dig him out, but the boulders were wedged in and too big for one person to move even in the low lunar gravity.

"Oh, my gosh!" Barbara choked back tears and couldn't believe what she was seeing. "Dr. Bright! Is he in pain?"

"He says no, but, I don't believe him. And he's been in and out of consciousness," Calvin replied. "I would have hoped he could tell me something brilliant to get us out, but he's been, well, out of it mostly. His left arm is trapped under those boulders. I don't know if it's crushed or not. I've been trying to get him out, but I can't do it alone."

Barbara let out a quivering breath. She could have cried. They were in an airless pit on the far side of the Moon, and her beloved mentor was hurt, maybe dying, under a pile of rocks.

"Pull yourself together," Pam said, in an expressionless tone. Just for a moment, Barbara understood why the others disliked her so much. "Breaking down will not help him. Analyze. Think of what you *see*, not what you *feel*."

Barbara forced herself to snap out of her funk. Dr. Bright was alive. His suit was intact, which meant it was feeding him oxygen and keeping him warm.

"Okay. We need more data about his health," she said. "That's the first priority. If there's an emergency, we treat it. Then we work on getting him out."

"Good." Pam's eyes were watchful.

Calvin squeezed in between the two big boulders and put his helmet against Dr. Bright's. He stood up again, shaking his head.

"He's pretty out of it," the bespectacled scientist said.

"Have you tried the hardware diagnostic port on his suit, Dr. Book?" Pam asked as she knelt next to Dr. Bright. "There is a suit system setup and diagnostic port under the arm."

"There's what?" Calvin asked.

"Of course," Barbara said, abashed. "We can hook into intrasuit communication. We had a briefing about that a couple of weeks ago. I should have thought of that. How do you know so much about this suit design? It's supposed to be brand new."

"I am part of the research and development branch that designed it." Pam reached up underneath his right arm to his chest. "The connection is just about . . . here! All right, I have it."

Pam spooled the small wire from the port and then set her PerDee on the ground next to him. She plugged the wire into the USB7 port and then toggled through a few menu icons.

Suddenly, Dr. Bright's face appeared on the tracker screen on Barbara's visor. His eyes were closed. Her heart sank.

"Dr. Bright! Dr. Bright, are you okay?"

Chapter Twenty-One

At the sound of his name, Keegan fought up through the pain and forced his eyes open. He couldn't move. His shoulder was killing him, and the arm below it was numb except for a few sharp tingles. Beyond the faceplate of his helmet was nothing but rock and stone, but on the inside of his helmet, Barbara's, Pam's, and Calvin's faces shone with concern.

"Hey, there," he said, and was amazed at how weak his voice sounded. "What are you two doing here? Why aren't you out there on the racecourse?"

Pam shook her head, an almost imperceptible movement. "In case Dr. Book hasn't been able to make you aware, this mine of yours suffered a blowout. You are trapped with your left arm under some rocks. Do you understand us?"

"I sure do," Keegan said. He swallowed. His throat was dry. "How's everyone else?"

"Three found so far, two of them injured."

"The shuttle got buried in the explosion," Barbara said, "but the two crew remaining on board are alive. Jan and Shiro, Pam's teammate, are trying to get through to the four downslope of here, but we can't reach them until we get you out and move this avalanche out of the way."

"Barb and the Sparks have a plan," Calvin put in. "I have to say, I'm impressed by the idea. It's so easy, it just blows my mind."

"I know you kids can do it," Keegan said, putting all the energy he had into a smile. Barbara's face was so full of worry. Jackie was right: He did put too much responsibility on those young shoulders.

"All right," Barbara said. The image behind her head changed. He assumed she stood up. Her face turned toward the side, addressing others in the room. "We're going to have to dig out a little around that one big boulder, but we have to make sure it doesn't shift at all."

"I got it," Dion's voice said. Keegan felt pebbles brush his shoulders. It was inconvenient, to say the least, not being able to look around and watch what was going on. He could see only those three faces and the stones under his face.

Gary sounded out of breath. "Here's the emergency habitat tent," he said. "I've got pressure hoses and sealant to attach them to the CO2 canister."

Another male voice, unfamiliar to Keegan, added, "And we contribute ours."

"Thanks, Riku," Barbara said, giving the unseen speaker a smile. He listened as she explained to her makeshift rescue team what she wanted them to do. And Calvin was right; it was an easy, elegant solution. It ought to work.

It would, he just knew it.

His arm spasmed, overwhelming him with pain, and he almost faded out of consciousness again.

"Watch it! No! Those stones are moving!" Barbara cried.

Keegan gasped. Something hit his shoulder so hard it dislocated the humerus from its socket. Pain radiated through his body like being struck by lightning.

"Cal—" he began. Then everything went black.

"Dr. Bright, can you hear me?" Another unfamiliar voice, this time a woman's. A rush of dry air hit him in the face. He squeezed his eyes tighter, and a cool cloth dabbed at the lids then his lips. "You are awake, sir. Can you speak?"

Keegan pried his eyes open. He flinched against the glare of a work light shining in his face and tried to raise his arms to shield it. His right hand came up, but the left one seemed to be immobilized.

"Your arm is broken," the young woman said. When his vision cleared, Keegan saw the speaker, Tomiko Nara. She still wore her spacesuit, but her helmet and gauntlets were off. Instead, she had on purple plastic gloves. Keegan realized he wasn't in his suit any longer, but in the undergarment, and the left sleeve had been cut off at the top of his arm. Below that was a thin but stiff cast all the way to his wrist. "I'm a doctor. I was able to set it and relocate your shoulder, but I don't have the equipment here to see if there is further damage. How does it feel?"

Keegan squeezed his fist.

"It all seems to be working," he said. "Hurts like crazy, though."

Tomiko smiled, though her broad forehead creased with worry.

"You were very lucky. There doesn't seem to be a crush injury, but symptoms of that can arise later. I didn't numb it because I want you to be able to tell if there were any parts you can't feel. You also have bruises almost everywhere but your neck and head. Please take care. This is what you call 'meatball medicine,' emergency treatment in the field?"

"Something like that," he said, with a grin. He remembered her bio from SolStar's application. She worked as an air-sea rescue volunteer on her days off. "Thanks, doctor. I think you saved my arm."

"I didn't," Tomiko said, with a gesture to her right. "This young team did, with their marvelous work."

He glanced around. From his brief look at the finished vehicle just before the race, he realized he was lying in the lower bunk behind the pilot's compartment of *Spark Xpress*.

Dion and Barbara hovered anxiously a meter away, their eyes fixed on him.

"Hey, kids," Keegan said, lightly. They rushed to his side, their eyes shining with unshed tears. "This is what happens when you let me go off unsupervised."

"We're so glad you're okay!" Dion said. He swallowed.

"Freak accident," Keegan said, trying to make light of it. "This kind of thing can happen when you are dealing with any kind of mine. We were just unlucky to get a moonquake at that moment. I didn't realize the buildup would be so quick. How's the rest of the mining team?"

"Gary and Jan are digging through to them now," Barbara said. One little tear rolled down her cheek. Keegan's heart went out to her. "Calvin's supervising. They're okay. Everyone's okay . . . ?"

That responsibility again. Keegan shook his head.

"I'm fine. Where's Leona?"

"Your PerDee was crushed by the landslide." Barbara held out Fido. "You're going to need another one right away. Everyone wants to know how you are."

"Dr. Bright!" Neil's face rose from Fido's screen, followed immediately by Daya's.

"I can't read your vital statistics without your suit diagnostics," Daya said, her small face screwed up with worry. Keegan glanced up at Tomiko.

"Forwarding current readings now," she said. "He needs more medical care, in a proper facility."

"My mother will be there in five hours," Daya said, firmly, after a glance at Keegan's chart. "She will bring him home."

"Keegan!" Jackie's face appeared. "Are you all right?"

"Better than I deserve," Keegan said, with a dry chuckle. "You're gonna get some spectacular video once you get here."

"You're hurt! That explosion could have killed you all."

"But it didn't," Keegan said. He winked at Barbara. "Today was my lucky day. See you all soon."

"Aargh!" Jackie said. Her face disappeared from the PerDee screen. Keegan shook his head, even though everything hurt.

"Dr. Bright!" Leona's avatar popped up on Fido. That day, she was a blue-skinned female in a lab coat with yellow hair in a tight chignon. "I have been unable to reach you. I have reviewed the data sent from this unit to Jackie and Sparks Central. I am concerned for your health. Damage was not significant, but I am tremendously inconvenienced by not being able to monitor you directly."

"Missed you, too, Leona," Keegan replied. She was developing a mother hen complex. They were going to have to have a real talk when he got back to Armstrong City. "My PerDee is smashed up and buried somewhere in the mine. I'll need you to activate a fresh unit for me from the electronics cupboard."

"Done," Leona said. "It will be programmed and waiting when you return here in approximately fourteen hours. I will continue to listen in on units in your vicinity until then."

"Counting on it. Now, tell me!" Keegan said, turning to the Sparks. "I was out of it. How did you get me out of there?"

"You tell him, Barb. It was your idea." Dion grinned at Barbara.

"Well, I used a similar technique to the way we lifted the transport off that rock on the way to Aldrinville," Barbara began.

"You put a jack underneath the boulder?" Keegan asked. He whistled through his teeth.

"Kind of. We used the emergency shelters from both *Spark Xpress* and *Blue Streak* as high-pressure airbags to lift the rock off your arm. We inflated both of them very slowly to make sure the boulder wouldn't bounce up and come down again, until we could pull you free. It was scary, but it worked."

"The habitats are no longer usable, but this was a good purpose to put them to." Pam appeared behind Dion. Keegan watched him carefully to see how he responded to the former Spark. No hostility showed in his expression. Dion even seemed a little friendlier than indifferent. Keegan felt cautious optimism. Maybe the ice was thawing at last. If it took him breaking his arm to accomplish that, it was worth it. He was proud of all his Sparks.

"Excellent improvisation," Keegan said. "Thank you, all of you, for stepping in to help. I'm sorry you got pulled out of the race, but I don't know what we would have done if you hadn't."

Ada, Pam's PerDee, erupted with an angry male voice speaking Japanese. Pam nodded an excuse and squeezed around to the pilot's compartment to take the call.

"Do you want me to translate?" Leona asked.

"No," Keegan said. "She is entitled to her privacy. It doesn't sound good, though."

"Hey, Dr. Bright!" Paul's voice came from above him. Keegan tilted his head out of the sleeping compartment. Paul grinned down at him from the upper bunk.

"What happened to you?" Keegan asked.

"Aw, I got knocked down," Paul said, looking sheepish. "It's nothing but bruises. Boy, what a mess! All of shaft number four cratered like a giant pothole! I overflew this area with the judges when they were plotting a course for the racers. I almost dropped one here. Good thing I didn't. A lot more people could have been hurt!"

"Dropped one what?" Dion asked.

Paul looked appalled at himself, and clapped a hand over his mouth. "I didn't say anything."

Dion looked suspicious. Keegan was pretty certain he knew what Paul was talking about. He looked down at Fido's screen and saw that the M-Tracker game was running in the background. Barbara noticed it, too, and shut it off, then gave the screen a double take. She was too smart not to figure it out.

Keegan tipped her a wink.

Pam returned, snapping Ada firmly into her sleeve pouch.

"We must go," she said. "Our employers are annoyed with us for stopping, but I assured them we can get out ahead again. We certainly will try."

"Thank you for your help," Barbara said. "I won't forget this."

"Once a Spark, always a Spark," Pam replied, with a kindly glance. "You have no room left here on the *Xpress*, and will have less once the miners are freed. We can take the shuttle crew as far as the next pit stop. It is one with medical facilities. The rescue shuttle can retrieve them from it later."

"That's great, Pam," Keegan said. "You and your team have gone above and beyond for us. I really appreciate it."

"Dr. Bright, Paul, I hope you will be all right." Pam glanced at Dion. "Goodbye."

"Thanks," Dion said. He couldn't seem to get any other words out, but Keegan knew she didn't expect anything. A real warrior. Pam gave them her thin smile and put on her helmet. She and Tomiko cycled out through the roof bubble.

"You should get going, too," Keegan told Barbara. "Help me and Paul suit up, and we can wait with Calvin in the mine."

"No way," she said, firmly. "We'll stay until the rescue shuttle gets here to take you home."

Keegan glanced at the chronometer on Fido's surface. That would be at least another four and a half hours.

"You're going to lose this whole day, Sparks! That will pretty much put you out of the race. I can't apologize enough for that. After all the hard work you've done to stay in it."

Barbara exchanged a nod with Dion.

"No, sir, we're not out," the big youth said.

"We're not out of the race," Barbara affirmed. "We all talked about it, all six of us. It's a setback, not a failure."

Keegan looked from one Spark to another, even the two younger

Sparks on Barbara's PerDee. He felt a smile spreading on his lips. "You're going to keep going?"

"Heck, yes," Barbara said. "We got this. But we want to make sure you're all right. We're behind, maybe, but we will keep going."

"Your life is more important than winning," Dion added. "Where would the Bright Sparks be without Bright?"

Keegan reached out with his good hand and squeezed theirs. His throat tightened. These kids cared about him as much as he cared about them, so much that they sacrificed their chance to win that race. He was the luckiest guy in the cosmos.

"Well, kids," he said at last, after a hard swallow to clear his throat. "I don't know what to say."

"Wait a minute," Paul yelped, from the upper bunk. "What time is it?"

Dion turned Candy toward him. Paul's eyes widened.

"Keegan, we've got fifteen minutes before we have to go on air!"

"He can't do that," Barbara said, shocked. "Flat on his back on a stretcher?"

Keegan had to laugh.

"You have no idea what kind of great video that's going to make," he said. "It's what really happened. I keep telling the viewers that life up here is dangerous. Even I'm not immune to that."

"But your lens is busted, Paul," Dion added, holding up the video unit. "You don't have a camera."

Paul looked dismayed for a moment, then his long face brightened.

"Can I use one of your PerDees for the show?" Paul asked. He swung down from the shelf, and started fiddling with the side touchscreen of the big camera. "I got some footage of the blowout. I can take it off the SSD drive in my camera, since you're already linked into it. I've got all the intros and graphics stored. We can upload directly from it to one of the BrightSats and hit the broadcast antenna in Armstrong City."

"Hey, no problem," Dion said, looking excited to be involved in the production side for once. "We've got nothing but time until Jackie and Dr. Singh get here."

"Professional to the last," Keegan said, pleased. Everything was falling together. It was as good as it could be, under the circumstances. "Daya and Neil, are you ready to go with today's interview?"

"Yes, sir," Neil said at once. "I . . . I mean, *Daya* has Mayor Petronillo coming in to talk about the racers hitting the halfway point. But everyone wants to know about *you.*"

"And we'll tell them," Keegan said, beaming at Barbara. "They'll hear that I'm the luckiest man ever to set foot on the Moon."

Holding Dion's PerDee over Dr. Bright, Paul watched the rear chronometer reading. He flashed three fingers, then two, then one.

Leona appeared in the video screen in her lab coat.

"This is *Live from the Moon*, with Dr. Keegan Bright!"

Keegan had done unusual shows before, in strange places, and with unexpected guests, but he had never done one lying on his back with his arm in a cast, no makeup, and his hair all over the place. It went better than he had hoped. Like integrated circuits, the kids had come through as the professionals they were growing up to be and did their parts seamlessly.

". . . So, it'll be a little bit of a setback to our plans for exploitation of minerals here on the far side," he said. "We'll have to reestablish the sealed compartments, but add in valves and releases in case of future buildups of gas and better fire control. Because we had firm safety protocols in place, there was no loss of life, just a few bruises and broken bones. I'm here able to talk with you now because of some pretty neat improvisation by our own Bright Sparks. Barbara Winton, why don't you tell our viewers how you got me out from under those rocks?"

Behind Paul, Barbara looked shocked, and Dion looked as if he wanted to laugh out loud. Keegan beckoned to her. He knew she would come through. By the time Paul turned around and aimed the PerDee at her, she was ready to go. Her cheeks were burning red, but her eyes and her voice were clear.

"Well, Dr. Bright, we had some experience with having to move heavy objects on our last major project. . . ."

He asked some questions culled from the information he had, adding to them from the expanded text that scrolled up in the air from Sparks Central and the vloggers. Barbara responded like a trooper. He let her go and had Paul turn the camera on Dion. They checked in remotely with Calvin, Jan, and Gary, just as the borer machine was on the verge of breaking through into the chamber where the miners were trapped. Jaime Petronillo added a few encouraging words.

"And we're praying for the safe return of all of you, Dr. Bright," the mayor concluded.

"Thank you, sir," Keegan said.

He signed off, and Paul lowered the PerDee.

"And we're out," the cameraman said. "Not bad for roughing it." He tossed Candy back to Dion, who caught it on its long, slow arc.

"Not bad at all." Keegan let his head drop back on the pillow. "I wouldn't be half surprised if that turns out to be one of our most popular episodes ever!" He glanced at Barbara and Dion. "We're going to have a bunch of company in a short while. They'll need water, number one. Then food, and moisturizer for their skin after being on dry, recirculated air for hours. Can you help?"

"No problem," Dion said. He glanced around at the cabin. "Now I really wish the Nerd-Twins had made this thing bigger!"

Eleven in a compartment intended for four was indeed a tight fit, but the miners and the team weren't put off by it. They sat three across on the upper bunk, wedged themselves between the pilots' seats, or squatted wherever there was room.

"It's a whole lot better than being trapped underground," said Tulip Carrera, the manager, a burly woman nearly as tall as Dion, with ebony-dark skin. She tipped the water bottle the big youth had given her to him, then drained it in one long drink. "Ah! Last time we had that happen . . . where, guys?"

"Nigeria," one of the men replied, in between bites of emergency ration bars. "At least we had air there. I stink from my own sweat!"

"You kids want a job?" Tulip asked Jan. "That was some good work, cutting through to us without bringing the rest of the spoil heap down on our heads."

"Thanks," Jan said, "but we've got jobs with Dr. Bright." She turned a warm look toward Keegan.

Gary nodded his agreement but kept chewing. *That boy has a hollow leg*, Keegan thought, with affection.

"I'd hire them away from you in a minute, Keegan," Calvin said.

"There you are!" Jackie's voice came over all the PDEs. "We're coming in for a landing now!"

Keegan looked up at the Sparks. "Well, what are you waiting for? Get ready to go! You have a race to run!"

Dion threw him a mock salute. "Yes, sir! I'll drive first."

"I'll copilot you," Barbara said, reaching for Fido. "Starting the departure checklist, now."

Jackie, Dr. Singh, Tom Beddingfield, and Yvonne, LFTM's other camera operator, added to the cramped state of the cabin, wriggling their way into the crowd. The colony chief physician looked Keegan over, clucking her tongue with concern, then helped him into his spacesuit. Jackie had a temporary link that she put into Keegan's helmet until he could get a working PerDee again. Yvonne took video of the cabin of the *Spark Xpress* and the damaged mine adit for the news channel in Armstrong City, and hit UPLOAD.

"Good episode," she told her colleague.

The miners suited up and cleared out as soon as the atmosphere had cycled out of the cabin. Tom and Calvin helped Keegan out the door and down the ladder to the ground. Keegan threw a salute to the Sparks, who waved at him from the door of the *Spark Xpress*. Yvonne stood behind him, recording.

"Go on! Race well, and I'll see you all at the finish line!" Keegan called.

"Let us know when you get back," Barbara said.

"I'm fine," Keegan assured her. "Now, get going!"

He waited until they dogged down the door and the *Spark Xpress* rolled away.

Jackie grabbed his arm and pulled him toward the shuttle.

"Those kids are going to lose the race because they couldn't help but rescue you. What do you think of that?"

"What do I think?" Keegan echoed, watching the *Xpress*'s running lights disappear over the lip of the crater, leaving the mine in near darkness. "That I couldn't be more proud of them." He laughed softly. "But don't count them out yet. They're more resourceful than you can imagine."

Tulip loomed up next to him, a powerful spotlight in her hand.

"I had a look at the shaft. This looks like a total loss, but we're insured. We'll have to rebuild the sealed-atmosphere chambers."

"Not a total loss," Keegan said. "We've got samples, and charts showing where the most promising veins of ore are located. Now we know what the terrain is capable of producing, we build in valves for the pressure so that won't happen again. And there's this." He gathered up an armload of the crystals from the mess on the surface, and dumped one into her arm.

Tulip grinned, running her gloved hand through the collection. "At least, there's that."

Keegan gathered up another armload and kicked at Jackie's equipment bag until she opened it. He let the pile of rough crystals sift down into the container, then fastened it awkwardly with his good arm.

"Why are you putting those dirty stones in there?" she demanded.

Keegan grinned. "Because it's an ill wind that blows nobody any good."

"Dr. Singh dropped off a fresh habitat unit and a ton of supplies," Calvin said, helping Keegan over to the shuttle. "I've already got it inflating. It'll be ready for the crew in an hour."

"Are you sure you're prepared to stay?" Keegan asked. "I put you in charge, but you can tell me it's too much and come back with me."

Calvin shook his head, and Bertie crawled out of his collar to adjust the scientist's glasses. "Why? I have your checklist. I think we can get the dig back on schedule pending your return. We'll just have to work in full suits until we can close off the chambers again. That ought to be within a week."

Keegan glanced off into the darkness, in the direction the *Spark Xpress* had gone.

"I am so proud of those kids. Including you, Calvin." He trickled the last of the crystals into Calvin's hand. "An early reward. You were getting a share anyhow."

Calvin looked at them, then up at Keegan, his eyes shining.

"Holy cow!"

The businesslike Dr. Singh strapped Keegan to a gurney in the rear of the shuttle next to Paul. In minutes, Major Beddingfield launched the shuttle and headed back toward home base. As soon as she could unstrap, Jackie came back and sat down on the edge of the bed. The movement made Keegan's battered body ache, but he was so glad to see her he didn't care.

"How *are* you doing?" she asked, worried.

Keegan ran a mental checklist. The new habitat had been inflated, with food and medical supplies on hand. The mining crew had been examined and pronounced fit to remain. Calvin had taken charge like the natural leader he was. Keegan was bruised to heck and gone, but he was alive. The Sparks and Pam looked like they might be heading for a détente. And the Sparks had gone back to the race with fire in their eyes.

"Everything's going to be just fine," Keegan said. "I have the best people in the solar system working with me."

"Well, settle down," Jackie said, closing her hand on his. "You're going to be on your back for at least a week."

Chapter Twenty-Two

Barbara woke up from her two-hour nap and peered over the pilots' shoulders out the front screen. That side of the Moon was in full darkness now, but it was also very late. Jan had the controls. Gary spoke in a low voice to someone on Turing's screen. If Barbara wasn't mistaken, the glimpse of red hair meant it was Tracy McGuinn.

"How's it running?" she asked, moving up to the seat behind Jan.

"Not great," the Asian-American girl said. "Speeding in on frustum power wasn't good for the buckyballs. Having to compensate for the disabled one meant the whole buggy pulled to the left. That was hard on the mechanisms for the remaining balls. I hope it's not going to slow us down even more."

"I wonder if Neil can program around that," Barbara said. She rotated her neck, trying to get the stiffness out. Her shoulders were sore from hauling heavy equipment and moving rocks, and her body still hadn't recovered completely from the extra gee force of the overland run.

"I asked him. He's on it, but he's having a hard time concentrating until Dr. Bright gets back to Armstrong City."

"We're going as fast as we can in the dark," Gary said. "I'm navigating by the topographical charts, but it's no substitute for being able to see what's out there."

"We'll make it," Barbara said, with determination. Behind her, Dion let out a loud yawn. He stood up to stretch. "Time for us to take over again. You get some rest, now."

The open channel used by the racers to talk among themselves had fallen completely silent, meaning that every one of the other teams had checked into the pit stop, and were talking to one another in real time. Barbara just concentrated on driving. She worried that the *Xpress* was now too battered to make it all the way to the finish line, but more importantly, she was concerned that Dr. Bright be able to recover without any lasting injury.

Until she was faced with the possibility of losing him, she didn't realize how much that would devastate her. Dr. Bright and his science show had been a part of her life since she was little. Now that she worked with him every day, he was more important to her than a figure on a screen. He called her and the other Sparks his "kids." Though she had parents and relatives she loved, she was glad and honored to be part of his extended family. She thought of Calvin, stepping forward to take over on the mine site, and Tom, who pulled himself away from his meetings to fly halfway around the Moon to bring Dr. Bright back. She knew she would have done the same. She let out a sheepish chuckle. She *had* done the same, as had Dion, and Jan, and Gary.

And Pam.

Almost as if he had been reading her mind, Dion spoke up.

"I wonder how far back *Blue Streak* came in to the pit stop." He didn't sound resentful or angry, just mildly speculative.

"I bet they stepped on the accelerator and made it in first," Barbara said. She hesitated for a moment, then plunged in. "Dion, I can't stand the pressure any longer. What is it that Pam did that upset all of you so much? This is the most tolerant group I have ever been a part of. I don't understand."

"You weren't there!" Dion snapped, then looked rueful. "I'm sorry, lady. That Pam just makes me want to break something. Even though she stopped to help Dr. Bright, it doesn't change the past."

Barbara watched his face. It looked as if he was finally going to let go of what had been bothering him.

"Please tell me about it. Fido, silence my microphone. No recording, no transmission until I tell you."

"Yes, Barbara," the PerDee said.

"Candy, you, too," Dion said. He sighed heavily and slumped forward toward the controls.

"Anything you say, Dion," the sultry voice said. Barbara couldn't help but giggle.

"Okay," Dion said. "We had a chance at a project Gary found, for a major Earth corporation, to design new memory storage that could make use of even ordinary organic matter, like DNA, or the cellular structure in plants—just about infinitely expandable. If you were on the edge of running out of RAM, you could attach a connector to the potted plant in your window, or even the skin of your own arm. Until the matter started to deteriorate, which I admit was pretty quick in some cases, you had a temporary backup. It would be great in emergency situations. It was the Nerd-Twins' idea, but I was primary researcher on the project, with Daya as my tester, and Neil and Pam running computer simulations to see what we ought to try next. Pam had some alternate ideas that we listened to, but decided they were dead ends for our purpose. We were really excited about it when we went to propose it to the company . . ."

"Echo Chamber," Barbara remembered. "They're the leaders in organic memory."

"That's them," Dion said. He sighed. "So, it shouldn't surprise you that when we booted up our demo, they said they had seen something a lot like it before, and had bought the prototype for that from someone else."

"Pam? But didn't you say something?"

Dion's jaw was tight with remembered resentment. "Sure, we went to her to complain. She said we rejected her ideas, so she was free to shop them herself. But she never mentioned the Sparks to Echo Chamber, or vice versa, or credited the work we had done to get to the point where she had her breakthrough. She said that a lot of what we were claiming as our original work was based on previous research that anyone could have drawn from, which is what *she* did. We should have been part of that project! I still think our prototype was better, but what really burned us was feeling we had been sandbagged by someone we really trusted and thought of as part of our group. She said if we had wanted even the bad ideas to stay in the group, we should have made a formal contract with a nondisclosure agreement. We never do that, not in the Sparks. We didn't think we'd have to.

"After that, we knew she was just out for herself. None of us talked to her any more. We couldn't wait for her to leave. I felt like throwing roses at the shuttle when it took her back to Earth."

Barbara was taken aback. She sympathized with the Sparks. Any research that had come out of their sessions ought to belong to all of them. On the other hand, she got it that rejected ideas might be considered to be outside the final project. Pam must have known that their minds didn't work the same way hers did, and they might be upset by her actions. On the other hand, and she knew she was up to at least four hands, it was unlikely that such a thing would bother her. The phrase *doesn't play well with others* went through Barbara's mind.

"But she did come to help," Barbara said.

Dion sighed. "Yeah, she did. Even knowing how we feel about her, even though it could have put *her* out of the race, she came. It was the right thing to do. I saw that, even if the other Sparks wanted to dump her down the mineshaft and leave her. It's just going to take a while before I trust her farther than I can throw her, and that's not counting Moon gravity. A lot longer before I ever could *like* her again."

"Thanks," Barbara said. Her heart went out to him. "I know that had to be hard to tell me."

He gave her a smile. "Sorry that it took so long. You didn't deserve to have to tiptoe around us. We're really glad you're here."

"Me, too," Barbara said, warmly. She glanced at the chronometer projected on the inside of the screen. "I'll take over now, if you want."

"Sure," Dion said, putting his hand on the switch. "Transferring control in three, two, one. . . ."

"We're here," Jan said, turning on the cabin lights as the *Spark Xpress* coasted to a halt. Barbara pulled herself up out of the depths of the upper bunk and peered over the pilots' heads. The brilliant light of the pit stop's lampposts made her eyes water after the endless darkness on the road. They blazed down on fourteen vehicles, the only buggies left in the race. Nothing moved in the lot. "We're eight hours behind even the last car. We'll have to sneak in so we don't wake everyone up."

"If they don't mind the sound of my feet dragging from exhaustion, it'll be okay," Gary said. He stood up and stretched, yawning wide enough to swallow his ears.

Dion was already awake, snapping on his gloves. He reached for his bubble and sealed it in place. Barbara jumped down and fastened her own gauntlets. Dion handed her her helmet.

"I don't care what they say," Barbara said, sealing the neck gasket. "I want a hot meal, a long shower, and a chance to sleep in something that isn't moving."

"I bet they left out cold cuts for us," Jan said, slapping Ms. Scruffles into her sleeve pouch. "Anything is welcome. I could eat a truck tire."

They waited until Jan cycled the door and bounced across the lot to the entrance.

"Enter, Jan Nguyen," the AI said. The rest crowded into the small airlock behind her.

"There you are!" Joe Ward said, meeting them as they came through the inner door. "We sure are glad to see you!"

He stepped aside, and a roar of voices almost sent Barbara stumbling backward. Every single racer was there in the dining room. They sprang up from the low tables and burst into applause. Team Podracer steered their wheelchairs in circles and started them bouncing. Most of the team members were clad in pajamas and looked as bleary as Barbara felt, but they grinned and cheered. Even Team SolStar, situated at the rear of the room near the sleeping chamber, stood up and clapped. Pam gave Barbara a nod, warrior to warrior. Loud music blared, and the ceiling lights strobed like party lamps.

Charlton Mbute raised his arms in the air.

"Yay, Sparks! Yay, Sparks! Yay, Sparks!" The others joined in his chant.

Barbara felt embarrassed.

"Oh, come on," she said, patting the air to quell the noise. "Anyone would have done it."

"But no one else did," Cantia said, coming forward to give each of the Sparks a big hug. "You saved everyone! We saw the video. That cave-in would have scared me to death!" The rest of the racers followed suit, hugging or high-fiving or just shaking hands with the team.

Joe got the Sparks settled at a table, and a couple of the other support staff brought plates of food from the service area.

"We could have done something fancy, but we know this is what you like best," he said, with a big grin.

"Pizza!" Gary crowed, grabbing the first fragrant platter. "This one's for me."

Cantia laughed, taking plates from the servers and putting them down on the table in front of the other Sparks. "Yes. And this one is for Barbara, and Jan, and Dion. Eat up, Bright Sparks. We made a special dessert for you. No one wanted to go to bed until they got their share, but you're first."

"I don't know what to say." Barbara looked around at the eager faces. The other Sparks looked just as astonished as she felt.

"Don't say anything," Alicia de la Paz said, pushing pizza into her hands. "It's rude to talk with your mouth full."

Dessert turned out to be a fancy dish Barbara had never seen before, with whipped cream, ice cream, real fresh fruit, and a white crust like ethereal marshmallows. Francine, from Australia, called it a Pavlova.

"This is amazing," Dion said. He wiped a streak of whipped cream from the side of his jaw.

"Oh, my gosh, I haven't had real strawberries in months!" Jan exclaimed, biting into a ruby-red fruit. She smacked Gary's hand as he tried to steal the next one in front of her. He affected mock outrage, then snatched a berry from Barbara's plate instead.

Despite her appreciation of the special feast and celebration, Barbara felt herself almost falling asleep over her food. The next thing she knew, someone was helping her toward a sleeping tube. She shook herself awake enough to look for her teammates.

"Four hours," she said. "We'll make up for it on the road. We've got to keep going. We promised Dr. Bright we would."

Jan moaned. "I guess so."

"All right, four hours," Gary said, hoisting himself up and sliding his legs into the top tube. "But you're driving first."

"Four hours from now, everyone else will be gone," Dion grumbled.

Chapter Twenty-Three

Barbara groaned as Fido's alarm went off. She fumbled around for the light stud near her head. Four hours was not enough time to rest. Her whole body ached.

"Second call," the PerDee said, brightly. "You slept through the first one. So did the others."

"Thanks, Fido."

"You are welcome, Barbara. Would you like some music while you dress?"

Every joint aching, Barbara pulled her clothes on and climbed out of her sleeping tube. She was glad she had taken a shower the night before. If she got under a stream of hot water, she knew she'd fall asleep again.

Tow-haired Joe Ward was waiting in the dining area, along with Dr. Lena Johnson, but to Barbara's surprise, so was everyone else. Team PolymerAce grinned at her over cups of coffee as she slid into a chair at their table.

"What are you all still doing here?" she asked, staring at *Rover*'s team in disbelief. "You passed your mandatory sleep period. You ought to be out on the road."

"No one's leaving until you do," Teddy Davis said. Like his teammates, he was suited up except for gloves and helmet. "It's the least we could do, since you were such big heroes."

"We weren't heroes," Barbara said, feeling tears prick at her eyes. "We just did what was right."

"That's what heroes usually say," Nev replied, with a smile.

The show of good sportsmanship from the rest of the racers made Barbara's throat tighten so much she couldn't say anything. She just smiled and hoped she wouldn't cry.

"Guys, you're the best," Dion said, looking around the room. Everyone else sent them friendly nods and thumbs-ups.

"Just trying to live up to your example," Aldonis Maranha said, clapping Dion on the back. "Hurry up so we can get out of here, yes?"

"It is still a race," Pam added from a nearby table, though she looked apologetic about it. "We're all here to win."

Gary and Jan rolled their eyes, but didn't say anything. Barbara shook her head. What she had said was true, but maybe not the most tactful thing ever. Pam certainly wasn't trying to make it easy for the Sparks to reconcile with her.

After the Sparks gulped down a quick breakfast, Dr. Johnson read the Sparks' vital signs with her medical scanner. It blipped for each of them, but she frowned.

"All right, I'll pass you, but just barely," she said. "Rest when you can. Make sure you drink enough water. Good luck, Bright Sparks."

"Thanks," Dion said.

Joe handed them a big reusable bag clattering with food containers and a big jug of coffee.

"Self-heating lunch, dinner, and a bunch of snacks," he said. "We'll see you at the next pit stop. Be careful out there, kids."

Barbara and the others sealed their helmets and went out into the starry night. After a quick check of the drive systems, they boarded their racer. The rest of the teams jumped into their buggies and activated their drives, but waited for the *Spark Xpress* to pull out.

Barbara took the pilot's position first. Overnight, Neil had sent them the most level route. Except for one brief run when they would have to double back east and north to avoid a chasm, it looked relatively straightforward. The *Xpress* switched on as it should have, but Jan's worry that the rush to rescue Dr. Bright had done more damage seemed to be borne out. The pull to the left felt more pronounced, especially on relatively smooth sections of terrain.

"I hope we're not going to lose either of the left-hand buckyballs," she told Dion.

"Neil wrote a new program to compensate," the big youth said, but he looked worried. "Baby it. We'll check in with them when they wake up."

Though the rest of the racers had disappeared out of sight within the first hour, the open channel was full of friendly interbuggy chatter.

"That dessert was so good, I am going to dream about it!" Lois said, raising her hands in rapture. Beside her, Rodin Senasate was piloting *Cheetah*. "My mother makes it for us on special occasions. I would not admit it, but this might be better than hers."

"I have to find out how they did that," Dion said, chatting while Barbara drove. "Up here, your taste buds are less sensitive, not more. My grandmother makes up really hot spice mixes for me to compensate for the bland flavors."

"Look ahead!" Svetlana said. "A TurnTable lies ahead. Is it a sign to take this way?"

"Did you hear? They are opening up that mine again. Dr. Book has been uploading pictures. They found impact diamonds in the crater!"

"How is Dr. Bright? Has anyone heard?"

"Not yet," Dion admitted.

"Neil Zimmerman posted a video of Dr. Bright last evening," one of the racers said, adding a link that glowed blue on the screen. "He has arrived back in the city. His arm is in a cast all the way to his shoulder!"

Barbara reached for it, feeling abashed. She had been too tired to check on their mentor. She shared a guilty look with Dion.

In the clip, Dr. Bright walked out of the shuttle, waving his good arm. Daya was right beside him with her medical scanner, her forehead wrinkled with concern, but their mentor seemed strong and steady on his feet. Even Dr. Singh didn't look as worried as her daughter did.

"I'm sure he'll tell us all how things are going on this afternoon's show," Barbara said.

"Yes!" Francine said. "We loved your interview, Barbara. You Sparks are so innovative."

"Hey, when all you have is a jack, everything looks like a flat tire!" Nev DeLeon chortled.

"Hey, anyone want to have a Battle of the Bands?" Charlton Mbute asked.

Dion glanced over at Candy's screen. He had the game up, but the question mark in the upper right corner instead of the directional arrow meant they were too far away to play.

Barbara stared at the churned-up soil visible in the twin beams of their headlights. They were kilometers behind, and falling further back. The *Xpress* would arrive dead last, as usual.

She gave Dion a half smile.

"We're still in the race," she said.

Dion shook his head.

"We can't keep up," he said. "We started, so we'll finish, but it's going to be tough on my ego."

"Hey, guys!" Neil said, popping up in all the Sparks' devices. "How's it going out there? I'm tracking you with BrightSat Three. You ought to be moving faster than that."

"I'm pushing it," Barbara said, checking her scopes, "but I'm not gaining any velocity. The *Xpress* is pulling to the left. Jan told you about that, I think."

Neil looked upset. "My update to the program should've fixed that," he said. He looked down, then back up at Barbara with a guilty expression. "I didn't upload it. I can't believe it! I'm sorry, Sparks! On its way now."

"You were thinking about Dr. Bright," Dion said, with sympathy. "So were we. How's he doing?"

"He's had a million interviews," Neil said. "He attracted reporters like a gravity well as soon as he landed, but I got the first Q and A session. Hey! A bunch of them want to talk to you guys, too."

"Not 'guys,'" Barbara said. It was a running joke among the Sparks.

"Fine!" Neil said, throwing up his hands in exasperation. "Self-rescuing princesses. But you rescued the king yesterday, too. They're all really impressed."

"We didn't do it for them," Barbara said.

"I know," Neil said, grave for once. "Daya and I are really glad all of you were there. Even Pam." He made a face.

"She was a big help," Barbara said, cautiously. "She didn't have to stop, you know."

Neil looked thoughtful. "No. I guess not. Well, forget her! Can I put the bloggers and reporters through to you?"

"Why not?" Dion asked. "It'll take our minds off what we're doing."

Even with the updated software, the *Xpress* continued to fight them. Barbara looked with dismay at the blue power line on the screen. Now that they were running purely on battery, with input from the friction caused by the dragging buckyball, the only way to maximize their power was to run slower than ever. Barbara did her best to distract the Sparks from their bleak situation. Every time they looked out the windscreen at the endless blackness, it brought their moods down again.

"We ought to be out in front," Dion said, gloomily, as he rose to make way for Jan.

"You don't have to keep bringing it up!" Gary said, his brow lowered. "We know! I'm sorry! How many times do I have to say it?"

"Until you can teleport us up to the front of the pack," the big youth said.

"Stop it!" Jan cried. "Look, we've been in bad situations before. We got through them."

"But not with so many people watching us," Dion shot back. "That hurts. Let me alone for a while, okay?"

Gary opened his mouth, but Barbara held up a warning hand. Her temper wasn't too far under the surface. She had to be careful in case she snapped at them.

"We're all tired. We need some good news."

Leona's avatar popped up on the scopes. That day, she was a purple unicorn, with long white curls of mane framing her long horsy face and spiraling silver horn.

"And I have some, Sparks!"

"Leona!" Barbara exclaimed, relieved. "How's Dr. Bright?"

"He is doing well," the AI said. "His humerus suffered a clean break, but it will heal quickly. He just has to finish with an examination from Dr. Singh, then he wants to talk with you. He has a new PerDee for me. It's very nice. I still have to hang pictures and paint some of the rooms, but it is very homey."

Barbara laughed. Leona did seem more like a real person every day.

"Wait, here he is!"

The unicorn vanished, and Dr. Bright's face appeared. Barbara scrutinized it to see if he was suffering any ill effects from the accident, but he looked normal. His only worry seemed to be for them.

"Sparks, I just can't apologize enough for putting you behind like that. I hear you've got some technical issues on top of everything. I can't make this easier for you. I wish I could, but then the other teams would expect outside help, and that defeats the whole purpose of this race."

"We don't need it, but thanks," Dion said.

"We got this," Barbara assured him, projecting confidence she didn't really feel. She looked at Jan and Gary to see that they were with her on that. They were, if just barely. "We're Sparks."

Dr. Bright smiled at them.

"I believe in you. I'm going to check in with all four of you at show time. Keep us posted in the meantime if there are any problems. I know your ingenuity and strength of purpose will make it work. Bright out."

"You heard Dr. Bright," Barbara said, as their mentor's face disappeared. "We go on. He believes we can do it."

But even his confidence in them started to feel like a thin shield against despair. By a quarter of the way to the next pit stop, it became evident that the left rear buckyball was showing signs of the same heat buildup the right one had. This time they did stop to examine the mechanism. Thanks to the passage of the other fourteen teams, they had a flattened-out surface to work on.

Barbara had the team disembark and run a series of tests on the mechanism. It was on the edge of failure, too.

She clapped the wrench she had used to tighten the buckyball in its socket and shook her head.

"It's no good," she said. "We'll have to run in on two wheels instead of three, unless you Twins have a workaround."

Jan and Gary shook their helmets in unison.

"There's no substitute for that piece," Gary said. "Like the other one."

"Why didn't you order backups when you had the chance?" Dion asked, looming next to them. Gary closed his hands into fists.

"Are you bringing that up again?" the young man asked. "We thought these would work! And we couldn't afford more. The rush shipping alone cost almost half what the components did!"

"I hate to lose!" Dion snapped.

"So do we!" Jan said, pushing herself in between them. "You think we sabotaged the pieces on purpose?"

"All right, all right," Barbara said, fighting her own temper. "We're all on edge, but we're out here halfway around the Moon! We still have to get back, even if we're out of the running. We promised we would cross the finish line."

"I know," Jan said. "All right. Count ten, everybody."

They got the *Spark Xpress* going again, this time using Neil's updated program to run the most efficiently it could. From the rear seat, Barbara watched the power consumption with a worried eye.

"We have to keep the velocity lower," she said, pointing past Jan to the storage indicator. "Using only two buckyballs and the two behind spinning free for balance, we can accumulate power from the friction they generate, but we're still consuming more than we would have on four good wheels."

"Can we make it on the power we have left?" Dion asked.

Barbara peered at the scope and did some calculations on Fido.

"I think so," she said cautiously. "I don't know for sure. If nothing else goes wrong."

"That does it," Gary shouted. "Take over for me, okay?"

Barbara swapped seats with him. He stalked into the sleeping area, and connected to a communications channel. From the sound of it, he was on a satellite link to the company on Earth that had furnished the components.

"I don't blame him being mad," Jan said.

"Neither do we," Barbara said.

"I want an explanation for why these failed!" he insisted. The muffled voices from Earth sounded apologetic. Barbara heard the words "partial refund" and some more platitudes.

"That doesn't help!" Gary yelped. He sounded as upset as the rest of them felt. He slapped Turing's screen and hunched over in misery. Barbara let him have his privacy.

"How about some music?" she asked. "Fido, crank up playlist number four."

It felt like days later when they followed the tracks from the other buggies toward the coordinates for the next pit stop.

"A little company might help cheer us up," Barbara said, as they crested a crater ridge toward the blazing light poles.

The lot was empty.

"I'm really sorry," Joe Ward said, as he met them by the door. His kind face was sympathetic. "Everyone had dinner and slept their shift. They left only a little while ago. They all said they wished you had been here."

Chapter Twenty-Four

The Sparks made it through their mandatory rest period, but Barbara knew none of them got much real sleep. She was too upset to relax. Instead of lying there staring at the ceiling, she dressed and went out to exercise in the dining area. Gary was there, sparring with a holographic opponent.

"I just had to work out my frustrations," he said, between feints and jabs.

"Me, too," Barbara said. She threw herself into a hard workout, raising a real sweat. After a long shower, she took a short nap and rose feeling better physically, if not emotionally. Eventually, Jan and Dion crawled out of their sleeping tubes, their eyes bleary.

Joe and the staff put together food packages so the Sparks could have breakfast on the road, as well as lunch and dinner.

"We'll catch up with them," Jan said, though she looked as if she knew that was whistling in the dark.

"We'll try," Barbara said.

The next several pit stops were just as bleak. The *Spark Xpress* was alone at each one of them but for the support crew.

"It feels like we arrived just after a party ended," Dion said.

That was true. Piles of dishes, tubs of cutlery, and bags of laundry waited near the door, ready to be loaded into the support shuttle. Most of the tables and chairs were stacked up against the walls. Only a couple of staff remained, including Dr. Johnson. While she gave the Sparks their checkup, the others swept accumulated regolith out of the corners and sanitized the bathing area. The Sparks realized they had made these volunteers remain at an empty facility until the last team arrived.

"We're really sorry about keeping you here," Barbara said, her heart in her boots.

Joe smiled.

"We're not upset about it," he said. "You're the *home team*. We'd wait for you for days, if we had to."

Barbara felt her eyes tear up.

"That's really nice of you to go to all that trouble."

"We mean it," Dr. Johnson said, with a broad smile. "You're the Moon's own. Everyone else is just visitors. Now, go on, get some sleep. *Really* sleep this time. I'm monitoring you for Dr. Bright."

Their warmhearted encouragement gave the Sparks the energy to continue. Every morning, Joe gave them a substantial picnic basket for the day's run. The support staff had split itself so part of them could keep each facility running just for them. The shuttle carrying the first half of the team came back for them once the *Xpress* had left. Barbara and her teammates slept the mandatory four hours in the pit stop, then ran as fast as the *Spark Xpress* could carry them overland. They were still substantially behind, but they were sure they could catch up. The two faulty buckyballs didn't seem as important as the fact that so many people cared about them and wanted them to make it over the finish line.

"Do you want to answer this blogger?" Neil asked, passing a comment over to Daya's screen in Sparks Central. He made a face. "I'll just tear a piece out of him if I say anything."

Daya read through the text, studded with emojis and exclamation points.

"It is one long gloat, isn't it?" she said. "But what do you expect from a commenter called PamRules?"

Neil glanced up at the feed from BrightSat 2, now making a long arc over the peloton. Four of the racers were bunched up on the run toward the tenth pit stop, with *Blue Streak* slowly but inexorably moving into the lead.

"I bet your boyfriend is gloating, too," Neil said, sourly.

"Charles is not my boyfriend," Daya replied, for the hundredth time. If Neil was not jealous, as he kept assuring her he wasn't, why did he keep throwing Murayama up in her face? "He is my friend, and perhaps an admirer of the Sparks, nothing more."

"Well, he doesn't seem to want to spend any time with *me*, and I'm a Spark."

"Have you been polite to him, even once?" Daya countered. "No. He hopes *Blue Streak* will win, naturally. The design is excellent; even you must admit that."

"Yeah," Neil said, at last. "I just keep thinking that the *Xpress* developed more problems after *Blue Streak* was close to it, with no one watching them."

"Neil! Stop being paranoid!"

"You're not on Pam's side now, are you?" Neil asked, his tone a challenge. Daya opened her mouth and closed it again. Why couldn't he be reasonable? But she didn't know what she thought any longer about Pam.

Leona popped up on the main screen on the wall, a big yellow and red monster with massive brown spectacles.

"It is almost time for the fan forum," she reminded them. "Are you ready to take questions? I have nearly ten thousand in the queue."

Neil squared his shoulders.

"Let it rip."

For the fifteenth or twentieth time, Daya fielded a question about Dr. Bright's rescue and ongoing recovery.

"Please see responses above yours," she said. "We have posted a message from Dr. Bright himself on the website."

"What do you think about the Sparks falling into last place?" a vlogger inquired in a video clip. "We thought they were going to do better!"

"We hoped they could," Daya said, forestalling Neil's undoubtedly sharper response. "Accidents happen. Component failures happen. Their design is sound. If you have not seen Neil's schematics of the *Spark Xpress*, please take a look. I was very impressed by it."

*The *Spark Xpress* looks like a piece of junk!* came a nasty comment from Captain86, a longtime correspondent and permanent curmudgeon.

"It's not what's on the outside that counts," Neil said. "How many racers have *you* sent out around the Moon?"

The audience seemed to like that reply a lot, judging from the laughing emojis and high-fives that poured in.

Daya kept an eye on *Xpress*'s progress, and shook her head. The buggy relied now on Neil's mashup of programming and Barbara's careful shepherding of the power system. Not without reason, the Sparks' online fans despaired of them making it home after spending more than eight hours off the track and the nonfunctioning buckyballs; and the Pam fans were holding that possible failure triumphantly over their heads.

"Please remember that the Moon is a dangerous place," she said, swallowing her own troubles with the former Spark. "We want everyone to return safely."

"This is Dr. Bright we're talking about," Neil put in, after looking at Daya for permission. "They had to save him!"

Is he okay? A thousand queries, almost all the same, rolled up the screen.

"I'm better than okay," Dr. Bright said. He leaned over between Neil and Daya to look into the camera. Daya felt a wave of affection for him. "Thanks for all your questions, but I have to steal these two back. We're live in ten minutes. Thanks for coming, and tune into the show!"

Leona shut down the forum, but not until Daya watched hundreds of goodbyes and thanks rolled in.

"How are you two doing?" Dr. Bright asked, looking down at the two youngest Sparks with a warm smile.

"That was hard," Daya admitted.

"It went by a lot faster than I thought it would," Neil said. He glanced up at the map. "I wish we could do more for the team."

"You're doing a lot of good right here," Dr. Bright said, patting each of them with his good hand. "You're holding down the fort for the others, giving them news when they need it, and handling the online presence with style and grace. Now, go get to Ann for makeup. I want you to get a remote interview with Calvin and a follow-up on the repairs to the damage caused by the moonquake. The race is not everything that's happening up here!"

Daya smiled at their mentor. Still, her heart went out to their colleagues.

✧   ✧   ✧

"No, no, they can't take that away from me. . . ."

A single thread of music met the team as they trudged into the next empty pit stop. Jan half-heartedly swiped at it with a flat symbol from her game. It exploded in a burst of blue and swirled down into her PerDee.

"There's a TurnTable right here," Gary said, showing a flicker of interest despite his exhaustion.

Barbara barely glanced down at Fido's screen to look.

"Hi, Dr. Johnson," she said, mustering a smile for the people waiting for them inside the airlock. "Hi, Joe."

"Hey, Sparks!" Ward said, waving them in. "Good news! The rest of the teams left only an hour ago."

"That's great!" Dion said. "We're catching up."

"It's too bad we have to stop," Jan said, but she yawned so hard she staggered backward.

Waving away the offer of dinner, Barbara hunched toward the showers. The schedule they were keeping was beating all of them up. In terms of time, it was midafternoon in Armstrong City, but the team had to take their mandatory rest. Like the others, she was all too aware that the rest of the teams were closing in on the finish line, but she was so tired, she found it hard to care. Barbara dreamed of being towed back into Armstrong City behind *Blue Spark*. She knew the idea ought to disturb her. It just didn't. The end just seemed so far away.

The four-hour rest period flew by. It seemed to Barbara that she had only closed her eyes before Fido was barking a wakeup call.

"When we get home, I'm gonna sleep for a whole week," Dion said, clasping a gigantic cup of coffee in both hands at one of the café tables. Along with her coffee, Barbara gulped down vitamin C and B-12 to try and get going.

The Nerd-Twins seemed to have raised energy from somewhere. Jan and Gary almost frolicked around the big empty room, gesturing over their PerDees at the musical notes that rose up from the very floor.

"Tequila!" a hoarse voice growled, followed by a blare of horn music, almost underneath Barbara's feet.

The Nerd-Twins leaped toward her. Barbara drew her feet back in alarm.

"Sorry," Jan said, with a wide grin. She stood up, admiring the scarlet swirl of notes bouncing up and down on Ms. Scruffles's screen. "That's a rare one!"

"Are you packed and ready to go?" Barbara asked.

"Everything's in place," Gary said. The thread of music seemed to elude his fingers. He threw everything at it: a sharp, two flats, and a whole rest, but it vanished. "No! Well, I'll wait for it to respawn. That'll only take another fifteen minutes or so."

Barbara put her empty cup down with a snap on the tabletop and stood up.

"We don't have time for you to wait," she said firmly. "That would be a complete waste of time. I don't know about you, but I don't want to spend any more time out here than I have to. Come on! Our four hours' rest is up. Let's get moving."

The Nerd-Twins looked at each other with something like despair.

"But we have identical songbooks!" Gary said. "I have to get this one."

Barbara put her hands on her hips and glared at him. Gary looked sheepish.

"We're partly responsible for this," Jan admitted. "We blew the build. We thought we were such shooting stars we could do it all by ourselves. We were wrong."

"Okay," Gary said. He shouldered the bag of food and headed for the airlock. "Sorry. I let myself get carried away. We've only got a couple of days left. Let's go."

Chapter Twenty-Five

"... And, yesterday, when we finally rolled into the pit stop, I caught a part of the old rock classic, 'Tequila,'" Jan said, with a sympathetic grin for her partner. She was at the controls of the *Xpress* after one more uncomfortable, lonely night in an almost empty habitat. "Gary missed it."

"First time ever that we don't have the same playlists in our PerDees," Gary said, looking mournful.

On their screens, Neil was almost hopping up and down with jealousy. "I could have used that one! Why are all these great tunes turning up out there and not here, Cisca?"

The programmer sat back in the chair between Neil and Daya in Sparks Central and gave the camera a conspiratorial grin.

"We had to put together some specials for the racers. Don't worry. They'll be released to the general players. Eventually."

"I hate waiting!" Neil wailed. Daya looked long-suffering. Barbara knew she had been hearing for almost two weeks about Neil's displeasure at not being able to go out on the racecourse. Being deprived of special M-Tracker tracks was just one more injustice for the crime of being too young.

"I know," Cisca said. "I would, too. Come on, you'll have all the fun of gathering them over the coming months."

"Months?" Neil echoed, outraged. Cisca's eyes twinkled with mischief.

Daya cleared her throat.

"Thank you, Jan, for that update. Let us move on to the teams in the front of the pack, Team Podracer in *Moonracer*. Francine, you are only five hours out from the finish line and currently in third place. How do you and your team feel about winning this race?"

The Australian's nasal voice filled the speakers.

"Excited! Everyone's jockeying around for position to get ahead. It's not a sure thing, but we're gonna try."

"You know what?" Gary said, slamming his hands on the controls. "I hate waiting, too."

"What do you want to do about it?" Barbara asked, leaning forward to look him in the eye. "We're running on two wheels. I'm afraid of overheating the ones we have left!"

"We could kick in the EMdrive again."

"Brother, that was one heck of a rough ride!" Dion reminded him. "And we only did that to save Dr. Bright."

Gary's face twisted in frustration.

"I know! But I hate being all the way in the back. I know we can't win. We've lost the prize money. I just don't want to drag in dead last. Let's get far enough up to finish with the others. We could do it!"

"How about it, princesses?" Jan asked, with a quick glance over her shoulder. "I like it. I'm willing to try."

Barbara stared out of the windshield. For the first time in a week, she saw the gleaming of lunar sunrise, faint sunlight glimmering on the edge of the horizon. By the time they made it to Armstrong City, it would be planetary dawn, just enough to feed a trickle to their solar batteries. Her companions were brimming with hope.

"I don't know if it's fair . . ." Barbara said.

"Oh, come on, Barb!" Gary pleaded. "We could cut five hours off our time."

"I'm not sure. . . ."

She was interrupted by a burst of excited voices over the common channel.

"Did you see that?" Tomiko exclaimed.

"Idiots!" Svetlana said.

"Oh, my God!" cried Charlton. "They flipped right over!"

The Sparks looked at one another in alarm.

"Barb Winton here," Barbara said. "Who flipped over?"

"Team PolymerAce," Pam said, calmly. "*Rover* was well out in front, then just ran off the road to the left."

"There is TurnTable visible there," Svetlana said, so upset she was losing her grasp on English. "I speaking to Teddy. He wants go there. I said no, do not blow air on your lead. Static burst on the channel. Now, I cannot hear him at all. Something is wrong!"

Barbara leaned forward in alarm.

"Teddy, Nev, Cantia, Stephen, what happened?"

She strained her ears to hear over the static. No answer.

Dion set his jaw. "A TurnTable, off the path in the rocks! See it?"

"How did one get all the way out there?" Gary asked.

"Paul," Dion said. "He almost admitted it when we rescued Dr. Bright. He's the one dropping whatever makes a TurnTable work."

"Paul is?" Neil squeaked. "I want those tracks!"

"Never mind the tracks," Barbara said, impatiently. Neil was incorrigible! "We need to know if *Rover* is all right."

"It's not responding to hails," Neil confirmed, glancing at his console. "Looks like their communication equipment went down."

"I am not getting vital signs," Daya said. Panic showed in her eyes.

"Do you think they could have lost power completely?" Gary asked. "They'd be running on battery, the same as the rest of us."

"It's possible to short out the system," Barbara said. "If that's the case, they could be in real trouble. Neil, is one of the BrightSats in position to make another run over the area where *Rover* crashed? Could you listen in on them for us?"

Neil went wide-eyed.

"Oh, so, this time you *want* me to eavesdrop?" he asked.

"Just do it, Neil!" Daya said.

"Okay," the youth said, with a decisive nod of his head. "I'll have to divert BrightSat Three to the location. It'll take about twenty minutes."

"In the meantime, we'll hurry to get there," Barbara said, sitting back and strapping in tightly. "Gary, you're going to get your wish. Fire up the EMdrive!"

"Why is this our responsibility?" Gary asked, making a face. "The rescue vehicle can't be that far behind them."

"We have to help because we're the home team." Barbara frowned. "I hope they didn't completely discharge their batteries. We don't have enough power to get home ourselves if we recharge *Rover*."

"Everyone hang on!" Jan said. "Here goes!"

Twenty minutes of having their kidneys hammered by the rough terrain brought them fifty kilometers closer to the site of the crash. Her muscles tensed with worry, Barbara kept her eyes fixed on the far horizon. She hoped Team PolymerAce had the sense to suit up and use their recirculators to give them air to breathe.

"I can hear them," Neil said at last. "BrightSat Three is within range. Their batteries are disconnected or dead. They hit a big rock, and it sounds like it shorted out their battery system. They sound really scared. They have about an hour on the emergency batteries before it starts affecting life support and temperature control."

"Download exact coordinates to our PerDees," Jan said.

"Sending now," Neil said. Barbara saw the topographical map with data appear on the forward screen.

"They must have put on their EVA suits," Daya said, sending them a quartet of health monitor readings. "Now, I can see their vital signs thanks to Neil's link. They are all right except for elevated heart rates."

"Fifty-two minutes to the site of the wreck," Gary said, reading Neil's data.

"That is cutting it very close," Daya said, fidgeting. "I wish we could tell them help is on the way."

"This is the pickup squad, *Spark Xpress*," a male voice said over the channel. "We're a couple of hours behind the main group. Neil, thanks for the location info. We're also a couple of hours from *Rover*'s position."

Barbara let out a breath in relief.

"We're closer. We'll get there and do what we can for them. We'll try to restore life support until you arrive."

"Roger, *Xpress*. Knew we could count on you."

Despite the tracks left by the rest of the buggies, the road was rough. Barbara hung on through the jostling. She worried all the way to the accident site. Neil had to realign the BrightSat's arc again and again to pass over *Rover*, giving the team frequent updates.

"There are no exterior lights visible," he confirmed, "but I'm still getting voices. Four. Everyone's still okay. They lost their antenna in the rollover, which is why they can't communicate with anyone."

Gary pointed through the windshield at a long swath of torn-up regolith and a big dark lump.

"There it is!"

✧   ✧   ✧

"Wow, we're glad to see you!" Teddy Davis exclaimed, opening the sealed hatch to Barbara, Dion and Gary. Jan stayed on board the *Spark Xpress*. Like the rest of Team PolymerAce, the curly-haired man had suited up. According to Fido's sensors, *Rover*'s interior had begun to cool off to lunar ambient temperatures, or approximately minus 170 degrees Celsius. Gary immediately hooked up a portable ceramic heater. In minutes, the enormous cabin warmed enough for the team to start moving around more comfortably. Barbara got her first real chance to see *Rover*'s facility. Compared with the *Xpress*'s modest interior, *Rover* was as big as a living room, with four padded couches, a video screen, even a game table. No wonder they weren't as maneuverable.

"What happened, as if I can't guess?" Barbara asked, starting to run checks on the power system.

Teddy dropped his eyes.

"Yeah, we were playing M-Tracker. I saw that TurnTable, and it was pouring out rare vintage spacepunk, stuff I've never even heard on Earth! We had such a great lead, I didn't think it would be a problem if we got close enough to snag a few tracks. Then we hit something, and all the lights went out."

Cantia looked embarrassed. She could barely look at Dion.

"I told you they were idiots," she said. "I warned them!"

"Sorry, Cantia," Stephen said. "It was too tempting."

Barbara shook her head. "Well, the chase car is on the way to pick you up, if we can't fix what's wrong. Fido, can you detect if the power loss is a catastrophic failure or not? Does *Rover* need a complete recharge, or can we solve this problem?"

"Woof!" Fido replied. "The batteries read eighty percent. The system cannot access that power, however."

"Sounds like a broken connection," Barbara said. "Can you handshake with our devices and give us schematics of your system."

Nev looked mulish. "You want access to our not-yet-patented design?"

"Oh, come on!" Cantia said, thoroughly exasperated. "The race is almost over! What does it matter if she knows how it's wired?"

Stephen swiped a gloved finger across his PDE's screen. "Here you are, everything."

The Sparks gathered around Fido as Barbara expanded the map of the power connections. The schematics rose up in three dimensions, turning over and over.

"A couple of the storage batteries are blown," Gary said, pointing to bars that were red instead of blue. "They lost a lot of power."

"There's plenty left to get them home, if they can back out of here."

"We can maneuver just fine if you can jumpstart us!" Teddy insisted.

Barbara pursed her lips, and made Dr. Bright's motorboat sound. She stretched the grid still further, following a line of connections that ought to have been firing on green.

"There it is!" she said. "It looks like the whole roof came down *crunch!* on that one circuit board. All of the components adjacent to it are off-line, too."

"What can we do?" Cantia asked, peering in between their shoulders. "Our engineers are back in Armstrong City."

"Fortunately," Gary said, gesturing to his teammates with pride, "we *are* our engineers."

"I think we can give you open access," Barbara said, thoughtfully, "but it'll be permanently on until you disconnect it again."

"We don't care," Nev said. "Do the Spark magic. It'll be just like being on the television show."

In order to get to the damaged section, Barbara had to climb up into a narrow access tube between the ceiling of the cabin and the massive solar panels on the roof. Dion and Nev passed magnetic tools up to her. Barbara hated being stuck in such a tight position, so she talked, as much to herself as to the others, while she was disconnecting the bad board.

"Whoa, look at that!" she said. "This thing is in pieces! Better disconnect that capacitor. Don't want it firing when there's nothing it can feed." She used a laser cutter on the printed circuit behind the component.

Suddenly, a burst of light dazzled her eyes. Barbara blinked, momentarily blinded, as small shards peppered her chest and bounced off her helmet.

"What happened, Barb? Are you all right?" Dion asked.

"It's okay," she called down to them. "The capacitor blew. Just making the connection now."

As she swung down from the ceiling into Dion's waiting arms, the lights in *Rover's* cabin came on, and the floor began to vibrate under their feet.

"Wow!" Teddy exclaimed. "You guys are amazing!"

Nev swung into the pilot's chair and strapped in. Cantia sat down beside him.

"Next stop, Armstrong City," Nev said, his voice hollow but triumphant in his bubble helmet. "You'd better get back to your own racer unless you want to come with us."

"What?" Dion asked, outraged.

"Git! Go! We've got time to make up."

The Sparks scrambled out and bounced back to the waiting *Xpress*. Barbara hadn't reached the ladder yet when *Rover* executed one of those wallowing moves that it had made on the first day of the race; its huge rollers digging into the regolith, it shot backward and did a bootlegger's turn onto the track left by the rest of the buggies. In a moment, nothing remained but a cloud of dust.

"See you at the finish line!" Teddy called.

"Ungrateful bunch of idiots," Dion said, disgusted. He kicked at a round rock, then stared as musical notes and notations began rising from it into the floating dust.

Barbara picked up the small object. It wasn't a rock, but a sphere-shaped electronic device.

"It's streaming music," she said.

"Another rare track!" Gary exclaimed, grabbing for Turing. "That's a TurnTable! So that's what they look like!" Gary gestured with rests and sharps to grab the bounding tracks. "Aaargh! Missed that one!"

Barbara held it out in the air.

"Fido, can you turn this thing off?"

"Yes, Barbara."

Instantly, the notes vanished. Gary looked frantic.

"But I can catch all that music!"

"No! Stop. No more M-Tracker from now until we get home. Turn off your games. We don't have *time*."

"But what if someone challenges us to a Battle of the Bands?" Gary asked.

"Are you kidding me?" Barbara asked, outraged. "Did you look at the map? We're tens of kilometers behind everybody. No one will be close enough until we get back, and then you can play until your fingers fall off. We need to concentrate now." Barbara waited until Gary swiped the program off Turing's screen. Jan followed suit just as reluctantly.

"Whatever," Jan said, as the other three climbed in and repressurized the cabin. "I'm ready. Let's get home."

"Let's make tracks. Get it?" Gary asked. "If we can't catch tracks, we'll make our own."

"The racers are all within hours of the finish line." He gave Barbara a hopeful look. "I don't really want to come in fifteenth out of fifteen. I know Jan and I are responsible for running behind, but can't we boost it now?"

"Yes," Barbara said, positively. She felt a little stung by Team PolymerAce taking off like that. "We've earned that. Let's do it. Run it as hard as you can. We've got nothing to lose now."

"Yahoo!" Gary shouted. Barbara belted in just in time as the gee force jammed her back into her seat.

"Now, aren't you glad I set up the laser system?" Neil asked from the windshield, with a cheeky grin. Daya rolled her eyes.

"I don't know whether to kiss you or kick you," Barbara said.

Neil waggled his eyebrows mischievously. "Do I get to pick?" he asked.

"No!"

With the help of the EMdrive, they passed *Rover* in a matter of minutes. Despite the pounding to her spine, Barbara felt a moment of guilty satisfaction. They weren't going to come in fifteenth of fifteen; maybe a lot better than that.

"And they're coming in toward Armstrong City now!" Neil narrated for the worldwide Earth audience and the population of the Moon as if calling a horse race. "It's Team Podracer in the lead! No, Team Solar Wind is edging them out. Here comes *Zhar-Ptitsa*! Hey, I said that right! Wait, look out for Team Amazonia—that *Piranha* is still fast. They're giving it everything they have! Oh, wow, look at *Blue Streak*! It's like a comet! Where'd they get all that extra power from? Podracer and SolStar are fighting for the lead!"

Out in the hallways, they could hear the citizens and visitors to Armstrong City shouting their excitement in the closing moments of the race.

Something caught Daya's eye. She pounded Neil on the shoulder and pointed. Neil looked up at the top of the big main screen, and his voice rose to a higher pitch than ever before.

"Oh, my gosh, I don't believe it! Here comes *Spark Xpress* out of nowhere! They're blasting in on EMdrive, folks, my own invention. . . ."

Daya ignored Neil's self-aggrandizement. Her whole heart was with the rest of her team in the buggy. She clutched her hands together, watching the small jeweled dot, willing the team to move up farther and farther, but the finish line was so close! Could *Spark Xpress* really win, even after all of its setbacks?

"Five kilometers to go! Four . . . three—no! *Moonracer* is spinning! I don't think they can recover—wait, they did! Awesome! Two! One! And *Cheetah* comes in over the line, followed by *Moonracer* and *Blue Streak*! They're the winners! *Spark Xpress* is in eighth place. *Jade Dragon* is next, followed by *Firebird*! Whoa, and way back there is *Rover*. Come on, guys! It's over!"

Neil leaped up and hugged Daya. She hugged him back, hard enough to make him squeak.

"Come on," Neil said, his face glowing. He grabbed Daya's arm and pulled her toward the door. "Let's go congratulate them!"

Daya followed, holding on tight to his hand. She had never felt so happy.

Rover finally made it into the shuttle bay and skidded to a halt, throwing regolith dust everywhere, including a shovelful all over *Spark Xpress*. Barbara fidgeted nervously until the bay sealed and green lights indicated that the atmosphere had been restored. She couldn't wait another moment.

"Open the door!" she insisted.

"I'm on it!" Gary said. He swiped his hand over the control. The repurposed airplane door descended. None of the four bothered with the stairs. They all leaped down onto the floor and joined the happy crowd, all hugging and slapping one another on the back.

"You did it!" Neil shouted, throwing himself into their arms. Dion picked him up and tossed him up like a doll, then leaned over to give Daya a kiss on the cheek. "You finished. We are awesome!"

Reporters surrounded them, all yelling questions. Barbara tried to smile at each of the hovering drone cameras in turn, but the movement and the moment made her dizzy. On the dais at one end, Team Solar Wind was being interviewed by a huge group of bloggers and journalists, all wanting to talk to the winners of the first race around the Moon. Ms. Reynolds-Ward was beside them, making them take turns. Team Podracer had made it all the way to the inner doors, where they held court with their own group of interviewers and Mayor Petronillo. Beside *Spark Xpress,* Pam took questions with quiet dignity, while her teammates beamed their excitement. Svetlana and the Russian team beamed at the Sparks. Barbara smiled and waved back. But there was only one face Barbara wanted to see.

Dr. Bright broke through the crowd and came toward them, his arms out. The left one was in a new cast, one that allowed him to bend his arm. Jackie, Paul and Yvonne came in his wake, cameras focused on the Sparks. He shook hands with all of them, but Barbara couldn't restrain herself. She gave Dr. Bright a big hug. He was all right!

He smiled down at her and patted her on the shoulder.

"Well, congratulations, Sparks!" he said. "I am mighty glad to see you now, but I admit I was a whole bunch happier to see you a while ago."

Barbara took a deep breath. Too many thoughts rushed through her mind, but only one made it out of her mouth. "We lost."

"You're winners in my book," Dr. Bright said. "And here's your consolation prize." From one of his myriad jumpsuit pockets, he took small plastic bags and dropped one into each of their outstretched hands. They contained a number of rough gray crystals. "You, too, Neil and Daya."

"What are they?" Dion asked, turning the bag over and over to look at his prize.

"Impact diamonds!" Dr. Bright said, with a big smile. "They were caused by a cometary collision with the Moon eons ago, and brought up to the surface by the explosion. You must have seen them on the ground near the mine blowout, but you didn't know what they were. Some of them might polish up pretty, but they're collector's items either way. Calvin got a share, and you sure earned one. Neil and Daya, your good work at home made my rescue possible, and kept the *Xpress* on track. Good job!"

Barbara couldn't be more proud. Even though she had missed out on the prize money, this little sack of diamonds would go a long way toward helping her family. She couldn't wait to tell her parents all about the race.

Jan put her hand in. "Team Bright Sparks!"

They all piled their hands on top of hers, including Dr. Bright.

"Bright Sparks!" they shouted.

"Hey!" Neil said, as musical phrases began to waft up from the floor. "There's a new TurnTable here!"

"It's the least I could do," Cisca said, squeezing through the crowd and coming up beside Dr. Bright. She held up a small device the size of a pool ball, twinkling with electronic components. "All the rare tracks are on it. Call it my thank you for making the race such a success."

"Wow!" Neil said, overwhelmed.

"I challenge you to a Battle of the Bands," Gary said, pulling Turing out of his sleeve.

"You're on," Jan said, her eyes gleaming.

"I'm next!" Daya said. "But first, you must have your medical examination. My mother insists! This way!" The smallest Spark herded her friends toward the shuttle bay door.

Barbara grinned and followed her friends down the hall.

✧End✧